DARQLANDS

deancracknell

Dean Cracknell has a degree in Electronics, but has never let that be a burden. He learnt to write long before he learnt differential calculus and has never looked back since. When not fulfilling his day job of writing test software for silicon chips, (aka 'paying the mortgage'), he is never one to sit still or allow lack of talent to get in the way. Over the years he has been known to paint, write, compose music (as The Cacophony Of Light), make furniture, musical instruments and pieces of Hi-Fi equipment, write computer software and magazine articles for Amstrad and Amiga home computers, create websites and he once managed a progressive metal band by the name of Season's End. He hasn't tried stand-up comedy yet, but it is only a matter of time, inclination and opportunity. When not doing one of those activities he can be found in the garden imagining how it would look if he had the money. (His goldfish have only recently moved from a very large plastic tub into the pond he promised them several years ago). He does all these while listening to his vast collection of vinyl LPs and polycarbonate CD's that span the years from way back then to the present day that cover just about every genre imaginable.

He lives in semidetached rural Hampshire with is wife Deborah, daughter Alex, four cats and an indeterminate number of Goldfish and White Cloud Mountain Minnows.

First print edition.

Originally published online as an eNovel in 1999 – lost in the ether 2007

None of characters in this story are real; any similarity to anyone you know of is purely coincidental, though rather neat. By the same reasoning, all situations and events depicted are also broadly described as fictional in much the same way as Salacity is not a real City. Most of the words contained here are in the average dictionary, some are not; the order in which they have been placed is mostly down to Dean Cracknell, however cosmic forces, chaos theory and random chance dictate that some phrases and sentences could possibly bear a passing resemblance to something that may have appeared in print before, however unintentional, it is possible that those authors were either remarkably skilled in predicting what would appear here, or were in the possession of some form of temporal transportation device. All doodles, scribbles and colouring-ins were also produced by Dean.

DARQLANDS

Contents

Chapter One: Apollyon

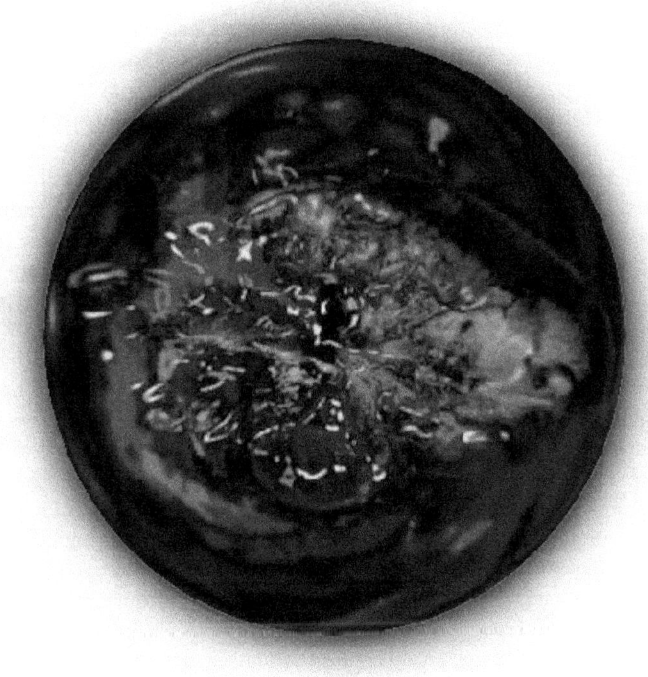

Page One: Into the Dawn

Snakes and carnivorous reptiles scurry about their nocturnal occupation, scavenging debris and litter from the decay of the night. As the fading Despair casts a diffused glow, a shadow moves tired and hungry through the city-wind, observing and discarding the possibilities and options in its wake, searching for the worthy prey. Only the weak remain and they will not do, they would be too easy, there would be no struggle and no release of energy...

Huddled in a doorway, wrapped in soiled layers of coats and woollens, blanketing against the biting winter cold, a girl clutches a small canvas bag, the remnants of a life. Sleep filled eyes gaze down at a small pile of unsold copies of 'The Big Issue' as the unseeing public, the Great Washed, file past uncaring or too embarrassed to care. For eleven hours she has sat here, watching the ebb and flow of the great human river, watching them flood into the West End and drain out again. Just shadows, all she sees of them are their shadows as they pass. Soon she would return to the bender to crash, but for now she waits for the last of the theatre crowds to pass, in the hope of one last sale. Maybe, then, a hand-out of weak soup and cake from the van on the embankment. Reflected in the darkened shop window she sees another shadow, the shadow of herself as others see her, a sad little run-away covered in grime with unkempt hair dyed in black and magenta, a poor imitation of a face she had seen on a record poster. She sees her self looking ten years older than the girl who arrived on the train last spring with dreams of freedom and hope. For the first time she is aware of how desperately miserable she has become - just another shadow, a shadow of her former self. Resting her head against the glass a single tear runs down her cheek, carving a river of grime free pink skin as it passes. The bodies continue to move by without breaking stride as a chink of coins in the burger-box at her feet cause her to look up. Sniffing back the tears and wiping her face with the back of her hand she voices a feeble "Thank-you". The pile of papers remain untouched and a body blends into the ever moving crowd. Reaching for the box she retrieves a single heavy coin, turning it over in her fingers its gleaming golden surface reflect the sodium street lights into her face and she is filled with an overwhelming feeling of warmth and affection.

...Undeterred, the Shadow traces the feculent River as it slowly bisects the City in a somnambulant procession. There is soul near, poised to enter the Darqlands, the Shadow can smell the sweet regret of tainted despondency germinating in the half-light between Hope and Despair. Heightened senses probe the fetid air, questing the prey over bridges and quays, through the wharfs and inlets. The scent is faint even to the Shadow's attuned perceptions that have been honed through æons of the Hunt, but Hope is fading and the trail is still warm. Soon it would be time...

If it was ever worse than this, he could not remember and contemplating it getting worse sapped his strength. The best part of a bottle of gin did little to dull his memory as the bitter events took precedent. He still had much to forget. It was as if an angel had touched his soul, burning and searing as it coursed through his heart, to cast a pain of love so pure, so absolute and yet so brittle. Like an exquisite Fabergé egg, too fragile to hold, too temptingly beautiful not to.

...Inevitable then, that he should let it crumble in his fingers...

Rocking back in the fake leather chair he pours the last of the gin into his mouth, swills it around and gulps it back. Squinting through one bleary eye, he studies the emptiness of the bottle, twisting and turning it to observe the glinting facets of glass distorting the already twisted world, in an effort to make every thing look right. He lobs the bottle across the office towards the wicker-effect waste bin. Then decides that bouncing it over the synthetic floorboards in the general direction of the bin was his original intention.

A noise from the street below, a car door slamming and voices raised, stir him from is melancholic thoughts. Through semi-blurred vision he scans the mock 1930's pastiche of his office looking for the window-remote. Seeing it perched on the imitation filing cabinet, he stands up abruptly. Two of his five senses follow several milliseconds later and the room spins in that peculiar, loping forward, rocking half backward and sliding off to the left, spin that only a spinning room can truly achieve. Angry at being taken on an impromptu roller-coaster ride, vertigo grips his inner ear and throws him deftly to the floor to lie unconscious in a puddle of juniper perfumed vomit.

...Even a Shadow has its pride and knows the unspoken rules. With trick and guile a Shadow plies his skill, the Darqlands are the bait and the trap, but each victim is a willing one. They come through choice and design, it is the Shadow's task to guide them on their way. Returning to stalk the silent streets the Shadow slides over rooftops in its vigilant pursuit. The light is growing and time is rapidly slipping by, now it must return to the Darqlands to rest. The Shadow begins to fade and drift into the nothingness when an instantaneous spark of Despair catches its attention and sends it off on the trail of a more likely prize...

In a candle-lit room a strong and youthful body sits naked on the edge of a bed, bathed in the flickering light. Nearly choking from the effort of containing the sobs that would humiliate him further his eyes brim with tears. The vision of perfection on the bed behind him coos comforting words, as the sound of the used condom hitting the floor interrupts her soothing tones. He wishes he was alone and the world would swallow him whole. He wishes tonight had never happened and he had never been born. More than this, he wishes that his staying-power had lasted longer than the moment she rolled the prophylactive over his erection. As he turns slightly to reach for a tissue the woman responds, her lithe body curling around his back until her head rests on his lap. He strokes her silken black hair, following its tresses as they flow over the subtle curves of her back as she gently licks away all traces of his impetuous shame.

...These are the waking times, the Despair will soon be gone and the ultramarine wash of Hope will sweep the predators into the hard shade of the dawn. Passed are the hunting times when the richest prizes fall to the Shadow's grasp, live souls with strong hearts and the will to live, the will to fight. However, they are long gone either entrapped into the Darqlands, or escaped back to the Waking Lands. Resigned to the endless cycle and the knowledge that Despair will return, the Shadow's aura shimmers in the cleansing light from the rising Hope and slips quietly back into the Darqlands...

Page Two: Awaken

Opening his eyes he could see the empty gin bottle neck on, like a giant glass eye staring back at him, accusingly. He tried to get up, but he could not, then the realisation that his face was glued to the floor by a paste of dried vomit. With a sharp pull and an accompanying yelp of sudden pain, he freed himself and raised his abused body to a sitting position. Straightening his left leg, which had become trapped uncomfortably beneath his right, he pauses a moment to take stock of the damage to his system. Surprisingly his head did not hurt, or if it did, it did not hurt nearly as much as his stinging cheek, still crusted with the desiccated remains of yesterdays lunch. Unlike the time he drunk a bottle of Chartreuse and his hangover lasted for days, defying the pharmaceuticals in the bathroom cabinet to dislodge it. He vowed then and there to never touch anything monks had messed with. This morning his mouth felt like a flock of Shitehawks had roosted the night on his teeth, so at least he had paid some penance for an evening of self pity and alcohol. He had no idea of the state of his liver but felt fairly certain it would survive, after all he could not afford to down a bottle of gin every night, even if he wanted to. Feeling stable enough to attempt to stand, he did so, and walked stiffly over to the water-cooler. His water-cooler was his pride and joy, the only bona fide genuine article in his otherwise fake office. It had cost him small fortune, colonial antiques were highly sort after and demanded extortionate prices; especially if they were in working order, but it was worth every penny now that daytime temperatures rarely dipped below 30° even in Winter. Swilling the chilled water around in his mouth, he picked up the window-remote and stabbed at the "open" button before spitting the now unwholesome water into the street. The dark stained splatter-pattern on the flagstones below nudged a grey cell, that tugged a synapse and caused a cascade of neurones to fire through his brain, coursing binary search paths through randomly stored memory fragments, piecing together scraps of data into a coherent message. An image of something very important that he must remember, a vital and pertinent piece of information securely locked away until the right signal keyed its release. Data retrieval was not his finest skill, in fact he flunked that module twice before scraping a measly pass, even his tutor joked that he could not retrieve 'Wednesday' even if he backtracked from 'Thursday'. With all the effort he could muster he concentrated on the shape: Mandlebrot? Julia? All he could think of was 'an elephant'. He smirked to himself at the thought:

'Yeah, one that had dropped three stories onto concrete.' He looked at the pattern, no longer elephant shape it slowly transmuted into smaller animals as the heat from the warming pavement evaporated the water. His attention sufficiently diverted, he gulped the last of the water, swallowed it back and tossed the freshly crushed paper-cup in the direction of the waste-basket. To have it bounce across the floorboards and land alongside the gin-bottle. His ablutions complete, his thoughts turned to breakfast and the idea of a large black coffee and cigarette.

...In the lair of the Darqlands, the Shadow has form and substance, it can feel the cold black nothingness all around. It can feel breeze from raging Despair as it howls through the land, whipping up vortices of Dismay in its wake. To dance and gyrate the ballet of the Darqlands to its æolian song...

In her makeshift shelter of cardboard and pallets, a girl sits watching the sunrise over the cityscape, casually rubbing the heavy gold coin between her fingers. She knows from its age that it is valuable and she knows it is not currency to spend over the counter, to readily convert into food, shelter and clothes. She knows can sell the coin and probably get a reasonable price from the right places. Places that won't ask endless questions of where she got it, or assume it was stolen and rip her off without asking questions. You learn a lot in a very short time here, you have to learn to survive. She also knows this is no ordinary coin, yet she does not know of its magic and cannot sense its power or feel its strength. But she knows it is hers and she would miss it if it were gone. A smile comes to her dirt rimed face as she thinks of Gollem and his little precious.

...In the Darqlands it can feel, it can feel remorse and it can feel hunger. With the tendrils of its mind stretching through the land it can touch and feel the souls of its inhabitants. It can feel their remorse and their hunger as it feeds on their despair. Something is wrong in the Darqlands and something is wrong in the Waking Lands. From the fruitless foray of the previous night, the Shadow is aware that the hunting is becoming more scarce with each passing. It was as though there was not enough Despair in the world to go around, let alone feed the Darqlands...

In lying naked on the vast expanse of silk sheets covering her oversized bed, Ashiya flaunts her sexuality. In her fashionable loft overlooking the equally fashionable apartments of her contemporaries, Ashiya flaunts her opulence. In raising her arm and signing "R-3" and "B-M-6" in Standard American Sign Language, Ashiya flaunts her modernity. Her flickering hand signals are captured and interpreted by unseen cameras that busily sets the Kitchenette preparing breakfast menu-6 as the stereo tunes into Radio 3. "R-V-5" and the volume raises to level five as Kurt Weill's The Threepenny Opera fills the room. Having set the day into motion, she slides over to the edge of the bed, relishing the silken caress of the bedclothes. Her feet touch the satin of the warmed wooden floor and the sensual feeling travels up her legs. Skirting gracefully around her minimalist furniture Ashiya heads off to the shower, where the pulsing jets of water can assault her body. To wash away the seedy remnants of the previous unfulfilled night. And to climax the erotic high from the designer drug that is connecting every nerve cell to her over-stimulated libido.

Page Three: the Naked Breakfast

...It was not that long since the Shadow could easily reach out and ensnare a willing victim. All that had changed. In a matter of a few periods of the endless cycle, the balance between Hope and Despair had shifted, something had disturbed the equilibrium and was now eating away at the fringes of the Darqlands...

Ashiya trembled and shook as the pulsing jets of scented water massaged her sensitised body, sending waves of ecstasy rippling inwards from her toes and finger tips to the centre of her being. Streams of water cascaded over her, caressing as they mingled with her own sexual fluids. With her eyes closed, her finger-tips sensuously traced her contours, lightly brushing as they passed, combing through tangled hair and slipping between moist folds. Rapt in pleasure her gentle moans grew in intensity, giving voice to the euphoria she was experiencing. As her orgasm reached its peak she let out all the air in her lungs in a low, hoarse grown. At this preprogrammed signal, the water stopped, to be replaced with blasts of hot perfumed air which began to soothe over her with the tenderness of an attentive lover, delicately evaporating the water from her skin. Sated, she slid slowly down the wall until she came to rest on her haunches, her fingers pressing into the soft flesh at the top of her thighs, her head resting on one shoulder, her breasts heaving as she breathed in harmony with the 'hum' of the dryers. After several moments recuperation, Ashiya stepped from the shower, refreshed and revitalised. Although perfectly dry, she proceeded to rub her body with a large bath-sheet, still enjoying the rapture of sensations from the remains of the drug. Dropping the towel untidily on the floor, she collected her coffee and warm croissant from the Kitchenette and sat at a glass table, knowing full well she was being observed by the occupant of the apartment opposite. As she is every morning as she sits, still naked, eating her breakfast.

...With the fabric being eroded it would only be a matter of time before souls started seeping back into the Waking Lands. As the souls departed the Darqlands would begin to fade and shrink. This the Shadow knew as 'truth', it did not require thought or deduction, it was the only 'truth' the Shadow had known since the endless cycle had begun. Rapidly equations collect and arrange themselves: The Shadow is a hunter, it has no other skill; The Shadow's only reason for being is to collect souls for the Darqlands; If the Darqlands ceases to exist, the Darqness would fade and the Shadow will also cease to be; The Shadow has not the skill to repair the rents in the Darqlands; The Shadow will search out the cause of the damage; The Shadow is a hunter, it will track down and destroy the enemy of the Darqlands...

At this time of the morning, the railway station is the only place open that sells cigarettes. It also serves fresh ground filter coffee which, to his jaded pallet on mornings such as these, could equal Java Blue Mountain for taste and aroma. Perching one bum-cheek in the specially designed loiter-free stools, he savours the coffee as he idly watches the commuters stream from the trains. Like a fresh transfusion of plasma injected into the veins of the city, the masses of individual corpuscles bring life to the bloodless heart, swelling the arteries of communications and adding flesh to the bones of commerce. Soon the whole city will pulse with activity. With each beat fortunes will be won and lost, careers will be made and ruined. In one beat lives will touch lives, friendships will be forged and romances will bloom; Another beat and lives will touch lives, affinities will be broken and loves will die. Like the mayfly, this new formed life will follow the arc of the sun and as it sets the lifeblood will drain away. To be replaced by a different breed of commuter, that will swarm over the city like a virus, devouring as it travels in an hedonistic pursuit of pleasure.

As his mind wanders, his concentration lapses and he slowly slips out of phase with the life around him. The constant flood of commuters blur as they rush past with ever increasing urgency, conversations speed-up and run together into a cacophonous babble of noise. The station concourse becomes an ever shifting river of grey and pink amongst which he is suddenly aware of other forms, moving at odds to the turmoil. These people are immune to the pace that normality leads, for they travel against the grain, ambling upstream. They are clutching possessions like secret treasure and shuffling without haste, purpose or direction, they are oblivious to the celerity around them. They are invisible to the morning's commuters, who appear not to see them, yet can magically sense their presence and effortlessly avoid touching. He knows he has seen these people before, yet in his guilt he realises that, like the commuters, he too had chosen not to. They are the city's unwanted: the city's invisibles; gravitating to its nucleus, drawn by some strange attractor for the promise of the charmed life, and on finding an empty nothing they bond together in Valence name. He continues to watch the melee as he sees a single figure confidently striding between commuters and invisibles alike, leaving a wake of bewilderment as it passes. The figure is cutting a direct path towards him, his heart skips and sinks. He knows he is about to meet an Angel. Again.

...Moving swiftly through the realm, the Shadow follows traces, searching for clues. And with all the senses and perceptions at its disposal it filters and analyses each and every disturbance and anomaly with precision and care. Each time the Shadow approaches an irregularity it moves away, repelled or repulsed, the two cannot touch. There is a power at work, a primeval power. A power equal to its own, but in every way imaginable, an opposite...

With the routine drudgery borne on countless days of repetition part 'B19283' fits into sub-assembly 'A19340' by inserting flange 'C' into mortise 'D' and is locked in place by a three-quarter counter clockwise twist of part 'B19283'. Item 'C19284' is attached with two crosshead screws from bin 'K12' using the No.2 screwdriver and secured using a single dab of the red locking compound on each screw head. The assembly is then placed on the conveyor belt in the first available space and the next assembly is started. According to the Company, this process takes, on average, exactly 19 seconds. Each employee must assemble a minimum of 170 units per hour, if productivity drops below this level then disciplinary action will be taken. If an employee fails to reach the daily target of 2,000 units then their wages will be docked a full days pay. Sam has been working on the line for three months and he is happy, he likes working inside, away from the rain. He takes pride in his work. He has never been disciplined and always takes home the full ¥$12 at the end of the week. Sam dreams of becoming the line supervisor. A position of respect, his six older brothers would not look down on him then. When Sam dreams he slows down, but since he can assemble a unit in 17 seconds he can afford small dreams.

...To the Shadow such things do not make sense, there is no logic or reason it can apply to explain it. Such distortions were against nature and by that were dangerous.

The Shadow feels threatened and vulnerable this close to so many tears in the Darqness. These feelings are alien to it, which is even more disturbing. It feels the need to head away from hinterlands, towards the centre of the Darqlands and safety. But first there is a much more pressing task to undertake...

From it's vantage point on the highest satellite dish on the tallest building, a raven casts a steely eye over the city. Ever watchful, ever vigilant, it is poised, ready to swoop on the weak, the dying and the lame. The city looks the same as it did yesterday, the same as it did the day before. It looks the same as it ever did, but even the raven is aware that something is not quite as it should be. It can detect the subtle changes in the wind, the flow of the river and the smell of life milling through the streets. The raven sits in silent contemplation, musing on the slight imbalances that disrupt the harmony. Then, as if heeding a far calling, it cocks its head to the wind and answers with a single "Kronkk!" before alighting from its roost. Swooping low over the roof tops it spies a collection of offal pilled high in plastic bins at the rear of a butchers, ripe and inviting. However, the raven chooses to ignore this prize offering and instead turns towards the grey topped building in the neighbouring street. It circles and spirals on thermals from the warming rooves, rising far above the city, higher than it would normally go. Once it has reached the cloud-base, it banks to the east and heads towards the decaying industrial belt.

Page Four: Reservoir Corvidae

...As a hunter, the Shadow was not fond of the scavengers, but they were tolerated because it needed them and used them. They, for their part were handsomely rewarded by the carrion that littered the Darqlands and were eager to assist if an easy lunch was involved. Even so, the pact was an uncomfortable one, borne out of necessity...

'So, are we a murder?' Asked the Jackdaw, scanning around the disused warehouse, eyeing his fellow conspirators with a single pale and beady eye. The Rook stared back with the measured aloofness the Jackdaw had come to expect and obviously had no intention of acknowledging the question. The little Chough was keep look-out by the window, while hooking ants from peeling paintwork with its flashy red bill, and acting like it really didn't want to be there. The narcissistic Jay was too busy preening to even partake in the conversation and fastidiously arranged and rearranged its feathers. The Magpie was clearly agitated and giving out signals that it more interested in plucking out the Jackdaw's tiny, irritating, little white eye to consider an answer. The Crow, however, was also getting impatient.

'Not 'till the Raven gets here.'

'And where the fuck is the Raven?'

'Quoth the Raven, 'Neverwhere'.' Deliberately miss-quoted the Jay, looking up from cleaning the electric blue feathers on its left wing.

'Eh?' Inquired the Crow, more than a little puzzled by the Jay's sudden out burst.

'Poe.' Was all the Jay offered in reply and turned to preen the right wing.

'Eh?' Inquired the Crow.

'Edgar Alan Poe, The Raven.' Snapped the Magpie, feeling even more irritated as the conversation took this mindless detour into the nether regions of the Crow's missing education.

'The Raven's called Edgar Alan Poe! Well I never, in all my years,' The Crow was off, there was no stopping him now, 'all this time I've been calling him 'Raven' and he's really 'Edgar'. I never had him down as an 'Edgar' though. Well fuck me sideways I never knew that, you could knock me down with a fea-'

'I'll fucking knock you fucking down with more than a fucking feather in a fucking minute mate, if you don't fucking shut the fuck up!' Interrupted the Magpie. Magpie was getting aggressive, its head bobbing from left to right like a prize-fighter squaring up for the killer punch. 'Edgar Alan Poe was a writer,' (bob to the left), 'he wrote a poem called 'The Raven'' (duck to the right), 'and all the fucking Raven can say is Never-fucking-more.' A sharp forward jab punctuated the final syllable, his jet black beak just missing the Crow's eye. The Crow reeled back in surprise.

'But he said 'Neverwhere'.' The Crow nodded his head in the direction of the Jay, who had since moved away from the crowd and was now picking ants with the Chough. 'The Jay said 'Neverwhere', not 'Nevermore'.'

'Nevertheless, the Raven said 'Nevermore', not 'Neverwhere' - it's in the poem...'Once upon a midnight dreary ... blah-blah-blah... Quoth the Raven, 'Nevermore'.'!'

'Cor.' Said the Crow.

''Balls.' Said Milligan.' The Rook, with a self satisfied smug grin, hopped back several paces, well out of Magpie's reach.

'Eh?' The Crow ducked as the Magpie lunged forward again.

'Puckoon, a book written by a human called Spike Milligan.' Said the Jackdaw, wishing that he'd never started this conversation. That set the Crow off again.

'Someone wrote a book about me once, well it wasn't a real book, it was a comic, well not a comic comic, but you know, one of those graphic novel things, well I suppose that's still a book though, anyway, it's real gory with loads of shootin' and stuff and they made it into a really brilliant film, except the bloke who everyone thinks is the crow, but isn't 'cos I am, gets k-'

'Can't you keep your fucking beak shut!' The Magpie cut in mid-sentence.

'Oh...' The Crow was well aware that the Magpie would not miss every time, so it did as it was told.

'So, what's his fucking problem?' Whispered the Jackdaw to the Rook.

'He always was one for sorrow' Quipped the Rook, a little too loudly, and the Magpie responded with its 'So don't fuck with me' glare. With that they all dropped into silence and stood there, waiting, looking at the ground and trying to avoid the Magpie's stare.

A tapping noise disturbed the uneasy silence. They all froze, then looked towards the sound. Fearing they had been trapped, they searched for a means of escape, but the door was the only egress and that was exactly where the knocking was coming from. The Jay was the first to speak.

'While I nodded, nearly napping, suddenly there came a tapping.'

- then the Jackdaw picked up the next line..

'As some one gently rapping, rapping at my chamber door.'

''Tis some visitor,' I muttered, 'tapping at my chamber door -'.'

- added the Rook,

'Only this and nothing more.'

- finished the Chough as the door swung open and in walked the Raven.

With barely a flutter of its wings it flew across the warehouse and settled amongst the crowd. Standing half as tall again as the Magpie, it towered over the ensemble, clearly their undisputed leader.

'Hello Edgar.' Said the Crow, seconds before the Magpie laid him unconscious with a swift peck to the back of the head. The Raven surveyed the scene, instantly assessing the possible causes of such an action before nodding to the Magpie and announcing.

'Okay Gentlemen, let's go to work'.

...And so it was, and so it would ever be. Such was the way of scavengers. With their task set into action, the Shadow can now head back to the Darqlands, to the centre. The Heart of the Darqlands, where Shadows are converging: to bicker and argue as disparate entities; That will congregate and assemble into cadres and cliques; Which will form and coagulate into factions and cabals; To finally merge and meld into a unified whole...

Page Five: Heart of Ancients

You have an ancient heart, the Watchmaker had told her as he reluctantly returned the gold coin to her grubby, outstretched hand. They had sat on a bench between the bridge and the theatre, overlooking the oily brown river as it sludged passed, where she now sat alone. The Watchmaker was one of the wise, he had the wisdom of years encrusted in the lines on his face. He was the first casualty of the silicon age and it had taken twenty years of destitution to carve those lines. She had brought the coin to him because of all the people she knew, he was the only one she truly trusted. Even then, as soon as the coin dropped into his shaking hands, she felt an overwhelming desire to snatch it back. And desire was the word he used to describe the coin. Although he had never seen its like before and could not even guess at its value, he concluded that it was desirable, very desirable indeed. It was the look in his usually rheumy eyes that disturbed her, a look she had never seen when she had brought him trinkets to value before. A look of greed that bordered on pure lust. She could not break eye contact as she held out her hand for the coin's return, for fear that he would disappear if she looked away. He continued to stare back, his pupils contracted to pin-pricks as they bored into hers. She felt like he was reading her, scanning her soul, searching for a reason to keep the coin for himself. Then he blinked as if startled and his features instantly softened as he carefully placed the coin in her palm.

'You have an ancient heart and this is ancient gelt. Keep it and it will keep you.' At that he stood up and walked towards the bridge, leaving her on the bench with more questions than she had arrived with.

...The Darqlands are infinite, but it still takes a finite time for the Shadow to travel from the fringes to its centre. A time that rewinds the linear time of reality so that at the Heart of the Darqlands there is no time at all. This is the most ancient place of all, the place where all time starts. As it travels back the Shadow can feel both its mass and energy increasing in a perverse distortion of Einstein's theory. Other Shadows that have been hunting in other parts of the Waking Lands are returning with their accounts of the threat to the Darqness. With each second that un-ticks another piece of the Shadow reconnects and another piece of information is added to its collective memory...

Meeting with an Angel was never what he expected it to be and, euphoria aside, it is not something he wanted to repeat. However, once again, he had no choice, when a Messenger chooses to talk to you, you do not get the option to refuse. He cannot remember leaving the station, or how they got back to his office, but now he is seated behind his desk watching the tall figure move around his office. The Angel is easily over two meters and without question superbly graceful, its face is thin with high cheekbones and a slightly hooked nose above a sensuous mouth. The Angel, carefully avoiding the mess on the floor, examines his reproduction antiques with more than a little disdain and finally stops by the sign painted on his glass door.

'Flip Mallow, Pirate Instigator. What is that supposed to mean?'

'It means, if you employ a dyslexic sign writer, don't take the piss out of his affliction.'

'Hmm,' The Angel crossed the room and seated himself on the chair in front of the desk before continuing, 'and the Eye of Horus?'

'A little joke.' Then noticing the Angels hawk-like features makes him wince and instantly regret saying that.

'Funny?' Enquires the Angel.

'I guess not.' There is a pause as the Angel waits for the moment to pass.

'Well Flip,'

'Actually, it's Philip.'

'Yes I know. That was my little joke. Well Philip, I understand you have met one of our kind before?' It asks with a comforting smile that is measured to have the same effect as a truth serum. However, Philip is far from comfortable, and far from relaxed. He has a guilty feeling in his stomach and an electric taste in his mouth, as if he had been caught doing something he should not have been doing. Was it a sin to make love to an Angel? Has this one come to exact retribution? He does not like this Angel's attitude and does not have a good feeling about telling the truth, never the less, he feels compelled to.

'Err, yes.' He hesitantly replies.

'We want you to find him for us.' That smile again.

'Her.' Philip blurts out.

'Pardon?' The Angel looks at him, a quizzical look replacing the disarming smile.

'Her, you said 'him', she was most definitely female I can assure you.'

'Yes.' The Angel draws the word out, letting it hang in the air for several seconds before continuing. 'I am certain you can. Him/her, whatever, it does not matter. As I said, we would like you to find 'her' for us.' Again that smile. He feels a little sick, it matters to him that she was a she. Suppressing the thoughts that were starting well up, he turns his attention back to the unusual request from this Messenger.

'Why do you want me to find her?'

'Because.' The Angel shifts slightly on the chair, it is now its turn to be uncomfortable. 'He,' The Angel throws him a knowing look, 'sorry... *she*,' another drawn-out word, 'has gone a little, shall we say, freelance and is creating all manner of problems. Since you know her, it should not be too difficult for you to find her.'

Philip leans forward, rests his elbows on the desk and stares hard at the seated figure opposite. Yes, even he can see it now, this is one very worried Angel.

...At the Heart of the Darqlands, the Shadow rapidly formed the intelligence gathered into a feeling. With this feeling, the Shadow could make deductions and speculations. Through interpolation and extrapolation it could turn these into plans and schemes. Empowered with this knowledge, the Shadow could now return to the Waking Lands prepared for the inevitable...

'So, things are a little tense in Heaven then.' Smirks Philip, feeling that for once he has the upper hand.

'Oh probably.' Alarmingly, the Angel relaxes, the balance shifts as it sits back in the chair and returns the smirk. 'I have not been in that forsaken place for quite some time.'

Page Six: People who Lunch

...the Darqlands were being eating away, consumed in small pieces; chewed and nibbled by an unseen hunger. The Shadow and the Darqness fed on Despair, and now something was feeding off them. As the souls escaped from the Darqlands, they took their Despair with them, leaving the Darqness famished. Like a voracious fledgling with its mouth agape for a constant supply of food, it implored the Shadow for sustenance. Its hunger urged the Shadow to return to the Waking Lands to replenish the dwindling Despair...

She had rapidly lost interest in events and conversations at her own table and was soaking up the atmosphere from adjacent tables. The restaurant was a buzz with noise, an avant-garde melody of chinking glasses and clattering cutlery that sang over a symphony of voices rising and falling in a babble of concurrent conversations. Staff dressed alike in black silk and denim, arms laden with plates of steaming food, or trays of mutlicoloured glasses filled with mutlicoloured cocktails, effortlessly pirouetted between the tables. At the bar, clutches of people met and parted with air-kisses and faux-hugs, carefully avoiding disruption to their pristine make-up and fine tailored clothes, before being guided to their reserved tables by an equally reserved Maitre'D. At small tables near the walls discreet couples practised their illicit intimacies within the unspoken restriction of eye contact alone. Their need to be secretive defeating their desire to be together as conversations dropped to clipped whispers of frustration and sweet-nothings gave way to sweet-nothing. While at larger central tables, groups engaged in the rituals of bonding were free from this guilt. Individuals exchanged morsels on fork-tips with the person sitting next to them, with tender offerings they fed each other, guided by a primeval instinct of sharing. Intimacies were openly proclaimed as finger-tips casually touched on arms or brushed faces in nonchalant friendship and heads touched heads in knowing laughter. With others, playful exchanges of risqué remarks between couples where loaded with coded messages, testing for the promise of something more. While her mind was focused on these scenes, Ashiya idly pushed the beautifully presented scraps of monkfish around her plate, her hunger for food replaced by a stronger desire.

No longer content with being a casual observer, she was slowly being drawn to the courtship rituals being displayed on the other tables. She was beginning to feel the need to participate in the game and yearned for the thrill of the chase. With predatory eyes, she searched for a suitable victim. She had already shared some degree of intimacy with most of the people she was dining with: longing kisses; passionate dances; nights of bliss and on one occasion, an erotic threesome. Yet they would not provide that tingle of the first tentative touch from an unknown lover that she desired. Of those she had not seduced, none appealed. She scanned the adjoining tables, most were filled with groups and couples but at one sat a lone girl, who Ashiya felt certain had been looking directly at her. Ashiya's eyes lingered on the girl's youthful body longer than is polite as non-verbal communication passed between them. Even though the possibility of sapphistic pleasures appealed, she felt the need for someone older and more experienced so broke the contact. Trapped within the social confines of her circle of lunchtime friends, she would have to wait until later to find someone to sate her appetite.

...the Shadow began the journey...

The girl sat on a small back-street vegetarian restaurant with the proceeds of yesterdays' sales clutched in one hand and the gold coin in the other. She had carefully scrutinised the menu and selected the cheapest and most filling meal she could afford. The staff here where kind without being condescending and did not appear to mind her presence, occasionally. Having cleaned herself in the toilets of a nearby department store and dabbed a couple of spots of cK-one from the testers on the perfume counter (under the constant watch of a floor-walker), she at least felt presentable. Even then as she sat in the darkest corner she was self consciously aware of everyone looking at her. To ease herself she took a sip at the glass of Coke, 'One-eighty for a soft-drink!', she though, 'I had to sell three crappy magazines for that and that one little sip was probably cost me 10-pages'. As she put the glass down she noticed a smudge of grime on the back of her hand that had missed the washing. Wiping a finger up the condensation on the glass, she rubbed away the smudge with the wet finger just as the waitress arrived with the largest bowl of steaming pasta she had seen for quite some time. The aroma of garlic and basil was intense, the shreds of pasta gleamed with olive-oil and tomato sauce and where slowly being buried as the waitress piled on layer after layer of parmesan cheese, waiting for the girl to say 'When'.

...slowly winding out time from the Heart of the Darqlands...

Feathers and scraps of flesh litter the grass as the Raven picks over the remains of a scrawny city pigeon. How the pigeon became lunch is of no concern to the Raven. It was probably the result of successful hunt by a one of the many cats that patrol the parklands. The Raven had nothing but disdain for cats. It was not because they presented a threat, the cat had not been born who was the match of the Raven. No, it was their callous waste of life that angered, killing for the pleasure and not for survival.

... slowly its mass and energy return to their normal levels...

What the fuck does that thing eat? Thought Philip, as he spat out another mouthful of dust encrusted cobweb. On hands and knees in the narrow crawl-space between eaves and loft, he was looking for the shoe box he had hidden there several years ago. Not normally afraid of spiders, well not afraid of normal ones anyway, the thought had been instigated when an extremely large specimen walked across his hand. Phillip froze. The house-spider was the largest he had seen of any kind outside a glass tank and one he had voiced the desire not to meet some moments back, as he crawled through its large and sticky cobweb. Undeterred by his hand, the spider continued on its away into the darkness and Philip continued on his, still pondering the possible sources of nourishment for such a monster. And what happens to all that spider-crap? He thought, After all, spiders must defecate and the shit must go somewhere.

Then he remembered the gritty taste of the mouthful of cobweb earlier and spat again. Apart from the spider incident, locating and retrieving the box was easy enough. Later, still covered in webs and dust, he sat at the kitchen table where he began to remove the wrappings of yellowed newspaper, followed by layers of oiled cloth to reveal the craftsmanship of a double barrelled 4-10 pistol. Barely ten inches in length, this was not the crude butchering of a sawn-off, but a purpose made weapon, designed for the gentleman farmer to dispatch vermin. Its compactness proved it to be highly popular with poachers as another tool of their trade, later it attracted the criminal elements for similar reasons, which lead to it final being outlawed. It was claimed the gun had been used in a notorious east-end gang war, but he had also heard that it had just been used it for poaching rabbits and recently only for taking pot-shots at rats by the dock-side. Philip had never fired it himself and was not sure he even knew how to. He also doubted it would be that effective against ethereal beings, even if he could get any silver buck-shot, if that is what was needed. Holding the weapon at arms length he took pretend shots at the door and various pots and pans around the kitchen, blasting away imaginary Angels as they infringed on his life. The without thinking, he slipped the barrel into his mouth, to taste the cold metal on his tongue and to imagine the effect of pulling the twin triggers. Suddenly realising what he was doing, he carefully removed the gun from between his lips and broke it open to reveal two cartridges still in place. Shaking, he pulled the brass end-cap of the first to remove it from the barrel. The rotted cardboard of the cartridge crumbled to dust and shot and gunpowder scattered across the table. The second had suffered the same fate and its contents added to the mess. After a very stiff drink of brandy, he re-wrapped the gun and place it back into its box. Through a combination of fear, inability and his own morals, he knew he could not use the damn thing. It was too illegal to own and even more illegal, if not dangerous, to sell. He did not really want it to end up in the hands of the kind of people who would buy it, only to come face to face with it one night in some dark alley. Whenever the police announced an armistice on offensive weapons, he was always too scared to hand it in just in case they decided to ask questions, or worse still - put him under surveillance. Depressed, Philip pushed the box into the middle of the table and resigned himself to hiding it back in the attic.

...slowly it moves forward through time to the present where it can sublimate the boundary into the Waking Lands...

The grease-proof paper crackled as Sam hurriedly unwrapped his lunch in the cramped room that served as the factory's canteen, rest room and coat-room. Often he would eat his lunch in the carpark, but today he was missing his quota and needed to eat quickly to return to work to catch up. He had daydreamt again. This time of his plans to send off for a wife. His six uncles would make all the arrangements, their wives would choose the perfect wife for him and use her dowry to smuggle her into the country. Then, at last someone to look after him, someone to prepare is lunch. But first he had save enough money and the only way he could do that was to become line-supervisor.

...effortlessly, the Shadow entered the city and fuelled with an increasing hunger, was ready to dispense with codes and rules...

Page Seven: Siesta

...nestling deep with the warming comfort of a downy bed, a supine shape dreams of early lives and lives to come. The dream spills out into the Ether, permeating the thoughts and day-dreams of souls at resonance. Connecting souls to souls in a network of tuned harmony, it envelopes the city, brooding and nurturing its children...

Languishing in the heat of midday, an over-fed cat curls amongst musty books and papers in the rear of an antiques flea market. Lazily it licks at the bush of its tail as it rests across it's fore-paws, then content that it has at least made a token effort of cleanliness, it dozes. With half it's senses still poised in readiness for flight should it be disturbed, the other half drifts into sleep and the feline realm of Bast. For in this domain the cat lives its life in a nether world of dream and spirit, where all manner of cats live and thrive in fellowship and unity with the ancient wisdom of Bast, Maldet and Diana. The domestic cat is on equal status with its feral cousins and they in turn the peer of the larger cats. And here, other spirits with cat-like souls can come and go as they please. As it enters the realm, the cat is aware of a non-feline, yet familiar presence reaching out to greet it. This spirit is far from equal, for it can command the cat, and the cat will obey through love and respect. The cat moves towards the spirit and soon is joined by others who have heeded the call. Before long, every cat in the city has gathered to hear the Sphinx spin its riddles. It tells them stories of times long ago, and prophecies of times to come. It warns of perils and danger in the city. It reminds them of deeds they have done and of duties they must now undertake. With a purring voice it rallies and musters the cats then sends them back into the Waking Lands.

...'Take care my chosen.' ...

Waking, the cat stretches and yawns before spring up and racing out of the door. Into the yard and off over the wall the cat enters the backstreet where it joins with other cats from the shops and houses in the neighbourhood. The group streams down the road to meet more groups from other streets. En masse, the horde pour through the streets and arcades, bounding over the crawling afternoon traffic and between of legs of astonished shoppers. Guided by the spirit of the Sphinx, the cats head towards the common land. They have a mission. As does every cat in the city.

...'Beware my chosen.' ...

Back at its roost on the highest satellite dish on the tallest building the Raven is as ever watchful. As ever vigilant, it has no time to rest as it surveys the cityscape. It felt the darkness as it slipped into the light and knows why it stalks the city. With it's keen eyes, it has seen the cats pour from the houses and into the streets and parklands, it can sense they have a purpose and feels certain that it will affect him. But the Corvidae too have a task to perform and the Raven is honour bound to ensure it is done.

...'Danger is close.' ...

Chapter Two: Asarte

Page Eight: Market Forces

The market was a constant noise of activity punctuated by shouts from the stall-holders. The urgency of their calls adding colour to the dullest of the mundane, offers too good to miss on goods to tacky to own. Philip wove a route through the crowds, by-passing china at knock-down prices and forgoing solid gold watches at less than retail. For a short while he was trapped by the audience at a mock-auction of electrical wares, unable to force his way through he stood and soaked up the barkers banter with the crowd, a near endless stream of...

'I'm not askin' twenny for this superb personal stereo, I'm not even asking fifteen. See it plays all yer 'holos' - yer discs, yer spheres an' yer cubes, in fact there ain't a polygon been invented that this baby won't play. Look, up the West-end youse be payin' over fifty for this little lot, but (an' believe me this is costin' me money, but youse seem a decent lot an' I had a good night at the cyber-dogs yest'dy), I'm going to throw in this high quality pair of 'eadjacks abso-bloody-lutely free and on top of that youse get the personal stereo all for twelve-fifty, no? Okay, yer breakin' me bleedin'art, a tenner and it's all yours. No, wait-up, tell youse what, Joe, 'ave we got any of them electro'ganisers left? Yeah? What Five? Right, youse get yer personal stereo an' high quality pair o'jacks and the first five to get yer money ready get an electro'ganiser thrown in all for a tenner. Okay Joe, that gentleman over there would like one an' this lady wants two...'

Boxes and money changed hands as more and more punters fell for the auctioneers' showmanship. Philip counted twenty of bundles of crude eastern-European packaging sold in the first minute and not one of them contained the fabled electronic organiser. By then the crowd had pushed forward, leaving a narrow gap he could just squeeze through, so soon he was clear of the stall and back on course.

...the Shadow too moved through the crowd, sensing and feeling the souls of the shoppers as they moved from stall to stall. Every now and then it would detect faint traces of despair, not strong enough to ensnare, but showing enough promise for it to tag them for later. Most of these taggings were easy: a dropped purse, missing keys, money spirited out of wallets. Then there were a couple that gave the Shadow's skill more of a challenge...

The Watchmaker was sat on one upturned crate with his tools laid out on a second crate in front of him. Each afternoon he sat there, within sight of the shop he once owned at the back of the market. Over the years successive market superintendents had heard of his story from the other stall holders, so turned a blind-eye to the Watchmaker's un-licensed pitch. Each afternoon he set up shop and a small trickle of people brought him mechanical clocks and watches to repair. Whether through eccentricity or alcohol induced senility, he charged them the price he would have charged twenty years ago and if anyone was foolish enough to place an electronic watch into his hand, he would growl and throw it into the gutter. Philip approached and held up a large gold coin.

'Mr. Small?' the Watchmaker looked up and there was a faint hint of recognition in his eyes, then he saw the coin and his eyes sparkled, reflecting the sunlight as it bounced off the coin into his face. 'I'm looking for someone.' Philip stated, smiling down at the Watchmaker. 'Have you seen one of these before?'

'Might have done,' his head dropped, and he started to fumble with the tools on the crate, trying to look disinterested in the shining gold coin, 'might not.' The Watchmakers non-committal reply was too late, Philip could tell that he had. He dropped a couple of crumpled notes onto the crate, which the Watchmaker carefully smoothed out so the sovereigns face could be seen. His fingers hesitated over the money, Philip knew that one of the notes would by a sizeable bottle of scotch and for all his eccentricity, the Watchmaker knew it too. Then he shook his head and pushed the money away. 'She's a good kid, she ain't done no wrong.' Philip crouched down to the Watchmakers' level and pushed the notes back.

'I only want to talk to her.' He looked into the old man's eyes, he wanted to tell him more, but could not. The old man was bordering on reality as it was and tales of Angels would undoubtedly tip him over the edge. If that happened, then Philip would get nothing but incoherent ramblings. He continued to look at the Watchmaker, but old man said nothing and just looked back into Philips eyes. 'Look, I'm a collector and I will pay good money for another one of these.' Philip lied as he slipped the coin back into the safety of his pocket, still the old man did not answer. Then the Watchmaker gave a startled blink and said.

'You have an ancient heart and carry ancient gelt. I cannot help you.' Philip cursed under his breath and stood up. He snatched the money from the crate and held it out to the Watchmaker. The Watchmaker ignored him and started to pack away his tools into their soft leather roll.

'Cannot, or will not?' Philip asked with annoyance in his voice as the old man stood and started to shuffle away. The old man stopped and looked over his shoulder.

'I cannot help you.' He said and walked away.

Page Nine: S & F

...the Shadow was quietly content. It sensed that the last two souls were special and the seeds of Despair it planted would soon germinate. Their Despair would grow and ripen. Then it would be ready to harvest. The Shadow left the Market, fleetingly touching more souls as it did...

The commissionaire greeted her by name as she approached the shop and with an overtly theatrical grand gesture, he unlocked and swept open the ornate door for her to enter. Inside, the cold polished marble in warm rust colours glowed with an autumnal radiance amongst the heavily gilded Romanesque decor. The sales area was flooded with contradictions. Translucent strands of gossamer fabric were draped over large blocks of roughly hewn stone in displays that would not look out of place in one of the near by galleries of Modern Art. Ashiya knew without looking, that the price tickets on the garments also had art gallery pretensions. The crisply dressed shop assistants stood unobtrusively by, motionless and emotionless, she knew they would not approach her unless she wanted them to. Through an unwritten rule, discretion and a tradition of aloof servitude, the assistants seldom spoke and never looked directly at a customers face. Ashiya strolled around the displays, touching and disturbing the clothes as she passed, she also knew an assistant would follow discreetly behind to retouch and rearrange them. Within half an hour, she had mentally selected several items, normally she would have taken longer and selected more, but the day had an air of urgency and this was only a diversion. Without having to call or signal, an assistant appeared by her side just as she finished, (their unfailing ability to read her body language always impressed and amused her). She was shown into the changing room, a large space furnished with two chaise-longues, an antique dressing table, several long gilded mirrors and a low table with fine china and a freshly made pot of coffee on a silver tray. The assistant poured the coffee and left. Before she had even sipped at the steaming cup, another assistant entered with the exact garments she had chosen. She never had to indicate which clothes she wanted to try on. The assistants' skill and training could instantly tell those she liked and those she did not. On several occasions she had tried to catch them out, pretending to take an interest in something she did not want, but she never succeeded. The assistant carefully laid-out the clothes, meticulously arranging them like precious works of art. When she had finished, the girl hesitantly turned to Ashiya and smiled. Ashiya smiled back and felt as if she had broken a sacred taboo. They continued to look at each other, not speaking yet relaying a clear message between themselves, but before anything else happened, or could happen, the girl smiled again and left. Unsettled, Ashiya spent another thirty minutes trying on the clothes in different combinations, without being able to decide which to buy, but finally deciding to take them all.

...from the Market to the high-rise tower blocks of the inner city. Never easy, the Despair always protected by an urban resilience forged from years of living on the border-line. But there are possibilities, fragments where the resistance is wearing thin, chinks in the armour of grim determination. The Shadow flows through the buildings seeking and probing through the concrete and steel. There is a soul, Despair tearing into its heart, images of suicide and death permeate its being - the Shadow strikes. Screaming and wailing, the soul wrenched from its corporeal host and is pushed into the Darqlands...

The conveyer-belt never ceased, gaps appeared, but it never stopped. Bin 'K12' ran empty of screws, but the belt kept moving. Red locking compound spilled over the work-surface, covered his hands and the No.2 Screwdriver, but the belt rumbled relentlessly on. Productivity dropped to 180 and he made mistakes. Then 170 and more mistakes, 160, still the belt moved on. His error-rate increased as his work-rate decrease. His hands were not his own - like a demon had removed his fingers and put them back in a different order. Components littered the floor at his feet, the faster he tried to work the more clumsy he became. The No. 2 Screwdriver slips. A deep gouge is ripped into the flesh at the base of his thumb. From panic and pain, beads of perspiration ran in rivulets into his eyes. He wiped them back with his hand, leaving smears of red locking compound and blood. His life rolled passed on the conveyer-belt, all he could do was watch his dreams disintegrate and his world collapse. Tears of grief mixed with the sweat, grime and locking compound streaked his face and T-shirt. The collapsing world spun, mocking him as he crashed to the ground.

...success breeds success. The Shadow ripped through the congested sweat-shops that packed the back-streets of the city. Row upon row of small factories of misery and mass production with Despair as a waste-product. In each factory, soul after soul was torn from desolate hearts and sent into the Darqlands...

She was sure some kind of magic was at work. She had sold her entire stock of magazines in an hour, more than she usually sold in a week. Rather than sitting crouched in a doorway waiting for people to buy a paper, she was on her feet, thrusting copies at people, urging them to buy instead of begging. Magazines and money changes hands with a smile and heart-felt thanks. Instead of mumbling and hurrying away, buyers asked how she was and wished her luck, some even gave her more than the cover price. Probably, she thought, this was because she looked less pathetic, having been fed and looking moderately clean. May be, it because she looked like someone just temporarily down on her luck rather than one of the flotsam of life. But just possibly, it was something to do with the heavy gold coin nestling in the secret pocket in her underwear. With nothing left to sell, and buoyed up with renewed self confidence, she had purchased an second supply and these too were shifted faster than proverbial hot cakes. Within the hour, having sold them all, she had to convert some of the coins into notes, to decrease their weight and bulk and to make her less vulnerable to the more desperate inhabitants of the cities under-life. On her way back to get more copies, she even bought a magazine from another girl huddled on the steps of the Underground station and then sold it on to a passing commuter. She felt alive and invincible and for the first time, in control of her destiny.

...even as the Shadow sent souls hurtling into the Darqlands, it knew the tears were still there and they would slip back. But not immediately, in their disorientation they would remain long enough for their Despair to feed the Darqness...

Page Ten: With Pride and due prejudice

The Raven caught the stench, for senses attuned to the rotting decay of carrion, the pervading sweet smell was repugnant - the scent of something benign invading the city. It relayed the message to the Rook, who passed it in to the others. Even without the Raven's ability they could sense its presence, they had already detected it and where agitated. They had not expected a force of such power and intensity. Like a thick fog, it pervaded every part of the city, covering everything so they could not locate its source.

...deep in the dreamlands, the Sphinx controlled the battle, directing and manoeuvring through the network. The Corvidae were arrogant and bellicose, but easy to track. Spirits of lion and tiger aided the instincts of the domestic and feral city cats, empowering them with the skill to hunt with stealth and as a pride.

The cats prowled and stalked the parklands and wastelands. In groups of ten or more, all over the city hundreds of cats were mobilised in the hunt. This was no longer play, this had purpose. In the central park, one group soon rounded on the Jay, pouncing before it had time for flight. In a frenzy, they tore the creature limb from limb, ripping its brightly coloured feathers from pale pink flesh, then deep red muscle from translucent white bone until all that was left was the litter of blue feathers on the red stained grass. By a converted warehouse by the rivers' edge, the Jackdaw was standing its ground, its broken wing hanging limply by its side. The bodies of two cats lay before it, blood streaming from their punctured eye-sockets. They too had caught him by surprise, but the ferocity of his fight had caused them to retreat and regroup. The cats circled the Jackdaw as it hopped and lunged at any cat who came too close. Slowly they herded it towards the wall of the warehouse, where two cats lay on a window-ledge, waiting. The Chough, now aware that its life was in danger, chose to leave the city and headed for the coast. The Rook also tried to leave the city, but met its fate at the motorway flyover, where the pincer movement of two groups of cats caused it to take flight into the path of an oncoming juggernaut. Alerted, the Magpie and Crow stayed airborne, circling over the city observing the fate of the others.

...the Sphinx returned to Bast's realm to summon the spirits of Jaguar and Leopard to join the fight. These too were sent into the network, to merge with the spirits of the city cats, to seek out and destroy the remaining enemy...

As the evening approached, the Crow began to tire. Cautiously it flew over the steeply pitched slate roof of an austere building, close to a city square filled with pigeons. The presence of the pigeons indicated that there were no cats around. However the Crow took no chances and passed over the building several times before deciding it was safe. As it alighted on the apex of the roof, a small grey tabby sprang from the cover of a raised sky-light and landed on the Crow's back. Extended claws dug into its flesh as sharp teeth sank into its neck. The Crow leaped and tried to shake the cat free, but lost its footing, tumbled down the slates to bounce over the guttering. The cat fought the instinct to save itself and clung to the Crow as it desperately tried to flap its wings. They plunged to the limestone pavement of the square, sending the pigeons to flight as they hit the ground. A dozen cats raced across the square towards the carnage. A large Persian was the first to arrive, the small grey cat had died instantly, but the Crow was still alive. Quickly the Persian ripped out its throat as it lay twitching, before crying for the Spirit of the Dead to carry its fallen sister to Bast.

...acceptable losses...

The Raven looked down from the relative safety of the preserved antiquity of the city wall. It had followed the trail back from the Corvidae through the Cats, feeling the energy pulse through the network. As each of them died the Raven got closer to the source, until the combined death of the Crow and its nemesis finally revealed the Sphinx. As it relayed the information into the darkness, the Raven became grimly aware that it too had become expendable. Below a pair of cats prowled back and forth, their eyes permanently fixed on the silhouette of the Raven. ‘Only two and never more’, thought the Raven, affording himself the luxury of a small joke.

Page Eleven: The Long Teatime of the Soul

...the enemy - cunning and cruel. The enemy - hiding in the city and destroying the Darqness. The Shadow knows its foe and knows where to find it...

The Watchmaker struggled back to his basement flat, forcing the door open against the mountain of free newspapers crammed through the letter-box and piled high in the hall. The delivery boys get paid by numbers and it's always easier to deliver them to one house than a hundred. Cursing, he kicked his way through the pile and closed the door behind him. Immediately the smell of fish and chips hit him as it permeated the hallway. Following his nose, the smell dragged him into the kitchen, where to his surprise, the girl from the embankment was sat at his table, drinking coffee from his mug.

'Sorry, I let myself in through the back.' She pointed to the poorly secured door, then slightly embarrassed, she got up moved towards the oven and retrieved a large paper-wrapped parcel. 'I've brought a fish supper, it's been keeping warm.' Depositing the parcel on the table, she ripped it open to reveal a large mound of soggy chips and two pieces of equally soggy cod. Hunger overriding his annoyance at her intrusion, he sat down and started to pick at the pile of food. Between mouthfuls, she related her good fortune in selling the magazines as he sat quietly, eating and listening. Then suddenly, she interrupted herself.

'Oh, oops! ' She stopped eating, stood up and went to the stove, 'I made coffee too.' As she poured him a mug of coffee, she asked. 'How do you take it?'

'White with.' She topped up the mug with milk and started rummaging around in the cupboards for sugar, finally finding a biscuit-tin filled with dozens of small white sachets with the familiar red and yellow 'M' logo. She passed the mug and a handful of sugar packets to him.

'Some one's looking for you.' He said, concentrating on emptying the contents of two of the sugars into his coffee and purposely avoiding looking at the girl.

'Shit!' He could not help but look up, the girl was seriously worried. 'It's not my fucking dad is it? Shit, shit, shit.' She was extremely agitated, pacing back and forth like a caged animal, ready to run at the first opportunity.

'I don't think so.' He replied, 'It's some Private Detective, may be your father sent him to look for you, but I don't think so. I tole him nothing. He had one of them coins like yours, but I tole him nothing.' She sat down, slightly calmer, but her hands were shaking as she wrapped them around her mug of coffee.

'What did he want?' She asked, her voice quivering, but tinged with a shade of anger.

'He said he wanted to talk to you, then he said he wanted to buy your coin.' He picked a chip from the crumpled paper.

'He can't have it, it's mine. You didn't tell him I had it did you?' He voice was steady and quiet, but he could tell she really wanted to scream at him.

'No, no, I said I tole him nothing and I tole him nothing. I didn't even say I knew you.' The chips were cold, but he continued to eat them.

'I've got to go. He can't have it.' She said as she got up and headed towards the door, before turning to him and adding, 'he just can't, it's mine.'

...the Shadow drifted across the city, now there was no haste, no hurry. The Raven's knowledge gave it all the time it needed. Patience would solve the problem and time was within the Shadows control. Time was just another base-element to build with. Now there was a more pressing need, gains needed to be consolidated and repairs made...

The tall, hawk-like figure stepped from a narrow doorway and walked into the evening traffic of pedestrians heading back to their homes. Sniffing the air, the Angel tested the wind for faint traces of its compatriot - it was still in the city, that much was certain. Concealment was easy for his kind, to blend into the background and disappear was first nature. They had walked among mortals undetected for tens on millennia. Solitary existences, avoiding contact with the human race and each other, had preserved and protected them. The renegade threatened this, meddling in the brief lives of these people, disturbing the balance. The renegade had assumed a female guise, at least that narrowed the search by more or less half, but further than that now relied on Mallow. Mallow was a failure: he was a failure to himself and had been a failure for the renegade. The odds were stacked, but he was a slight hope, even a dead loss can create surprises.

...guiding souls through the Darqlands, the hunter became shepherd. Disoriented and frightened, the souls whimpered and cried as they were herded deep into the darqness. Despair radiated in all directions and the Darqness grew stronger with every drop. Throughout the Darqlands, the Shadow repaired the damage caused by the Sphinx. Small rents and tears were sealed over with raw Despair, its essence fixing the torn edges with a desperate urge to grasp and cling. Larger holes in the Darqness where plugged with souls woven into its very fabric. The residual flesh of souls was torn and stretched, splinters of shattered bone pinned the hide in place as the Shadow ripped tendons and ligaments from the screaming bodies to stitch over the splits, a living patch of torment. Screaming and wailing as pulsing organs strained against taut skin, each soul was crafted by the Shadow, using threads of sinew to embroider a grotesque quilt. An undying tapestry, binding the soul to the Darqlands and the Darqness to the soul for an eternity of the damned and the depraved...

Page Twelve: Repast Riposte Re-post

Anticipating the old man's departure by the back door, Philip was surprised to see a girl leave the Watchmaker's terraced house and set off down the narrow alley between two rows of narrow back-yards. The girl walked at a near run, frequently looking over her shoulder and occasionally pushing herself away from the mosaic of larch-lap and corrugated-iron fence panels with her hand. From her agitated behaviour, he knew this was the girl who had the gold coin. He had followed the old man, knowing that he would try and warn whoever held the coin, but he never expected it to be this quick, or this easy. Now he followed the girl and the girl would lead him to the Angel.

...content in his handiwork, the Shadow took a moment for an uncharacteristic rest and to muse over its possibilities and options. The repairs where not perfect, but sufficient. This last was difficult and expensive, three souls to fill the fissure and the Despair from two more to hold it all together. However, once the major leaks had been fixed and when the problem of the Sphinx had been resolved, then it would be able to collect enough souls to rebuild the Darqlands anew...

The cat padded back to the Antiques shop, gripped by an overwhelming air of depression. Back amongst the familiarity of yellowing books, the cat slumped down in its den. Victory was not supposed to feel like this. At the centre of the conflict, adrenaline pumping, the euphoria of the chase and the kill was everything. As each of the Corvidae met its end, the power surge left the cats feeling invincible. There was no mercy, no remorse, only a primal drive to kill and vanquish. As the Rook impacted into the truck, a feral Ginger Tom had quipped something about the last thing to go through the Rook's mind was its tail. Now, the cat found nothing funny or amusing in this. Cats and the Corvidae were never enemies: cats were predators, Corvidae were scavengers. No one would claim it was a symbiotic relationship, the two just co-existed in nature, the cats killed and the crows cleaned up afterwards, but neither depended or relied upon the other. There was never animosity, never fear and never fighting. The cat had bonded with a Lion-spirit, releasing suppressed instincts from a forgotten past. Previous lives before they were tamed by the apes, lives where killing was survival, lives where a cat was not a kitten all its life. With this release, the cat became aware that this was wrong, only apes kill what they do not eat and through aeons of domestication, this is what they had become too.

...the Sphinx, an ancient foe. This was not the butchered visage of the Androsphinx of Giza, or Hieracosphinx the falcon headed usurper, or even the throttling, riddling Sphinx of Thebes defeated by Oedipus. No, this was the true Sphinx, the Watcher and the Guardian, a primeval spirit as old as the Shadows...

A spider scurried across the rough floor-boards of the attic. It does that from time to time.

...like the spider, the only riddle this Sphinx posed was 'Why?'...

The clothes arrived at her apartment by special courier within a few minutes of the specified time. With a casual indifference, Ashiya threw the packages on the bed and promptly forgot about them. Gazing out of the window towards the tower of glass and steel apartments opposite, her eyes focused on free space several meters in front of her as her mind wandered aimlessly over the city. In her imagination, the image of the shop assistant super-imposed itself on the girl she had seen in the restaurant, this double exposure then merged onto countless other images of young girls she had encountered until the composite resembled all of them and none of them. Slowly and imperceptibly, this image morphed into her own face and then vanished as a reflection in the building opposite caught her attention. Across the concrete and grass courtyard, the glass surface of the building reflected her apartment back at her. She moved her head so that the grid of frames matched, the subtle distortions in the glass bending and twisting the horizontal and vertical lines. Mesmerised, Ashiya played with the reflections, trying to see what had attracted her. In frustration at not seeing anything, she moved away from the window and went and got herself a large drink. Sitting at her large glass-topped table Ashiya stirred the ice-cubes around with her finger, the cold numbing its tip. She removed her finger from the liquid and placed it in her mouth to sucked it clean of gin and lime juice and to restore circulation and heat. Once again Ashiya found herself looking at another reflection of the building, now inverted in the glass of the table. As the sun went behind a cloud, the reflection vanished. Looking up, Ashiya could see straight into the apartment opposite. Her mouth dropped open in astonishment at the sight before her. It was as if she were looking into her own apartment. The furniture and fittings an exact mirror of hers, the layout and content of the flat mimicked hers in every detail except one. Ashiya quickly stood up, slipped off her clothes and sat down again. Smiling, she raised her glass in a toast to the occupant of the copied apartment. Now they matched perfectly.

Page Thirteen: Luck? I should be so unlucky...

...the Shadow continued plugging the holes in the Darqlands. Now the repairs where becoming more makeshift as the supply of captures souls dwindled. So it concentrated on the rips that threatened to grow wider. Perhaps a smaller Darqlands would be easier to maintain, but until now, it had never been a problem...

Philip followed the girl on foot for over an hour. She did not use buses or the underground, but chose to walk from district to district. For miles she trudged through the city, following an inconceivably complex route of twists and turns, frequently doubling back on herself and constantly looking over her shoulder to see if anyone was following. To begin with, Philip found the girls clumsy attempts to shake off an assumed stalker as amusing, her skill at being followed would never match his at following. Now it was plain irritating and he was getting tired. She had passed the same tube-station three times, each time Philip hoped she would duck inside and catch the train. He needed the rest, the thought of sitting down and enjoying the comparative comfort of a train ride seemed like heaven. But she kept walking. They hustled through crowds of busy shoppers, following close as not to loose her in the throng, close enough for Philip to catch the scent of cK-one. Other times, they travelled along near deserted streets, Philip keeping his distance and using every trick he had to blend into the background. Occasionally she darted into shops and malls and left by a different exit. A couple of times she just stopped and waited several minutes before carrying on. After and hour of these games, he felt like running up to her and shouting:

"Tag - you're it!" But he resisted. Once in exasperation, as she double backed and passed by him again, he almost grabbed her by the arm and dragged her into a café. Now, as they crossed the bridge and headed towards the derelict wastelands by the rivers edge, he wished he had. Perhaps it would have been easier just to sit her down and explain about Coins and Angels than to trek across half of the city.

...the incessant cries of the souls fed the Darqness and the Shadow could feel it grow stronger...

A myriad of thoughts raced through the girls' mind as she returned to the bender. Her only hope was to grab a handful of her most treasured possessions and leave the city. For the second time in her life she was running away. But this time she did not know where she would go, or from what she was running from. All she knew was that someone was after her coin and she could not let it go. Ducking inside the shelter, she quickly stuffed clothes and her washing gear into a small rucksack. She dragged the bedding to one side and frantically scrabbled in the hard packed dirt, first with her fingers, then with a can she had been using for a ashtray. Soon she had dug down to a small plastic container. Peeling back the lid, she peered inside to check the contents were intact. Content that nothing had been disturbed, she emptied out the contents. A small amount of 'emergency' money was quickly counted and stuffed inside the secret pocket in her knickers. Her passport, a clutch of photographs, her mothers' ring and a small notebook were crammed into the rucksack. That only left a set of keys. She sat back on her heels, holding the keys in her left hand, wondering what to do with them. These were the last link with her past, the keys to her fathers' house, his cars, his office... every key he owned. Of all the things she could taken, she knew that he would miss his keys more than anything else, more than his daughter at least. Tossing the keys into the air, she snatched them with her right hand and smiled. Crawling out of the shelter, she stood up and gave it a hard kick. The bender shook, but remained standing. Kicking it harder, she heard wood snap and the structure finally gave way, collapsing into a heap of wood, cardboard and cloth. Sadly, it did not look any different to when it was 'home'. The girl then hoisted the rucksack onto her shoulder and walked towards the waters edge. Standing square to the river, she threw the keys with all her might, only to hear them land with a dull thud in the soft mud. Then she realised the tide was out.

...strength, the Shadow needed the Darqlands to be strong. It would need strong Darqness to confront the Sphinx, to overpower and crush it. The Shadow laboured on, meticulously patching the Darqlands...

The Magpie caught a glint of something sparkling in the deep brown mud of the river. The temptation to swoop down and thieve the keys was great, but the fear of being trapped by the cats was greater. Safe in its temporary roost of a disused and rusting dockyard crane the Magpie was happy, though far from content, to watch the keys slip into the soft mud and disappear.

...the Shadow was reduced to its last soul. A sad and pathetic specimen, scrawny and cowering, reeking of piss and oil, its hands and face covered in a sticky red mess. The Shadow was dismayed at the quality of souls these days. This wretch had neither the energy nor will to enter a state of true Despair, it just sat there resigned to its fate, huddling its knees and whimpering. Perhaps that was the problem, the Waking Lands grew more like the Darqlands with each cycle, there was not enough Hope to convert into Despair. This soul was as good as useless for repairs and far too feeble to feed to the Darqness. With an ethereal sigh, the Shadow sent the forlorn soul deeper into the Darqlands. This soul probably thought it was lucky to be saved the grisly fate of being torn limb from limb to seal the Darqlands, but the Shadow had a special use for this one..

Page Fourteen: Segue

Rainbow Warriors

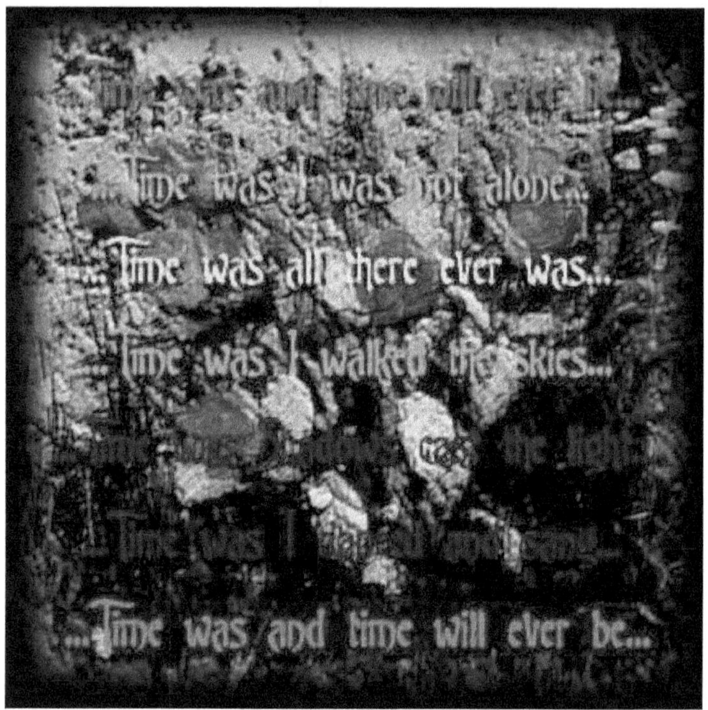

Chapter Three: Absinthium

Page Fifteen: Prime-time

The television trailed a constant flow of advertisements and news reports, the styles mixing and blurring so that it was impossible to tell one from the other. Sharp punchy reportage to sell soap powder, glitzy graphics and juicy sound-bites to sell world events. The main feature, a long forgotten war in a long forgotten country, was not moving: poor marketing and bad PR failed to stimulate buyers and sellers alike. In the studio, a debate on how the market had become saturated, stifled by public indifference to the suffering and carnage. Around a virtual table, computer-generated experts discussed how arms traders and dealers recognised the downward trend long ago and had moved into more lucrative areas of commerce. Location reports on how insurgencies, coup d'etats and uprisings were fuelled by thrift-shop economies and the pre-owned hardware (For Sale: Sherman Tank, fsh, careful lady owner, low mileage, Box 9836). On the Home-front, vox-pops reports of a plague of cats infesting the city; inter-cut with still-shots and downloads of pet supplies and discount neutering and spaying services. A maelstrom of meteorological textbook perfection was ripping a distant country to pieces, the large screen filled with bar-graphs of ¥$-rated economic damage. Satellite generated animations plotted its course as it weaved a path of destruction through holiday destinations and trade routes. Scrolling captions promoted souvenir info-packs, data-stacks and wall posters of the climatic event of the week with toll-free credit card hot-lines. An expensively coutured Braggadocio expounded the virtues of Biltong to a receptive and responsive audience. At a pre-ordained moment, an overly eager woman leapt to her feet to testify to the life-changing abilities of dried meat with the sincerity and enthusiasm of an evangelical lottery-winner. Around her, companions whooped and cheered applause in response. Through this, Ashiya watched but saw nothing, listened but heard nothing. The television blared its abuse of imagery and noise at her blanked face in an insistent barrage as she gave herself up to another designer cocktail of chemical escapism. She was immune to the broadcast. Absently she signed "TV0" and the television cut off, filling the room with silence. Her aural and ocular stimulation now provided by the narcotic elixir that screamed through her body. Lifting her consciousness to artificial levels that short circuited her senses and cross-wired pleasure and pain to create alien emotions and stimulations from the simple act of sitting. From deep within her throat a low murmuring sound accompanied the rising and falling of her breath. The thrumming softly reverberated in her chest like a shallow snore. Ashiya closed her eyes and the blank expression was replaced by a contented smile as she slowly slid down the large sofa and curled up into a foetal ball, still purring a gentle purr that no human can truly imitate.

...hidden and secure, the Sphinx reclines and relaxes, its mind caressed and comforted by the purring of a thousand cats, their silken voices creating a psychic symphony of celebration...

At the back of an antiques flea market, amongst the piles of books and papers that had been ignored and disregarded for years, a large tortoise-shell cat is far from content. Lying tense and irritated, its tail flicks from side to side, its large amber eyes stare out at a pair of tourists who have ventured too deep into the shop. A near endless stream of visitors has kept the cat awake and alert since it returned to the shop after the battle. Desperate to slip off into Bast's Realm to find answers to its feelings of remorse for the Corvidae, the cat considers finding another resting place, away from the constant interruptions, but the desire to stay and guard its territory is more compelling. Out of frustration it spits at the couple as they browse the low tables of trinkets and glass display cabinets. The woman looks up startled and grips her companion's arm. They both look at the large cat, still hissing and signalling displeasure with its tail, and visibly relax. For once the cat wishes it were black, humans seem more wary of black-cats. Symbols of good luck and omens of bad, witches familiars and shadowy demons. But it knows that nothing it can do will frighten these humans off, they have seen through its posturing and bravado. So it continued to glare, and occasionally hissed if they got too close, until they finally move away to explore another corner of the market.

...alone, so many souls, (so many spirits), yet still alone. Alone in a crowded world, so many mortals, (so many cats), yet so alone. Alone for so long, so many millennia, (so many æons), yet not countless time. For the Sphinx counted every cycle of its isolation since the deluge. It had not forgotten, it knew its antediluvian past, unlike the Shadow. Ah, the Shadow. The Sphinx had felt the Shadow's touch, felt its anger, felt its darqness. The Shadow did not remember the past...

Mr. Small sat in a battered, but friendly arm chair. A single bar on the archaic electric fire glowed in sporadic hot spots between areas of black where the element had burnt away and been badly repaired. Bathed in the orange glow from the fire and the meagre light from a forty-watt bulb in a single wooden standard lamp, the old man reflected on how his own life matched the glowing electric fire, intense and white hot in places, but mainly dull and warm and now fading and dying. He hoped he had done the right thing. He recognised spiritual aura of the man in the market, the Dreamer, a benign spirit. He was aware he had followed him back to the house. Finding the girl here was fortuitous, it meant he had not had to go out and look for her. In younger years, he would have mistrusted the girl, but her kind never meant harm they just did not appreciate the consequences of their actions. Or simply did not care. In later years he relished their meetings and did not fear her. However, he new they would never meet again. Now, he hoped, that the Dreamer would find the girl and they would help each other. The electric fire sparked and went super-nova, briefly shining with an intense bright white glow, then spluttered, fused and burnt out for the final time. With that, the Watchmaker closed his eyes and died.

Mr Small, the Watch-repairer Man,
Mended Clocks and Watches every day.
He didn't ask for much from from anyone,
And so he worked through both the night and day,
Repatching, listening, watching,
For the tiny particles of dust that busted
All the watches in the town.
People came from miles around
To see Mr. Small.
He'd not ask for much.

...Mr. Small, the Watchmaker, was buried the following Sunday. There were no mourners present as they laid him beneath the grass at noon...

Page Sixteen: Twilight Encounter

...as the sun sets over the city the Shadow's time is approaching. Hope is fading as the Waking Lands prepare for sleep. Soon Despair will grow, bloom and flourish in the twilight half-light and sodium glare of street lamps. The endless cycle continues and the Shadow is ready to slip from the Darqlands, now more vigilant and prepared for the powers of Light and Hope...

The girl stood in the Station concourse, watching the daytime commuters head back to their comfortable lives in the comfortable suburbs, with their comfortable families in their comfortable homes. If only that were true, she thought. No, life is not like that, it's twisted and dirty, it's cruel and vicious. Mean people forced to live meaningless lives. Like her father, they leave the city to take out their anger and frustration in the privacy of their own homes. Safe behind closed doors and drawn curtains they turn from sheep to tyrants. Spiteful people in spiteful homes. As she watched, she saw through their weary city-washed faces into their souls buried deep within, she could measure their lives and knew when they would die. In them she saw the repressed desires - an endless stream of would be abusers, addicts, pornographers, perverts, murderers, rapists and alcoholics. But like an oasis in the desert, she occasional glimpsed signs of hope: The Lawyer who donated half is salary to charity; the PA who wanted to grow orchids; the Accountant who wanted to expose corruption; a Private Detective who dreams; the Banker who would rather be a Bluesman and the Civil Servant who was rushing home to write romantic novels. A smile came to her face as she was reminded of the magical scene in The Fisher King, with the people waltzing through Grand Central Station. But these commuters would not do that, they would not admit their dreams. Even in her own dreams she could not image these people being so externally spontaneous, so visibly irrational and so openly honest. Honesty, that is what is missing. She looked at the money in her hand, she had enough to get her half-way to nowhere. And that was all she needed, to escape the city and start again in another where that was not here ~ a nowhere or even half-way nowhere ~ a somewhere that was someplace else. But she did not want to leave the city, she could not face starting again. She was not even sure she knew what she was running from, she just had an overwhelming desire to safeguard the coin and the only way she knew how to do that was to run away. So to be honest to herself, she turned and walked out of the Station.

...yet it is not ready to confront the Sphinx, it needs more souls, it needs the Darqlands to be stronger...

The familiarity of the Station and the pull of the coffee bar started to make Philip feel uneasy. The girl was obviously planning to leave the city, but she had been nowhere near the ticket booths. She just stood and watched the commuters fleeing the city. Neither looking lost, nor searching for anyone, Philip could not work out what she was doing. It could be she had come here to meet the Angel he had met this morning and that did not put him any more at ease. However, it was evident she was not going anywhere just yet, so he risked buying a cup of coffee from the near-by cart, which he did while constantly looking over his shoulder to check on the girl. If she moved, he would have to jettison the drink and run after her. Positioning himself by the boards of timetables, he sipped at his coffee and watched the girl watching the commuters.

For that instant, he was lost in the pleasure of the coffee. The hot dark liquid warmed as he drank, its aroma filling his nostrils with the bitter burnt smell of freshly ground beans. Looking up from his cup, Philip was aware that once more he had slipped into the ephemeral dream-state where the pace of normal life flashed past in a blur. Now he could see the city's Invisibles, the flotsam carried through the crowds by brownian motion, moving at odds to the general flow of traffic. He looked towards the girl, stationary in the pool of the concourse as the stream of passengers flowed and eddied around her. To Philip it seemed as if she too is out of sync with the rest of the world and ran in a different time-frame. Abruptly she turned and cut a direct path towards the exit, leaving a wake of bewilderment in the commuters and invisibles behind her. Temporarily off balanced by the déjà vu of the moment, Philip hesitated, then dropped the half empty cup into a waste bin and carved his own swathe through the crowd.

...so the Shadow rose out of the Darqlands and soared into the evening sky. With its senses tuned to the scent of Despair, ready to swoop down on unsuspecting souls and rip them away and feed the ever hungry Darqness...

Deeper and deeper, deeper still. The room sucked at Ashiya, drawing her deeper into its fabric, into its warmth. Deeper and deeper, deeper still. The chemicals cross-wired synapses and re-routed signals, short-circuiting neural pathways and basically fucked with her brain. Touch had taste, smells could be heard and sounds vibrated with colour; reality and normality muddied and merged like a child's' paint-box. Ashiya opened her eyes and saw herself looking at herself. Closing her eyes she gave herself up to the drug. Deeper and deeper, deeper still. The feel of finger tips on her eyelids danced like the dappled shadows of trees in the snow. The gentle caress of silk on her arm sparkled with the iridescent beauty of laughter. A light kiss on her lips fizzed with the electric radiance of satin. Firm, insistent pressure between her thighs sang to the enchantment of whale-song. Deeper and deeper, deeper still. She again opened her eyes and she was still there, now locked in an embrace with herself / the girl from the restaurant / the shop assistant / the woman in the apartment opposite. Once again she closed her eyes and now gave her self up to her new lover. Deeper and deeper, deeper still. Waves of pleasure engulfed her, beyond animalistic sex; it was pure, beyond love; it was devotion and beyond affection; it was trust. It elevated her to levels of bliss that only exist in poetry. This was fulfilment, her quest and her ultimate need, her delirium met by the desires of another. Deeper and deeper, deeper still. Committed to the release of all her emotions, Ashiya absorbed, and was absorbed by, her paramour, neither selfish or selfless they became one. Completeness. Deeper and deeper, deeper still. Then slowly they separated, without yearning or loss, for even apart they would forever be one. Lost in total contentment, Ashiya felt something cold and metallic being pushed into the palm of her hand and everything went blank.

...once again the hunting is not good, the city is under the spell of a protective spirit. Sweeping over the roof tops, the cowl of protection is imperfect, there are chinks and leaks. The Shadow follows the faint traces of Despair where then can be found, for they are here, in isolated pockets of dissolution and desolation...

Page Seventeen: Supper's not Ready

Ashiya woke still clutching the heavy gold coin, the strength of her grip leaving an impression of its surface in her palm. A grip so tight there could not be a force on earth that could wrench it free. She knew the coin held the answers to questions she had never thought to ask. And for that, she was determined to hold on to the coin. For to loose it go would be to lose everything, her whole life; her being, would cease to have meaning. Ashiya stretched out on the sofa, forcing the stiffness from her joints, slowly she straightened her back, unknotting her spine from the cramp induced by sleeping on the couch. She looked around the apartment, it did not surprise her she was alone, she felt saddened that her new lover was not there, yet she thought she could sense her spirit. Then, perhaps it had been a dream or a drug induced hallucination, repressed memories reformed as reality, nothing that perfect could be real, no reality could be that pure. Ashiya gripped the coin and smiled. She held it up in front of her face, turning it over in her fingers. It was devoid of writing or inscription, it just had an image of an Angel on one face, and was totally blank and smooth on the other. She gently rubbed her thumb over its surface, the coin felt sharp and freshly minted, yet something deep within her told her it was old. Very old. Grinning widely, she kissed the coin and tucked it into her pocket. Raising her hand, she went to command the apartment to prepare her shower and a light snack, but changed her mind. The Room-System responded to her half-completed hand sign with an insolent 'meep!'. Her extended middle-finger reply was met with silence as she got off the sofa and headed for the kitchenette. Culinary skills were not her forte, but after a few false-starts, she managed to make herself a drinkable cup of coffee. The carbonised remnants of a toasted waffle lay smouldering in the sink. Unable to find the controls for the garbage compactor, and the kitchen rapidly filling with the sickly smell of burnt sugar, Ashiya relented and signed the commands for the System to remove the evidence before the sprinklers kicked in.

...close, so very close, yet so far. The Shadow seeped through the walls of the Watchmaker's house into the evening air. The body was already cold when it got there, its soul already fled. A prime soul wasted, lost, too late to harvest the Despair. The old man should not have died. That was not how it worked. The Sphinx's meddling was disturbing the balance. Already the Shadow could feel other forces awakening, the struggle had started...

The girl appeared to have no idea what to do next. She had left the Station and made her way to one of the city squares, where she now sat watching the square fill with tourists and locals who had come to sample the delights of the city's night life. Philip sat on the other end of the same bench, trying to figure her out. All afternoon she had acted like someone who was preparing to run, but at the last minute changed her mind. Now she just sat. This close, he had time to examine her more intently and was beginning to doubt his instincts. Maybe she wasn't going to lead him to his Angel after all. Dressed like any other stray, in filthy jeans and layers of unwashed clothes, this bedraggled wretch could not possibly be connected to the woman who disrupted his life, tore out his heart and left a hollow husk behind. The girl brushed a strand of magenta-dyed hair from her face and looked directly at him. Realising that he had made a serious mistake and been caught looking, he thought quickly, trying to recover the situation, but it was pointless. The girl had had a good look at him now, he could not trail her any more, she would easily recognise him again. The only option was to try and talk to her, win her confidence and see what she knew of the Angel and the coin. There was the risk that she would run, but it was the only choice he had. So he meekly smiled at her. To his surprise she smiled back.

'The Dreamer...' She said in a mater of fact way, as if it was her normal way of greeting total strangers. Unable to come up with a suitable response, he met the statement with a puzzled look. 'I saw you in the Station, you're the Private Detective who dreams.' Philip's heart sank, his cover had been truly blown, another assignment crumbled to nothing. How had she known? She stood up. 'This is it', he thought, 'now she walks off into the crowd and I'm back where I started'. But instead she turned and waked to his end of the bench and sat herself down next to him. The smell of perfume did little to mask the stale earthy smell of the street. 'Mr. Small said you were looking for me and I assume, because we are here now, you have been following me. So, before I start screaming 'Rape' and 'Pervert' I'd like to see some credentials, then we can talk.' Philip reached inside his coat and pulled out his licensed identity card. 'Wrong. I already know you are a Detective. Or do you call yourself a Dick, you know - like Humphrey Bogart?' He shook his head. 'Hmm, no don't suppose anyone calls themselves a dick by choice.' She giggled to herself, then started to laugh. She laughed like she had not laughed for days, weeks maybe. She laughed a natural, child-like, infectious laughter that he found impossible not to share and soon he was chuckling with her, to the amusement of passers-by who smiled at them as they passed. 'So Dick,' she said through boughts of laughter, 'show me what you've got, and I don't mean your dick, Dick.' Her crudity made him wince and again he reached into his coat as she continued to giggle. Withdrawing his cupped hand so that casual passers could not see, he revealed the coin. The girl went silent and visibly blanched, her hand instinctively went to the right-side of her groin as if twinged with appendicitis. Then she smiled, the colour returning to her face.

'I've shown you mine, now show me yours'.' He smirked, now knowing full well she had it hidden in her underwear, the only logical place of safe concealment for someone living on the streets.

'No, I - I can't, not here.' She thought for a moment, biting on her lower-lip, before continuing. 'You must be on expenses, feed me and I'll show you. And you can tell me why you're looking for me.' The thought of taking this girl anywhere he was known was not that attractive, and he especially did not relish the thought of eating anything with her smelling as she did.

'I've a better idea. Why not come back to my office for a shower and then we'll eat and talk.' The shear gauchness of what he said had all the subtlety of a brick. *I should have just told her outright that she stank*, he thought. 'Sorry, I mean...' She laughed again.

'It's okay, I suppose I must be quite ripe. I forget, you get used to the smell after a while, but I guess we ain't time to waste waiting for you to get used to it.' She smiled reassuringly at him. 'Make it a bath and you've got a deal.'

'The office's only got a shower, there's a bath's at my home. It's not as 'neutral' as the office. Do you trust me enough to go there.'

'I'm not stupid enough to trust anyone, but my gut says you're harmless. Let's go.'

...close, so very close, yet so far. Infinity stretching in all directions. Time-lines radiated out in more dimensions than the human mind could cope with, travelling through the past, reaching into the present to disappear over the horizon that will be the future. Sam's twisted soul's own time-line was close to The Heart of the Darqlands, it could sense its presence, feel its purity dragging at his Despair, ever urging him to move closer, to travel further back in time, to become one with the Darqness...

A large black and white bird fluttered noiselessly over the city square. It did not know why it had followed the two from the river-side. It only knew that it had to, that it must follow them and under no circumstances lose them in the crowds of people. It flew to window ledges just in front of where they walked, and once they had passed, took off again, circling high over their heads before landing on another ledge. After two blocks, they hailed a taxi and the Magpie could follow at a more comfortable speed as the taxi crawled through the evening traffic.

Page Eighteen: Peachy Keen

...the Shadow continued on, probing and testing the chinks in the protective layer like a tree-creeper looking for larva, only occasionally plucking a choice rare soul from the hive of the dying city...

The hawk-like figure had watched Mallow lead the girl out of the square. Cursing himself for relying on a human whose only achievement today, it appeared, was in picking up an underage prostitute, he turned and left the square. Saddened and sickened by the state of humanity, he now had to think of another way.

...for this city was dying, the Shadow knew this beyond doubt. It had felt for centuries, through the years of rotting pollution; through years of plague; of flood and of fire; through years of depression and of war. The city endured and survived, but now it dies. All cities die, they grow, flourish and eventually choke themselves to death under the weight of guilt built up around them. They live a thousand years and die, to be swallowed up by the land around them. Some die for a thousand years, but still they die. The Shadow has known this since humanity began to cluster in tribes and communities, it has lived off their cities for æons. As one city dies, it moves on to another, slowly moving over the land. It had seen cities sink beneath the waves; cities consumed by fire; cities smothered by ice and cities buried in sand. As one city perishes, another blooms. This city, however, is dying...

The boxes and bags of newly acquired clothes where slung unceremoniously to the back of the walk-in closet. The space was a blur of flying fabric as Ashiya, dressed in nothing but a loose black T-shirt, rummaged head down in a large battered trunk, throwing discarded garments over her head to the floor behind her. Around lay enough labels to stock a select west-end shop for several years, yet still she dug deeper into the trunk until she finally emerged, her hair in wild disarray, clutching a pair of slick patent leather jeans. With much effort and rolling around the floor, she squeezed her way into the trousers, convincing herself they had gradually shrunk over the years and just needed re-wearing-in a bit. Standing, she smoothed the leather down her thighs and pulled at the hide as it rucked up into her crotch. Then she plucked a heavily adorned leather jacket from the floor and walked into the kitchen to attack it with a pair of offensive looking boning scissors. By the time she had finished, the work-surface was littered with an assortment of chains, sequins, buckles and scraps of fur cut from the once fashionable jacket. Carelessly sweeping the littered remnants to the floor, she returned to the bedroom, where she sat down at the dressing table and emptied the contents of several makeup bags over the table-top. With a long unpainted finger nail, she flicked through the pile of foundation, eye-shadow and mascara. Phials, compacts and bottles rolled over the polished ash of the table, but nothing caught her imagination. Frantically she pulled open drawers and riffled around through carefully arranged rows of colour matched make-up, finally settling on the little used section of deep blues, blacks and silvers. She looked at herself in the mirror, turning her head from side to side, as if seeing her face for the first time, before busily setting about herself with the cosmetics. After the best part of an hour, she again looked at herself in the mirror. Her back-combed and lacquered hair stood in soft jagged spikes like jet floss. Long braided strands hung down around her face, the hair entwined with lengths of velvet ribbon cut from an expensive evening gown. The new found volume of her black hair accentuated her naturally elfin pale face. Her eyes were delicately painted in blended blue and black, with hints of red below her finely drawn brow, her cheeks hollowed with a gently dusting of kohl. She snarled at her reflection, baring perfect white teeth framed in the thick black gloss of her heavily layered lips. Satisfied with her new self image, she pulled the leather coat on over her T-shirt and turned to examine herself in the full-length mirrors that furnished one side of the room. The final result was pleasing, but not quite right. Inside one of the jacket pockets she found a pair of plain black sunglasses, slipping them on she grinned as she caught her reflection mirroring a cartoon-drawing she had once seen.

...the Sphinx yearned to walk the Waking Lands, but now was not the time. Soon, but not now. There was still much to be done by continuing to travel the ethereal world. The Shadow had been awoken and alerted, yet had purposely avoided contact, the Sphinx would have to goad it some more...

The girl's thin arm extended from behind the bathroom door, holding out a bundle of clothes. Philip carried them at arms length straight into the kitchen where he proceeded to force them en-mass into the washing machine, caring not whether they were delicate or mixed fabric, hand wash or dry clean only. The machine lacked an incinerate program and did not include a fumigate cycle, so he dialled up non-fast coloureds and hoped for the best. By the time he had percolated a large pot of espresso and returned to the living room with two steaming cups of coffee, the girl was sat by the fire, engulfed in his dressing gown, towelling her hair rigorously with a large white bath towel. He placed the cups on a low table and sat in the chair on the opposite side of the fire. She momentarily stopped drying her hair and smiled at him from under towel, the bath has washed years from her. He could not help but notice that her skin was remarkably clear, she carried only a few spots and sores from her time on the street and her lips were not cracked or blistered. Her appearance gave the impression she had only been homeless a few weeks, yet her attitude and confidence told him otherwise. Dropping the towel to the floor, she raked her fingers through her hair, sweeping the damp strands back behind her ears.

'Why are you homeless?' Philip asked without thinking.

'Because I don't have a home.' Came the curt reply. She saw that his expression had not changed, so she took a large breath. 'And I don't have a home because I haven't got any money and I haven't got any money because I haven't got a job and I haven't got a job because I don't have a permanent address and I don't have a permanent address because I don't have a home.' Finally she stopped and looked at him, her eyes narrowed, her lips pursed and her head tilted slightly to one side.

'Okay, if you don't want to talk about it just say.' He laughed, holding his hands palms up.

'Can I see the coin now?' She reached inside the dressing gown and Philip grimaced as she pulled out a condom containing the coin, which she emptied into her hand.

'It's the only place I could think of to hide it while I was in the bath.' She said defiantly, seeing the look of disdain on his face. She held up the condom with her finger nail. 'I found this in your bathroom cabinet, and anyway, it's way passed its use-by-date.' She added, seeing him wince at that, she pinging the condom at him like a school-boy with an elastic-band. He dodged the rubber missile, letting it fly over his shoulder and hit the back wall with a *Phlat!* He held out his hand for the coin. She looked at his outstretched hand and chewed on her lip, obviously reluctant to part with the coin. Philip dug into his pocket, retrieved his and held it out to her in exchange. She hesitated for a moment then deftly made the swap, simultaneously they sat back and examined each others coin. To Philip the coins looked identical, the felt the same, they appeared to be the same weight, they were both very old but still looked new. Yet there was no feeling of belonging attached to this one, it wasn't his and he didn't want it. He looked up to see the girl must have reached the same conclusion, for she now stood before him both arms outstretched, one holding his coin and the other empty, waiting for the return of her's. After swapping back, Philip rubbed his coin between his finger and thumb and slipped it into his pocket. The girl had sat down and was holding the coin close to her heart, he quickly looked away as he found himself staring at her uncovered breasts. Noticing his discomfort and embarrassment, she pulled the dressing gown together with her free hand.

'Sorry. Living on the street you tend to forget modesty.' Philip gave her a quizzical look and she snapped. 'Don't look at me like that!' She leaned forward, her arms crossed protectively across her chest. 'Look! I don't whore and I don't thieve. I don't booze and I don't do drugs. I just get by. I buy magazines and sell them. It's not charity and it's not begging. I don't know how long you've been following me, but you must have seen how and where I live. I'm not a fucking whore, so if that's why you've brought me here you can just fuck off!'. With that, she sharply stood up to leave, Philip jumped to his feet to stop her as she brought her fists up to defend herself. He quickly stepped back and held his hands up, palms open in surrender and shook his head.

'Whoa! No, no, it's not like that. I didn't bring you back her for a cheap shag.' It was now his turn to get angry. 'As you have surmised, I haven't had sex for a while, but I'm not celibate nor impotent and I don't need to buy sex - from you or anyone! I just haven't felt the need since...' He was speaking rapidly, without thinking he was heading off into territory he did not want to enter and certainly did not want to talk about. He lowered his arms, his shoulders sagging and his head dropping so that he was now staring at the floor. After a short pause he looked up, she had relaxed her stance and was staring at him with her hands on her hips. 'I just want to talk. I'm looking for some one, the woman who gave you the coin. I need to find her and you might know where she is.' His voice slowed and trailed off, the dressing gown had fallen open again and he was now staring at a tattoo on her bare shoulder. A small tattoo of an elephant.

...behind a lock-up garage a pair of wild eyes shone out of the half light, unblinking they pierced the night, huge pupils dilated so far that the coloured irises had all but disappeared. The mind behind the eyes had gone, shattered and lost. Below the eyes, a nose bled blood, snot and cocaine into a cocktail of bile, alcohol and more blood that dribbled from a blackened mouth onto an Italian suit that a few hours ago would have been described as 'sharp'. The Shadow slithered down the wall and engulfed the body, wrapping and warping the weak flesh and probing the damaged mind for residual fragments; then deep into the heart for traces of a soul. But all it could find was blackness, deep and total back - a vacuum from which no light would escape - a

Blackness darker than the Darqness. And Despair, so much Despair. All the Despair there could ever be in the Universe contained in a singularity. Enough Despair to build an infinite Darqlands' for eternity. A concentration so deep the Shadow was pulled towards it with an insatiable appetite, compelled to consume and devour. To be consumed...

Page Nineteen: Just Average

The girl studied the man before her. Average. Not tall not short; neither slim nor fat; not handsome not ugly. Just average. The kind of person you meet everyday, and promptly forget you've met. 'Ideal Detective material', she thought, 'just blends in to the crowd'. She looked at where he was staring, and quickly covered her bare shoulder. He shifted and looked directly at her, then snapping out of a momentary dream, he gesticulated, almost randomly, his hands open and fingers splayed as if trying to pluck words out of the air. What had just passed, what ever it was, had completely thrown him, he was lost and did not know what to do or say. She watched him, unable to help, as he floundered. Finally, he swung his arms forward and gestured towards the chair,

'Sit. Please sit.' As he said the words he sat down in his chair and the she followed suit, carefully sitting back, so the over large dressing gown kept her covered and the sight of her body did not disturb him further. Even sitting, he still looked troubled, his left hand came up to his face, his fingers tracing the lines on his furrowed brow. 'Sorry, I -'. His eyes went to the ceiling and he noisily exhaled. 'Look, erm, sorry, I never asked your name. I'm Philip'

'I know, it was on your Licence. They call me Saffron.' She said, holding up a strand of damp magenta hair for him to see. ''Cos of my hair.'

'Oh, you're a retro then.' He was visibly relaxing, slowly coming into sync. with the rest of the world. She glanced around the room. All of the furniture and decoration was antique (or pastiche), exquisite black and coloured lacquer in sharp geometric shapes. He had obviously spent a great deal of time and money recreating this look.

'No, not really, it's a bit before my time. I saw an old poster once and liked it. You into Art Deco then?' He looked around the room before looking back at her and nodded. 'Is it a Bogart thing then?' He nodded again, slightly embarrassed, then lent forward and picked up his coffee. She reached for her cup and then sat back, cradling the warm cup in both hands. For a while they both gazed into their drinks, not saying anything. Eventually she spoke. 'I never saw who it was.' He shot her a quizzical look. 'This woman. I never saw her. I was selling mags near the Royal Theatre. The coin dropped into my tin, she didn't even stop for a mag. I couldn't even say it was a woman ~ it could have been a man.' He seemed to get cross at that, because he glared at her for an instant before taking a sudden interest in his coffee again. She was making him uncomfortable, and his erratic behaviour was making her feel uncomfortable too. 'Look, are my clothes ready? I should be going. I'm sorry I can't help you. If you get my stuff, I'll go.'

'Sorry, er no, they're still in the wash. I've some women's clothes in the bedroom, you can take what ever you want.'

'I don't think you're my size.' She said, watching him turn red as she started to giggle.

'No, no. They're not mine, the belonged to a friend.' She raised an eye-brow and giggled some more. 'A lady friend.' She giggled even more, almost laughing. Then he must have realised she was teasing him, because he started to giggle with her. Within minutes they were both laughing out loud. With tears running down his face he finally managed to speak. 'I promised you something to eat. Why don't you get dressed, then we'll go out.' With the ice broken, she felt more at ease and the idea of food was tempting.

'Or we could stay here and you could cook, or send out for a take-away, I don't mind.' He shook his head.

'My cooking is okay for me, but I wouldn't inflict it on someone else. I know a great Mongolian restaurant, we could go there.' He stood up and held out his hand, which she took and he helped her up from the chair. He then led her into the bedroom and showed her a wardrobe full of clothes. The wardrobe was meticulously laid out, with all the hanging garments protected in polythene bags and smaller items neatly folded in tissue paper and stacked on shelves. Boots and shoes with incredible heals stood in rows on the floor of the wardrobe. She picked one of the dresses and pulled it from its plastic protection to examined it. The cloth was unlike anything she had seen before, she draped it over her arm, the material looked like cotton, but flowed like silk. She could not believe how sensuous it felt. She checked inside the collar for a label, but there was none. She looked at him in total amazement. 'They belonged to the woman who gave me the coin. It's called *sommerfäden*, it's supposed to be made from angel's breath and morning sunlight.' He offered by way of an explanation. She just had to try it on. She handed him the dress, while letting the dressing gown drop to the floor and stepped out of it. Philip held up the dress for her, now oblivious to, or at least unfazed by, her nudity. It slipped over her head and poured over her flesh like double cream. It was so shear and so light she had to look twice to make sure she was still wearing it and it had not simply slid over her body and fallen straight to the floor.

'Wow! It's like I'm not wearing it.' She said in an incredulous tone. 'It's not see-through is it?' He shook his head as she spun round, peering over her shoulder, trying to look at her bum. He pointed to the mirror on the inside of the wardrobe door. At first she did not recognise the reflection. The dress transformed her from a waif to a woman, she could see the dress accentuating her curves without highlighting her bulges. Smoothing her hand over her flattened stomach, the touch was so sheer it was like she caressing her naked skin. She kicked her leg and watched the cloth billow like clouds and flow like mist. She had a million more questions, but doubted he would have any answers. So she bent down and searched through the shelves. 'What about underwear?'

'Er.' He paused. 'She never wore any.' She looked up with a mischievous grin. That did not embarrass him.

'Then I guess I won't be either.' And neither did that

...to be consumed.
A trap!
The Shadow fought the pull.
Like a fly caught in resin,
Each kick,
Each fight,
Pulling it deeper,
Suffocating,
Drowning.
Like a soul,
Caught in the Darqness,
Thrashing madly,
Clawing and scratching
In panic.
Then,
The Shadow stopped fighting.
Motionless.
Hanging still.
Frozen in amber.
It could sense it was no longer sinking.
'Every action has an equal and opposite
'Reaction'
Slowly and deliberately
It started to swim
With smooth fluid movements
It began to rise,
Rising,
Through the Blackness,
Rising up,
Reaching towards
The light of
The Waking Lands...

The elderly couple to Rochelle du Pont's left jumped slightly as one of the large candle flickered briefly, some impurity in the wick causing it to momentarily burn brightly and then spit with a bright orange spark, before continuing to burn with its usual dull yellow light. They clutched each others hands tighter, the two young women to her right giggled. 'Amateurs' she thought to herself, 'Still, I'll have to speak to Maud about those cheap wicks.'. Without moving her head and through partially closed eyes, she scanned around the room. With the exception of Maud who was off in a world of her own (again) and the new girl who just smiled and nodded, everyone else kept glancing nervously at the red and white banded candles. 'Then again it does add to the atmosphere.' she concluded. After a dignified pause, Rochelle continued with the incantation.

'Do you know Maud.' Rochelle would state later, after bidding everyone Goodbye, Safe-journey and Merry-part, as she sat in the parlour in silent communion with Maud, who will still be on planet-Maud, aided by the herbal pipe she kept sucking on.

'Something's not right.' She would reach out and top up her cup with steaming apple tea, then pile in three heaped spoon-fulls of sugar, making a hot sickly syrup to counter the healthy measure of brandy she will then add. 'I can feel it. I don't know what it is, but it's not right. We haven't had an attendance of that size since the eclipse. It takes a good earth-crisis to turn folk back to the old ways.' She would take a sip of tea, waiting for Maud to respond, before continuing. 'And that new girl's spooky, did you see her aura? Have you ever seen a blue that dark? What do they call it?'

'Indigo.' Would be Maud's single contribution to the conversation. Following that there will be a long period of silence. Rochelle in deep contemplation, Maud away with the faeries.

'Still having those cat-dreams?' Maud will nod and suck on her pipe. 'See, it's not right.'

But before then, Rochelle must finish the incantation and then serve tea and cake to the gathering, before sending them on their way.

...the Shadow surfaced in the alley. It's only thought for retribution. The putrid wretch had gone, or had never been there, just a manifestation by the Sphinx to bait the trap. Enraged with unfettered anger, the Shadow rose into the night sky, the clouds spitting bolts of lighting at the negative energy created. The Shadow roared back with thunder, shaking the clouds, causing them to panic and release their load in a torrent of rain over the city...

Poised in the centre, the spider felt a vibration in the web. It waited a while, balancing the vibrations as they travelled up its legs. Left side, third leg. It spun around by 135 degrees and ran off in the direction of the trapped fly.

Page Twenty: The Beat of Butterfly Wings

...the storm raged with the power of nature: simple, unguided and raw. The Shadow could appreciate that. The storm raged with chaos theory: pure, elegant and simple. The Shadow knew that. A power that mankind would never command or master - a power that could make them immortal - a power that would keep them mortal. The Shadow liked that too...

The Xanadu had excelled, as always. Saffron's appalled reaction to the display of raw meats was soon calmed when he explained that it would be cooked on a Mongolian barbecue after they had chosen their portions. Still, she chose a modest selection of sliced fish and seafood doused in the hottest most fiery concoction of spices and sauces they had to offer, while Philip hungrily had a bit of everything piled on his plate, with a similar searing cocktail. Over the meal, they laughed and joked like old friends, the conversation flowing with seamless ease as they slipped from one subject to the next while effortlessly avoided the one subject they wanted to discuss. They had left the restaurant still laughing, with her arm linked in his and their mouths tingling from the burning spices, to be caught minutes later by the sudden downpour. Rushing through the rain soaked streets, with Philip's coat held above their heads in futile defiance against the onslaught of wind and rain, they arrived back at the house drenched and shaking from the shock of the near freezing water.

...the Shadow knew. It sent minor events into the storm. Subtle insignificance's to fine tuning the atmosphere and minuscule variances to tip the delicate balance of forces. With delicacy and precision the Shadow manipulated the electro-magnetic energies within the clouds, carefully crafting a maelstrom from the raw material of nature...

The shop had finally emptied and the owner had closed up for the night, leaving the cat to the now darkened peace. The steady rain beat down on the plate windows at the front of the shop, but deep in the rear, all was calm as the cat settled down amid the piles of books and papers. A cracking bolt of lightning struck somewhere near by, flooding the shop in an intense blue-white light, momentarily blinding the cat causing its pupils to narrow to razor thin slits, before plunging it back into an inky black nothing. The cat's fur bristled as the surge of static electricity charged the air. The long florescent lights that delineated the ceiling also reacted to this free energy, emitted a dull glow as their inert gasses became excited, the energised electrons in turn jolting photons free from the phosphorescent coating of the tubes. Gradually the cat became re-accustomed to the diminished lighting, its nocturnal vision returning to its usual sharpness. Cowering, yet ready to pounce or flee, it searched the show-room. Something was there, but it could neither see nor smell it, yet the cat sensed a presence.

'You have questions.' The thought was warm and silky as it soundlessly entered the cats head. It jumped up, startled and very frightened, its ears flicking in all directions, searching for a sound that was never made. Yet it did not run.

'Who are you? Where can I run? How did you do that? Am I going to die? What are you? How big are you? Can I eat you? Am I dead? Where are you? Why?' It thought, a multitude of questions asked in parallel as its defensive instincts took over.

'Not those questions. Calm down. You know who I am.' The unspoken voice said. The cat relaxed. It did know the visitor, but not on this plane, not in the physical world. Slowly it cleared its mind of the clutter of questions, carefully answering each one so they would not resurface unexpectedly later. It sat down on its bed of papers and cocked its head to one side.

'Why are you here?' The cat thought.

'To answer your questions.'

'Oh sure.' The cat was not convinced. 'You could have done that in the Realm, why come here?' The soft chimes of purring laughter filled its head, not mocking laughter, but laughter of realisation. The realisation that this was not a stupid cat.

'Okay, it's not safe for you to come to the Realm.' A subdued orange glow enveloped a near-by armchair. 'I've been sending distractions to keep you away, but I cannot do that indefinitely. So, now I've come in person.' The glow gently vibrated with each word and with each vibration, became more solid.

'Your entrance was a bit melodramatic.' The cat said to the shimmering figure seated before it. The figure moved to look towards the shop window, then turned its now feline/human face back to the cat and smiled.

'The storm? Oh that is not my doing, but it has to do with why I am here and why you cannot got to Bast for now.' The figure leaned forward, it had now coalesced into a solid female human form, her feline features now muted into cat-like human features. 'That' the figure indicated to the storm, 'is the work of The Enemy.'

'The Enemy!' The cat spat at that. 'The Enemy! Sweet Bast - more melodrama! Half a dozen scrawny Corvidae against the entire population of the Realm. They never stood a chance.'

'They were not The Enemy, they were just the expendable ground troupes, sent to look for me.'

'So we slaughtered them.'

'Expendable. And Yes, you would do it again if I so wished.' And the cat knew it would too, such is the persuasion of the Sphinx.

'So-'

'-why is it not safe to go the Realm?' the Sphinx completing the question before the cat had even thought it. 'Because, before they died, the Corvidae selected you to guide them. Through you, The Enemy would reach into Bast's Realm with this Tempest it is creating and destroy us all.'

'So now-' The cat resigned.

'-I kill you? Now who is being melodramatic. There is no need for that, we do not kill our own-'

'-we don't kill scavengers either.'

'A fair point, but not exactly a precedent though.' The Sphinx paused for a moment, reflecting on the possibilities and options. 'Anyway, only three of them actually died, and they were regrettable 'accidents'. I only wanted to scare them a little, but they fought well and died an honourable death - for scavengers.

'No, all you need to do is not go the Realm for a while.' The cat gave a cat-frown, flicking its tail once to register its vote of disapproval. Outside, the storm appeared to be easing off, or at least moving away.

'And how-'

'-are you supposed to do that? Simple, just do not go to sleep.' The Sphinx smiled. 'And no cat-naps either.' It then stood up, revealing its tall slender body in all its glory, still glowing with the warm orange aura. The Sphinx examined itself, bending and flexing its arms. 'Hmm', it mused as it fanned its fingers, curled them into a fist and then flicked them out like a cat extending its claws. 'Now I have this body, I think I will keep it for a while.' The aura began to dim. She looked at the cat. 'It has been a long time since I walked the city. Let us do some exploring, that should keep you awake. Grab your coat then.' The cat jumped down from the pile of papers and padded over to the Sphinx. 'Oh good, you are already wearing it. Got any boots to go with that?'

...the Shadow stopped directing the storm, but let it rage on under its own will. The channel was not opening and the opportunity was lost. The aura of the Sphinx was shrouded, but still present. It could end this now, confront it now, but now was not the time, the Sphinx was too strong and the Darqness was not ready. But soon...

Page Twenty One: The Somniloquies

...The Lament...

A Dreamless Sleep,

No chance to dream.

But lonely voices like the wind,

In my dreaming head,

And distant voices like the rain,

In my sleepless thoughts.

All my Sleeping Dreams are Voices

Chapter Four: Meririm

Page Twenty Two: The Meadow

…wait…

The tall, unmown blades of grass undulated in gentle waves of deep garnet green, creating shimmering patterns in the afternoon sunlight. The cooling breeze played amongst the layers of celandine, cowslip and daisy that dappled the carpet in splodges of yellow and white. Shadows of wispy clouds raced over the field, chased by bright bands of sunlight adding to the patchwork of light and shade. A mist of dandelion seeds hovered over the meadow, looking more like a flock of faerie spirits than in any childhood fantasy. They swirled and danced in harmony with the rippling grass as their feathery sails caught the wind, drifting over the sea of grass as an ethereal cloud. An ancient stream meandered through the centre of the field, painting a broad stroke of deeper verdant green as the ever thirsty grass flourished in the sodden ground fed by the brook. Thin stalks of reed shivered by the waters' edge, casting fringing patterns of shadow. The warm summer air was filled with the heady bloom of pollen and intoxicating flower scent, as potent as any joss-stick or room-freshener yet lacking the overpowering acrid and artificial pungency. Rochelle's fingers dug into the earth as she sat cross-legged amid the grasses, drawing earth-power from the sun-warmed soil, enriched with the humus and silt that flooded the meadow each spring, bringing fertility and growth to the land. With eyes closed, she tilted back her head to feel the sun rays warming her face, its fire-energy feeding into her body filling her with a rich glow that fuelled the energy conversion within her body. The symphonic music of trickling water from the brook accompanied a soprano bird song, their melodic chorus drawing her closer to nature quicker and more complete than any new-age soundtrack of simplistic guitar or pan-pipe. Rochelle breathed deeply, sucking in the fragrant air, before releasing it back to the breeze in a slow, controlled exhale. The plants stripped the carbon from her breath, replenishing and revitalising the oxygen she breathed, together they nourished each other. Oxygen rich blood now coursed through her, purging the city's impurities and sustaining her with elemental energies. The symbiosis connecting them, she became part of the landscape, routed in the same primeval magick from where all life began. At last her mind was free.

…wait…

Rising high above the field she could see her body, lost in the lake of swaying green fronds. Her spirit flew over the landscape darting among the insects and airborne seed. Free from the confines of her earthly body. Swooping and diving over the thick blanket of meadow-plants, she could feel the renewing power of the land forcing growth into every cell of every plant, ripening the fruits and fattening the rejuvenating seeds. The Earth's gift of birth and rebirth. Smaller spirits rose from the land, others came from the wood and hedgerow. Soon she was surrounded by the life force of every living creature. Her mind spread, covering every inch of the field, enveloping the animal spirits, embracing them, exchanging gifts of love as her heart rose to join them. Then she reached out and grabbed an iridescent spirit, her mind became gnarled black claws that tore into the ephemeral flesh, ripping out its pulsing heart from its incandescent body to the terrifying screams of the defenceless creature. Its cries panicked other spirits, who turned to flee but were quickly scooped up into her arms and rent into a myriad of dying pieces. She carved a inky black wake through them, destroying and devouring each living thing in a demonic feast of destruction.

The air was thick with the stench of blood and foul detritus that now covered the meadow, soaking and poisoning its rich soil, killing and rotting its carpet of crass and plant-life as the tainted ordure swelled over the ground, polluting everything it touched.

…wait…

Rochelle watched in horror as her demented spirit savaged the land. She cried out in grief as each spirit was crushed and consumed. Her clothes where now drenched in the putrid decay of life. Fighting to control the energy she had released, it twisted and swirled, ripping at her flesh. It turned to face her, a mocking distortion of her own face grinned with staggered rows of jagged black teeth. Blood and sinew flowed from its gapping mouth, a sickly, nauseating reek caught in her throat, causing her to gag. She tried to scream as the jaws widened to engulf her head, but no sound emanated from her mouth as the demon bit down and everything went black.

…yes!…

Page Twenty Three: The Lauren Bacall Routine

When the scream finally arrived, it burst from her with an intensity that could shatter glass. The harmonic distortion of the sound scrapped at her vocal chords, the serrated peaks of the tone scratched deep into the flesh so that blood flowed back down her throat. She wretched and vomited a spew of blood, bile and digestive-acid, covering her legs in a slick, sticky slime. Spent and drained, she collapsed into the mire that flooded the bed. The terror had emptied her stomach, bowls, bladder and glands. Every excrement the body could expel now soaked into the mattress. Menstrual blood, sweat, urine, faeces and mucus mixed with the contents of her gut, drenching her in the foul excreta as she lay quivering and sobbing.

…'pah!' Thought the Angel, 'Witches! They know nothing of Magick!' Shaking his head with disdain, he crossed the road outside Rochelle's house and moved off down the road, towards the main street of the dirty city borough. He did not need to have been this close to invade her meditation, yet he felt it necessary. He wanted to draw on her energy and feed off her life-force, but he could have done that from anywhere on the Earth. And probably several places off of it. He need not have travelled across the city to stand outside her basement window, waiting for her to begin her meditation, yet he did. He wanted to feel her terror and hear her scream, yet he could have achieved that simply as he took over her mind, her thoughts and feelings becoming his as he distorted her visions. There was nothing to be gained by standing at the foot of her bed as he perverted and manipulated her mind, yet he did. He could have been more subtle in conveying his message, but he enjoyed this more. After the fruitless encounter with Mallow, he needed to find another to continue his search. But more than that, he wanted to extract a little revenge for his wasted time from the 'Useless Fuck-up' known as Mankind…

They had talked into the early hours of the morning, slowly emptying a bottle of Armagnac and devouring a box of cheese-straws Philip found in his larder. The girl became more animated and laughed almost continuously as they talked of art, music and vintage films. He was impressed by the depth of her knowledge, her intelligence was natural and eager to show off in his company, with out appearing egotistic. With time he drew her life story from her, melancholy gripped her as she dwelled on a dark region and she started to close up. He carefully manoeuvred the conversation around to a slightly different subject, before edging back to nibble at its fringes. As the story of her years of abuse by her father unfolded, it made him feel uneasy: he wanted to hug her, to comfort her; yet he dare not, afraid that his familiarity would trigger the wrong response. There were long pauses of reflection and tears welled up in her eyes, yet she fought them back, trying not to look weak before him. But she was far from weak in his eyes, if only he had half of her courage. Eventually she looked up and smiled.

'Tell me of Angels.' She said still smiling at him. He was taken aback. He did not recall mentioning Angels and was certain he had not. She had caught him off guard and he flustered.

'A-Angels, H-how do you mean?'

'You said the dress was made from angels' breath, and it certainly wasn't something you got from Marks and Sparks.' He smiled uneasily. 'And the coins have a picture of an Angel on them. So tell me, what's this all about?' She lent forward, he lent back in response, maintaining the distance between them. Philip swallowed, she had been honest with him, now it was his turn, but he did not know whether he could. He did not know where to start, or how far he could go back without hurting himself. Eventually, he gave in to his cowardice and relayed the story of meeting the Angel in the Station, of how he tracked her through Mr. Small and how he had hoped that she would lead him to the renegade Angel. She listened intently, not saying anything, just nodding occasionally. As he finished, she smiled the same smile as before. Fuck, he thought. He knew he hadn't got away with it.

'Okay, I guess you now want to know how I knew the hawk-like man was an Angel and how I got the coin.'

…so the Angel strode through the city with arrogant confidence, 'At last,' it thought, 'now we're getting somewhere.' The raw earth-energy that Rochelle so carefully gathered bolstered his confidence, the short-lived spirits of the creatures he demolished fuelled his arrogance. As he walked he grinned a wide, manic smile at people who were foolish enough to look directly at him. And grinned even wider as they quickly averted their eyes and scurried off…

'Saffron' lay cramped and uncomfortable on the sofa, covered in an unnecessary quilt, more for Philips modesty than her warmth. He had volunteered to take the couch, offering her his bed, but she had sworn at his misplaced gallantry, insisting that she had slept on worse than his aged couch and had literally pushed him into his own bedroom. Now she swore at her stupidity. She had never slept on anything as lumpy as this forsaken sofa, anywhere. Who ever thought that a construction of wood, leather, spring-steel and horse-hair would be considered 'comfort', (by any definition of the word), needed to spend a restless night trying to sleep on one. Unable to sleep, she lay thinking over the story Philip had told of his Angel. At first she thought it just his term of endearment, but soon came to the realisation that he actually believed. Philip had shuffled nervously in the chair, almost squirming, before continuing.

'I met her by accident, well I suppose a lot of meetings are accidental.' He pause for a moment, possibly reflecting on any number of accidental meetings, or possibly just for effect. 'She had come into my office building looking for a firm of accountants that have offices further down the corridor, but she was intrigued enough by the sign on my door to simply want to look inside. My first sight of her was a head peeping around the door. She took one look at the fake 1930's decor and slipped into a Lauren Bacall routine...'

'You know how to whistle, don't you...'

'Yes, that one. Anyway, we just hit it off immediately and before I knew it we were doing the boy-friend/girl-friend thing.' He glanced towards the bedroom. 'Well. Err.' He cleared his throat with a cough. 'You know, the usual things. Everything seemed pretty normal. I thought she was the most amazing creature I'd every met. A perfect angel.' He smiled. 'So, anyway. A few months into the relationship, we were in a bar. Nothing special, just a bar with loud music, fancy drinks and inedible food. The place was full of small groups business people winding down from a days work. You know the usual city types, stock-brokers, insurance assessors, bankers.' He stopped for a moment and started to giggle. 'Do you now the collective noun for a group of Bankers? - A Wunch, d'yahgeddit? A Wunch of Bankers' He laughed raucously at his joke, a side effect of the brandy. He saw she wasn't laughing, so quickly composed himself before continuing. 'One group were celebrating something, a major contract, Mickey Mouse's birthday or something - I don't know, anyway, they were getting very drunk quicker than anyone else and were being extremely noisy. Something happened, I forget what exactly, I must have knocked into one of them, spilt his drink or just looked at them in a funny way, because they turned on us, jeering at me and leering at her. One of them starts telling her she should dump me and go with a real man, one who would fuck her good and proper, giver her a right seeing to, (and other such primate remarks). She looks him in the eye and quietly says that he should watch his tongue or it will get him into trouble. He replies that the only place his tongue should be is up her snatch. Next thing I know this guy is rolling around the floor, clutching his throat, gagging for air like he is choking on something. His eyes are bulging and his lips are turning blue, his arms and legs are thrashing about so much no one can get close enough to help. Not that anyone tried, we're all too stunned to move. Then he lies still. He's dead at our feet. I panic, grab her arm and get out of there as quick as we can, everyone still too shocked to stop us.

'Later, back here, sat in these chairs, I'm still shaking, drinking brandy, trying to work out what happened and she just says.

'Oh, he swallowed his tongue.' in a matter-of-fact way, like it happens all the time.

'What!' I go. 'People don't just swallow their tongues while they're standing in a bar.'

'No.' She says, 'I made him do that.' And she smiles at me, (just like that other Angel smiled at me), and I instantly believe her. I'm nearly pissing myself. I've spent every possible hour with this woman over the last few months, screwed her in every room in the house, in the office, in the car, everywhere imaginable, and some unimaginable. She's done things to me I never thought possible and I've done things to her I've never thought I was capable of. And she could kill me without touching, just by thinking, if she willed me dead - I'd die. She kneels at my feet and takes my hand in hers and tells me she is an Angel.

'Angels don't kill people.' I tell her, but she just shakes her head.

'Read your Bible,' she tells me, 'Angels killed people all the time, we once were God's hit-men after all.'

'Were?' I ask her.

'Were.' She says, patting my hand. From that night on, things turn sour and after a week she leaves me, but before she goes she gives me the coin. I've scoured libraries and databases, but can't find anything about it. I've read just about every book that's ever been written about Angels and I think I understand less now than I did then.'

'So, was she your Guardian Angel?'

'No, I think I was just a passing distraction.' The conversation ended there, Philip was not offering any more information and she did not want to pry deeper. Now the couch had seemed to have developed more lumps and was digging into her flesh. She tried lying at different angles, but could not get comfortable at all. She tried sleeping on top of the quilt, but that did not help. Sleeping rough was never this uncomfortable. She considered slipping into Philip's bed, but that would send the wrong signals, so was not an option. Eventually she spread out cushions over the hearth-rug in front of the fire, covered them in the quilt and lay herself on top.

Page Twenty Four: the Bar Ba Black Sleep

…seething with hatred, the Shadow sulked with the ultramarine clouds. Both deprived of their release, they skulked high off the city peaks. The storm was no longer confined or controlled, with no restraints it began to disperse into the night, breaking into smaller clumps of dense vapour and drift on the wind and air-currents. To shed its torrent in minor storms far into the countryside. Or in a futile attempt to dilute the sea.…

The cat followed the slim feline/feminine figure of the Sphinx as she strolled through the rain cleansed streets. The electric glow of neon, halogen, tungsten and sodium reflected in the mirror surfaces of puddles slicked with a molecule layer of rainbow. The city soundscape of night traffic was punctuated with alien rhythms pulsing from bars, clubs and restaurants. As they approached a brightly lit entrance, the exuberance of laughter and merriment rose in peaks and then cascaded back down in rumbling avalanches as they passed. The Sphinx relished in the atmosphere, her aura growing stronger, throbbing in time with the beat as they walked. The cat revelled in her presence, basking as the penumbra to her nimbus and walked fearlessly in her wake as she sliced a path through the jam of bodies queuing for one entertainment or another. After walking half the length of the main street, they settled on a basement bar of bright lights and deep shadows, loud music and layers of smoke. The Sphinx moved swiftly past the line of black-clad people waiting patiently to get in. Ignored by the threatening pair of bouncers that guarded the doorway, they entered the hidden lair. The cat paused at the top of a shallow flight of stairs, hesitant and unconvinced. The Sphinx turned and scowled, then stooped to pick up the cat before descending into the thick ambience. As they moved deeper in, no one spoke and no one looked directly at them. No one appeared to notice a naked woman carrying a cat in a crowded bar, yet they were allowed free passage to a low table on the edge of the room. The Sphinx gently placed the cat on a red velour covered chair and disappeared back into the crowd. To return moments latter with a vivid blue drink that fluoresced under the black light from UV tubes secreted around the bar. Aided by the Sphinx's protection, its apprehensions waned and the cat began to enjoy the new found experience. This was another world, a darker side to apes it had not seen before, buried in a subterranean cave of throbbing primeval noise and harsh pulsing lights. All around they had thrown off their pretence of civilisation and reverted to their animal origins. As if they were enacting some mystical ritual, trying to reclaim their own spirit world through a rite of intoxication and dance.

'Do they have a Realm?' Thought the cat.

'They did have, but they left it long long ago. They make up stories and myths to delude themselves. Stories of battles and trickery. A fall from grace. But the truth is they simply forgot. Some try to get back but very few succeed. Some reach other Realms by mistake or accident and that can be a problem. However the spirits of those worlds have learnt to swiftly deal with them. Some come to Bast, and she welcomes them if they are honest and pure. Or she breaks their spirit of they are not. Some try and create new Realms, but they lack the belief to make them real, or the faith to sustain them and they fade and die. One day, maybe, they will find their way. Except this physical world is too seductive for them for now, its claim on their souls it too great for them to release it.'

'I never realised. They must be very unhappy.' The cat had other thoughts, but it kept them to itself, holding them as feelings and emotions, preventing them forming themselves as coherent thoughts the Sphinx could interpret. 'I do not envy them.'

'No. But you must admire them.' The cat gave a quizzical look. 'Take a good look at them.' The Sphinx gestured towards the melee of revellers, her arm tracing a broad sweep, its arc encompassing more than the contents of the room, but the whole of mankind. 'See, even when lost, they fight to enjoy their lives. Every spiritual pleasure they forfeited, they now strive to recreate in a material form. They are quite remarkable, such resilience. I doubt that we would fare so well.'

'But we would never loose Bast's Realm.' The Sphinx nodded and did not continue the conversation, but preferred to sit and watch the bar vibrate with the material-fuelled pleasure of the humans. Satisfied with the answers, the cat had no desire to know more and was content to just sit in the company of the Sphinx.

...the storm dissipated, taking pieces of the Shadow's anger with it to dispense to the unsuspecting and the innocent. A sudden downpour to flatten the sole crop of a struggling farmer. A single bolt of lightening to shred a tree into the path of an oncoming car, widowing a newly-wed bride on her happiest day. A flash flood to dilute the hopes of trout-farmer. Another lightening strike to take out a power substation, to create mayhem in a small community hospital. Everywhere the storms-fragments would discharge the Shadow's vengeance in small pockets of germinating Despair...

Philip felt the bed move, the unmistakable tilt of the mattress as someone slipped under the covers beside him.

...the Shadow continued to float high above the city. It knew the Sphinx was abroad. Somewhere in the maze of soul and spirit that co-existed with the flesh and blood, concrete and steel of the city. But something had changed, shifted, phased. It could no longer isolate the spirit that the Corvidae' sacrifice had revealed...

Ashiya blinked and looked twice. But she was mistaken. The bar was full of young people, partying and carousing like a demented horde at a theme night on Halloween. A party that had been twisted beyond recognition by every horror writer that had ever picked up a pen into an unbalanced parody of a good time. All around were bodies covered in black and purple velvet; latex, leather and lace; punctured and punctuated with surgical steel and silver; adorned in flowing and jagged designs scratched and inked into the surface of skin oiled in sweat. Their litheness gyrated to thumping rhythms of once forgotten gloom masterpieces. Sombre lyrics and melodies played over the counterpoint of uplifting guitar riffs and body-moving bass lines motivated latex-sprayed bodies to strut and pose. The electro-kick of industrial noise modulated into dance beats grated in contradiction to the flowing movements it inspired in the bodies moving in time with its pulse. Ashiya sighed. In spite of their outlandish dress and behaviour of designed shock, all of the young bodies were quite normal. Nevertheless, from the corner of her eye she was certain she had seen a naked woman carrying a cat walking through the crowded bar.

…the essence of the Sphinx was lost in a blur of other, younger, spirits emerging from the chaos. The Waking Lands were waking, stirring, rising. The Shadow puzzled over this, contemplating its meaning from high over the city. It was incongruent that the Sphinx, so bent on destroying the Darqlands, would be arousing these other spirits. What other explanation? Another power interfering with the balance, disturbing the Endless Cycle? One it had not felt before, perhaps, darker than itself, concealed in a darker Darqness. It searched the minor radiances, sniffing for a hint of this other nemesis. All it could trace was a faint golden after-glow of the Sphinx that diffused through the night…

Page Twenty Five: The Wrath of Grapes

Philip stirred. Turning on his side, he found the bed empty, devoid of any trace of anothers' presence, the sheet smooth beside him, the pillow undented. His heart sank with the realisation and cursed his dream-world for deluding him once more. Then he was thankful that the fantasy had not corrupted the reality. He sat up in bed and blinked at the sunlight streaming in through parallel slits in the charcoal black blinds. Oriented to the hour of the morning, he swivelled to sit on the edge of the bed in the semi-fog of a hangover. He foolishly shook his head, trying to dislodge the several layers of stale brandy that clouded his mind. But that only served to aggravate them, causing his temples to pulse with a dull ache as the spirit of the grape vent its wrath. Absently he reached out and plucked the lone cigarette from a crumpled packet and lit up. The glare of the match fuelling the pain behind his eyes, he almost gagged on the first drag of the first cigarette of the day, the bite of tar and nicotine rasped with the phosphor-burn of the match. As his lungs filled with smoke, he fought to contain the accompanying cough, then conceded to a racking blast that gurgled with the phlegm and fluid in his throat. Oh Fuck, he thought, I'm starting to sound like my father.

…a stray thought drifted up from the city and caught the Shadow. Wry amusement welled from deep within as it twisted and perverted the thought to its own design and sent it back down from where it came…

Saffron stirred. The sound of a hoarse cough dragging her from the edge of sleep where she had spent most of the restless night. The familiar hack disorientated her, throwing her back into another nightmare. Images of the bloated form of her father leaving her bed, leaving her soiled and violated, leaving her sobbing and crying. The pain and blood in her vagina and rectum no match for the hurt she felt in her heart. The self loathing crushing her with the weight of sin that caused her father to treat her so badly. The filth crusting her young body and staining her night-clothes the physical evidence of the filth and vitriol that emanated from her father's mouth as he cursed and swore while punishing and defiling her. No! She screamed at the images in her head, It's over, it's better now, it's gone away, he's dead, gone away, gone away, go away! She curled up and dragged a jumble of cushions and quilt over her head, smothering the sound and drowning her tears.

By degrees, the disturbed childhood echoes abated, forced back into the secure blackness and covered in thick strata of blankness, burying them in a sepulchre of forgotten thoughts. The vacuum left by the subsiding waking-dream was gradually filled with the comforting embrace from deep clouds of nothing, the lilting peace drifting her off into a shallow sleep now purged of its calumniatory spectre. The mist of non-existence washed over her, she swam in a lake of purification, cleansing her body and absolving her soul. Gliding effortlessly she at last felt at ease, the cushions that had formed her pillows and snuffled her crying where pushed away and in her sleep she was smiling. Her dozing was disturbed again, now by the telltale creek of naked feet attempting stealth on ancient and unforgiving floorboards. Slowly she raised the covers enough to see out and catch the sight of Philip caught mid-stride, creeping on tip-toes between the bedroom and bathroom doors. She tried to suppress a giggle at the comical sight, but failed. He froze, whipping his head around towards her, a shocked and guilty expression broke the concentration that had gripped his face and he started to glow, his cheeks turning a bruised red. Now laughing openly, she bolted up, the cushions and quilt scattering as she pointed at him.

'Is that an erection, or are you just pleased to see me?' She joked, as he swiftly tried to cover his embarrassment with both hands, his face harmonising with the deeper shade of red of his engorged member as it peeked between his fingers.

'I need the bathroom.' He blurted before completing the dash into the bathroom and slamming the door behind him. Saffron continued to giggle until she was distracted by the thought of her uncovered breasts bouncing as she laughed. Then a stern look came over her, she looked down on her own naked body, and to the closed bathroom door, wondering just how long he had been looking at her to get into that state. Bemused, she shook her head and smiled.

…(fuck)…

Philip lent back on the door until he heard the catch click and then he let out a long sigh. The excess blood slowly drained from his face and penis. He cursed mother nature for giving men a mechanism that prevented them wetting the bed, one that caused so much amusement to women.

Page Twenty Six: The Grilled Grapefruit

…come on my pretty. Shake a leg. Rise and shine. Breakfast is on the table. Hot buttered toast, freshly squeezed orange, half a grapefruit, sugared and lightly grilled and a steaming pot of hazelnut coffee…

Of course, in younger times, as a teenager Rochelle had scared herself. In a friends bedroom, with red paper taped over the table lamp and a solitary joss-stick to mask the smell of a joint they had smuggled in past parental eyes. A group of three school friends crowded around a low desk laid out with an arc of Scrabble tiles and an up-turned glass for a planchette. As is typical, it did not take long for the giggling to turn to blanched fear as overactive imaginations took hold of the makeshift Ouija board. Of course, now, Rochelle could offer a million and one explanations for events of that night, most of them well documented in the rows of books that decorated one wall in her living-room, a few of them in her own self-published books and pamphlets. The adolescent mind was an untamed and undirected power, trapped in an ever changing body it was capable of many wonders. But this was different and Rochelle was truly scared. Nothing in her learning and reading could have prepared her for that - elemental forces so dark, so obscene that they tainted everything they touched.

After two scalding showers, she now felt clean enough to soak in a deep scented bath and not have the water tainted by her own filth, to allow the emulsified essential oils to work their magic. However, she still did not feel fully clean, 'the physical filth may have permeated my body, seeped through my skin by osmosis, percolated through every pore, to taint my blood, rot the ichor. Tish! Hysterical nonsense.' Nevertheless. 'I have been abused, my mind has been despoiled, sullied ~ raped!' She felt sick at the thought, as if she had insulted every rape-victim in the world. In her self-pity, her heart went out to them, apologetically seeking comfort and solace in the sisterhood. She felt the link, a connection, the act was different, but the cause and effect the same, a will greater than her own had forced itself on her - deflowered her virgin thoughts.

Laying back, she inhaled the soothing perfume as she systematically analysed the disruption of her meditation, discarding wild notions and fanciful ideas as logic routed out the cause and reason. 'The most rational: self inflicted, overworked tiredness took over her meditation and she just fell asleep, to dream. And in dream, a nightmare, personal anxieties carried through to her subconscious to conjure her worse fears. But what of fear? The most powerful and potent of emotions. The most base of the basics, the one used throughout countless millennia to control and subjugate. Ah, control… Perhaps, someone, or something, was trying to control her, force her to do its bidding. A option. Something very strong, stronger than herself. A power capable of raping your thoughts? Violating your inner most dreams? Now, that's frightening. But who, or what? The strange new girl from last night? A possibility…'

Rochelle mused on these options as she lathered the soap between her hands and rubbed the smooth white foam into her arms. The image of the girl transfixed in her mind, deep blue eyes, deeper than midnight, looked back at her, smouldering, probing, hypnotic. 'Limpid?' Rochelle smiled, 'Limpid-pools, such a poetic phrase.

No, not limpid, but dark and impenetrable. A thousand lives behind those eyes and not one of them reachable. She must find this girl.' An overwhelming and uncharacteristic feeling washed over her, one of complete smugness. In the steam rising from the bath, the fragrance caught her, intense and inviting. Rochelle's only thought was of grapefruit as she bit down on the bar of soap in her hand.

…the Angel scooped out a lone segment and spooned it into his mouth. 'Manner from heaven' he grinned, crushing the polyps of juice between his tongue and palate, relishing the release of sharp citric acid bursting into his mouth, permitting a slight leak of liquid from the corners of his mouth to dribble down his chin, before swallowing it back deep into his throat…

The sun broke over grotesque carvings of gargoyles perched below a slated steeple. Distorted heads chiselled from raw limestone, blackened through decades of fossil-fuel pollution. Decorated and defaced by the accumulated marl through centuries of roosting starlings and poxed by the starburst growth of pale yellow lichen. The sharp rays picked out time-eroded detail, elongated shadows distorting their cruel features into comical caricatures of sadness, forlorn sentinels forever pondering the fate of the city from their ecclesiastic lookout. Amid the silent horde of petrified demons, a lone shape, alabaster white contrasting against coal black, the feathered prince of pathos, a piebald clown in a circus of sorrow, huddled down in a solitary vigil on the rain-washed balustrade. Watchful intent focused its ink-spot eyes on the three-storey Georgian town-house opposite. The couple had entered the building in the late evening. Lighted windows switched on and off as they moved from room to room, finally settling on large bay-window on the second floor as a warm orange flicker, subdued through thin curtains. There they remained throughout the night as the Magpie stood guard. Reward, there would be reward in this.

…the acid touch of the morning beams bit like lasers searing the edges of shadows, cutting them into crisp, hard edges, sharply defining the threshold between day and night, Hope and Despair. The black silhouettes of tower-blocks slowly stole across the city streets like ghosts of the skyscrapers cast by the power of the sun. A power that gradually ate them away as its strength increased. Like vampires, the shadows succoured no life from sunlight, only death. Yet one shadow refused to be intimidated, undaunted by the killing radiation it stood resolute and defiant, the persistence of the sun unable to touch the indistinct edges of the Shadow…

Ashiya sat crosslegged on the floor looking over to the prostrate body sleeping on the bed. Diffused light from the muslin draped windows accentuated the undulating curves, softened the hard edge of muscle, blending them into healthy regions of fat as graceful hints of toned perfection. A delicately rounded stomach rose and fell in time with shallow breathing. Pale white skin tattooed with rosettes of red fringed bite marks connected by parallel runs scratched into the white flesh. She knew similar markings adorned her own back, like tribal markings of affiliation. An affirmation of lust. Faint smears of blood diluted with saliva etching cuneiform poetry of passion all over her body. fleeting poems that would last longer than the feelings she held for the girl on the bed. A transient love that would heal faster than cuts and lacerations. The floor, like the bed, was littered with the toys from the nights play, soft imitations of instruments of torture recreated for pain as pleasure, their effect as short-lived as her love for the girl. Ashiya sighed. A sadness prevailed. Passion had become a routine, an act of trivia to be turned on and off at a whim. And there was a feeling of loss, as when something had been stolen. Each of her lovers had left something behind, locked in her heart, a shared gift. But from this girl, nothing. Not even a name.

…unfettered and unrestrained. Untouched and unmoved. The Shadow stared into the golden unblinking eye of the heavens. It had watched its birth, sixteen trillion cycles ago, (so long, yet only a heartbeat). Witnessed its heat and light fuelling the cooling and coalescing of matter into planets and moons. And the rising of life from simple nucleic acids into the complex and confounding artefacts of flesh and blood that teemed the land and sky and seas. The blazing beacon that flamed the endless cycle. The Shadow contemplated the Light, not so different from the Darqness: trapping souls in 'earthly bodies', a purgatory of Hope and Despair. Without Light there can be no Darqness, without Darqness, what point has Light? Without us there would be no life and without life who would dream? We are the stuff that dreams are made of…

Page Twenty Seven: The Stuff that Smiles are made of

Hastily provided explanations over breakfast appeared to do little in convincing Saffron, yet they went some way towards relieving Philip of at least some of the associated guilt. Her knowing smiles were more disconcerting. As were the fleeting touch of hands as they reached for the same piece of toast, or the accidental brushing of her foot against his leg under the cramped confines of his tiny kitchen table. Or the way her eyes coyly peaked from beneath her scarlet fringe whenever she looked at him, or how her fingers played and lingered around her mouth when she spoke, or the way her tongue was always visible when she smiled, its tip teasing the edge of her teeth. Each seemingly unintentional action was accompanied by that knowing smile. Philip silently cursed to himself, he doubted there was a man alive who could correctly interpret female signals, *Am I seeing what I wanted to see or being blunderingly obtuse to the obvious? Why can't we be more open, more blunt, more direct? Why are there always games to play and rituals to dance?* He smiled back. She smiled back at his smiling back. *And? …what does that mean? How many faces had been slapped or friendships shattered by a man's ineptness in these rites?* He frowned and returned to spreading butter on his toast.

'What's up?' She inquired on seeing his perplexed expression.

'That-a-away.' He replied in total dead-pan, gesturing with a butter-loaded knife towards the ceiling, a pat of butter falling from the warmed knife onto his knuckle, which he absently licked off before continuing with the chore of layering more butter onto his already generously covered bread. She chuckled as she reached out and scooped a missed knob of butter from the back of his hand with her index finger. He looked at her, watching as she popped it into her mouth to be sucked clean in either the most salacious way he had ever seen or the most innocent. He instantly wished he was that finger, or that mouth, then scolded himself for the thought. She removed the finger with an obscenely wet kissing sound that created a movement his loins that he would not be able to explain away as the safety mechanism of an over-full bladder. A movement that threatened to produce a tenting in his dressing gown that the table's edge would fail to hide. He tried to ignore his thoughts as he took a bite out of the toast.

'Now I'm all wet.' She pouted in a put-on childish tone, wiping her finger on the lapel of her borrowed dressing gown, inadvertently revealing a youthful breast crowned with an exceptionally awake nipple. Once again he tried to shift his thoughts elsewhere while uncomfortably crossing his legs. A singularly awkward movement that slid his foot up round the soft curve of her calf and into the tender crook at the back of her knee and simultaneously smacked his own knee into the hidden cross-brace on the underside of the table. He grimaced as the reflex knee-jerk stubbed his toe into the hard edge of her chair. Before he had chance to rearrange his clothing, she had ducked down below the table to see what the commotion was about. There was a gasp and a thump that shook the table as she cracked her head against its underside. Slowly she righted herself, her brow furrowed and a seriously wicked grin on her face as wide as Tuesday. 'Randy little fucker aren't you?' He squirmed, trying for all the world to pretend that nothing had happened. 'Do you ever go down?' She smirked, rubbing the back of her head. He coughed, almost choking, uncertain whether the remark was a retort or an innuendo, and gulped down a mouthful of half chewed toast.

'Er, um, it's not what you think.' *Liar,* he chastised himself, *it's exactly what she thinks it is!* 'How's your head?' He asked, trying to change the subject.

'Oh, no complaints so far...'

…so, what now my son? A rhetorical question, the Shadow knew the answer and it knew the Sun would not give it. It would continue in its arc, rising higher in the sky as it journeyed to the west, a gentle deception on a tilted and spinning world that beguiled mankind for millions of cycles…

The cat felt the ever increasing pull of sleep as tired muscles moved aching bones through the city. Each pad-fall on the relentless flag-stones jolted pain into its joints. Its head hung low as it fought to keep its eyes open. It could go no further, it needed to sleep and would happily do it here, now. The cat stopped and sat down, giving a weak cry as the Sphinx continued to walk on. After a few strides, the glowing figure stopped and turned round, then walked back to where the cat had given up. The Sphinx crouched down and gently stroked the cat, her long slender fingers rubbing the fur at the back of its head and around its ears. The cat had no choice but to purr, an innate reaction that the cat could no more control than a baby its giggles at being tickled.

'~ sorry ~ ' the cats thoughts were drowsy, clipping the margins between sleeping and waking '~ I ~ can't ~', but as the Sphinx continued to stroke, energy flowed from her aura into the cat, soothing the pain and easing the aches. The cat purred louder, rubbing its head against her hand. Then gently she picked up the cat, cradling it in her arms and tenderly placed a kiss on the top of its head.

'No, my apologies, it is my fault.' She cooed, emanating heart-felt love to the cat. 'It has been so long since I was flesh, I forget that these primitive bodies tire so quickly. And yours is so much smaller, but then it must take less energy to sustain it'

'Something like that. It's our carnivorous diet - high protean so we do not have to eat continuously. But it does mean we sleep a lot.'

'That must be why I feel hunger.' She raised her head, jerking it in different directions, sniffing the air. 'Where shall we hunt?'

'We could try a restaurant.' The Sphinx made a noise approximating to a laugh as she stood up, still carrying the cat. They did not have to travelled far before they found a suitable café down a narrow side-street off the main high road. Soon they were seated on a hard, red vinyl covered, bench-seat at a chipped wood-effect Formica table layered with a thin layer of grease that left swirling patterns when you touched it. A stained and worn card that represented a menu was wedged between crusted plastic sauce bottles in red and brown, surrounded by chrome topped glass bottles of salt, pepper and sugar. They studied the menu while waiting for the waitress to approach. When she finally arrived, the cat was disappointed not to see a half-burnt cigarette drooping from crudely painted lips and a broken ball-point pen tucked into badly tied-back hair, still, the soiled apron that served as a uniform did not inspire cleanliness. The waitress appeared not to notice anything unusual about a glowing naked woman and a cat, but simply raised an eye-brow and stood with pen poised over her tattered note-pad, waiting for their order. The Sphinx gave hers first, a bowl of muesli, an orange juice and a large black coffee, and then turned to the cat. As the cat thought, she instantaneously spoke the words to the waitress.

'Fish, lightly grilled, no butter and bottled spring water, the non-fizzy one - Oh, in a bowl.' The waitress raised both eye-brows.

'Kippers, we've only got kippers.'

'Then kippers it is then. Thank you.' She went to pass the menu to the waitress, who had already turned and walked towards the kitchen, then placed it back between the two sauce bottles. 'Spring water? A little refined for a cat is it not?'

'Just a precaution, would you drink the tap-water in this dump?'

'Fair point, however, I thought you would have a saucer of milk.'

'Nah, that's a fallacy, actually we can't digest lactic acid, we don't produce the necessary enzymes or something. Anyway, it makes me yak.'

'…And butter?'

'Yak.'

'…And Yak's milk?'

'Oh-hardy-har-har! Anyway. Muesli? Ha! Rat-food! Wait 'till they hear about this back in the Realm. Eek-eek, look at me I'm a sphinx, eek-eek!' The cat chuckled to itself, shaking its head from side to side. The Sphinx scowled at the cat.

'I am a vegetarian by choice, not that I have not eaten meat. I am easily capable of killing, and not just animals smaller than myself,' she looked down on the cat, 'unlike others I could mention.' She lent towards the cat, emphasising the height difference between them and grinning as to bare her teeth, revealing long sharp canines that the cat had failed to notice before. The cat cowered.

'Okay, okay, I get the message. I won't say another word. You've made your point, now back off and give me some light down here.' The cat wriggled, trying to create some more room for itself. She lent back and tenderly stroked it between its ears, then patted it on the head as the waitress deposited their food and drinks on the table, together with a scrap of paper meant as the bill. 'And how are we going to pay for this?' Thought the cat.

'There is no charge.' The Sphinx replied.

'Huh? There's no charge.' Repeated the waitress, picking up the bill and scrunching it in her hand.

'Wow, Cool!' the cat exclaimed in wide-eyed disbelief.

'Woh, Kule!' The Sphinx mimicked, not quite matching the inflection. 'How twentieth century.'

'Well, I never had you pegged as sarcastic.' The cat mumbled as it peered over the edge of the table at the steaming golden fish on the plate, framed by a knife and fork. It almost leapt onto the table to devour the food, but thought better of it. It looked at its fore-paws and then to the cutlery and shook its head. It raise a paw and considered hooking the fish off the plate, then decided that that would be chastised too. So it sat back and looked at the Sphinx.

'You are dribbling.'

'I'm not dribbling. I'm drooling. I'm hungry.'

'I thought only dogs drooled.' The cat responded by thinking a fair approximation to a bark and raised its paw again, like it has seen countless dumb dogs do, which caused the Sphinx to smile. Swiftly, she diced the fish and placed the plate on the bench beside the cat. As they ate and chewed they continued to talk, something that is not politely possible by verbal communication alone. At some point the cat realised it did not know what the Sphinx was called, never having opportunity to converse with it before, it was always refereed to as The Sphinx, and usually in hushed reverent tones with that odd head-turned-one-way-eyes-looking-the-other gesture that is used when passing on a secret.

'What's your name anyway?' it thought, as nonchalantly as it knew how. The Sphinx laughed, in thought and out loud, causing several heads to swivel round to look in their direction, then it told the cat that it already knew and that there was nothing to be gained in the telling. The cat went quiet for a moment as it tried to remember, then shook its head. After much goading the Sphinx promised to tell if the cat went first. The cat looked as embarrassed as a cat can get. 'Cat-name, or', the cat almost growled the next bit, 'what the apes call me?'. The Sphinx took a deep breath through her nose, as if pondering the question.

'Umm, Human name first I think.' Ratshit! thought the cat to itself. 'I heard that.' the Sphinx grinned.

'Oh Sweet Bast, this is so-o-o embarrassing.' The Sphinx was struggling to suppress a giggle, the cat scowled at the Sphinx, She knows!, then it took a mental big breath and blurted 'Tiddles!' The Sphinx surrendered to a fit of giggles. The cat waited, sulking. 'Finished?' She nodded, trying to compose herself and then shook her head as the giggles overcame her again.

'Humorous bastards are they not.' She joked through fits of giggles.

'Once that's all, just once. I was just a kitten, that's all. I didn't know you weren't to piss in their dens, but I didn't know were else to go.' The Sphinx made sympathetic cooing noises, stroking the cats head. 'I got a generous dose of ginger up my snout for that - couldn't smell a bloody thing for weeks!'

'So, what is your cat-name then?' The cat slumped and shook its head. 'Oh please, I will not laugh again.' She implored, tickling the sensitive fur under its chin. The cat reluctantly gave a series of low growls and mews, finishing with a flick of its tail that she instantly translated into Human. She burst into spontaneous uncontrolled laughter. 'Lard-arse!' She almost screamed through her laughter, so that a couple dressed in work-a-day clothes on the next table turned and threw her an admonishing look over their shoulders before returning to their breakfast.

'L'Darce' the cat indignantly corrected. She finally reclaimed her self-control and apologised to the cat, who was now in a deeper sulk. They ate in silence for a while, the cat pawing at the fish more than eating it. Eventually it looked up and asked. 'We've had a good laugh at my names, so what so special about yours'?' The Sphinx's thoughts dropped to a whisper, as if to guard against eaves-droppers.

'To Humans I have many names, as many names as there are stars in a night sky, and as many as the grains of sand on a beach. To some I am the cycle of seasons. To others the cycle of life. I am known as Isis, Asarte, Hecate, Demeter, Kali, Inanna,' She paused, waiting for the cat to process the name-list, allowing each title to slowly sink in. She faced the cat and fixed her golden eyes on the cat's amber eyes. 'and Diana.' The cats wide eyes went wider still and its jaw dropped.

'Oh Sweet Bast!' There was near terror mixed with total awe in its thought.

…the Shadow was beginning to sublimate, blending the boundaries between the Waking Lands and The Darqlands, as it picked up the faint unguarded cry from the cat. Unable to halt the transmutation between realities, it slipped into the Darqlands cursing, knowing it had missed the Sphinx once again…

'Yes my child?'

Page Twenty Eight: SalaCity

Sala City lives

The City breathes. But the City is dying. A slow rhythmic respiration sucking in plump rich life, exhaling dry spent souls. The all consuming City. But the City is dying. To the west wealth begets property and proximity, the developers' City-Garden of privilege, the urban suburbs of mews and lofts, conversions. Status increasing as it moves closer to the centre, the prestige of zip/post codes collected as loyalty points. To the east wealth begets property and distance, the re-developers' Garden-City of reclaimed dereliction and poverty, tenements and terraces. Ever creeping further east, spreading out into the Green-belt of agriculture and Grey-belt of industry, The Black-belt of progress leaving a wake of debris and detritus. Between them: The Centre. A demarcation-line where opulenCity looks down on the pauCity. The poor unable to follow the tide, are left stranded on the shore, to pick over the waste and squalor. Where the greed of developers' created a sham by skating on the thin icing of a putrid cake. Where deals within deals cut the corners of prudence, increased the margins for the benefit of the bottom line. The legacy of the fast-buck is the slow rot of decay. A facade hiding the accumulation of a scam within a scam that ate away at the foundations, crumbled the bedrock, causing the Heart to tumble into the waiting hands of the underworld. A No Man's Land where commerce and trade relocated to greener pastures, taking the life-force with it. Leaving a vacuum, pockets of nothing inhabited by the flotsam of life, the forgotten and the invisible. To fall prey to the undertow of Morning. The most dangerous of times. Where pimps and pushers prowl in the open, in the light, unrestrained and unfettered. Ever seeking the likely candidate, the new recruit to the parasites' game of living. Picking up the destitute and the desperate, press-ganged into the service of the black economy of the City. Earnt by night, but invested by day. The City lives.

Chapter Five: Ishtarah

Page Twenty Nine: Feeding Ducks

…deep within the swirling vortex between long ago and soon, a stirring…

Ashiya walked in a daze. Unaware of where she was going, or how she was to get there. Like an automaton, she placed one foot in front of the other and lent forward, transferring her body weight onto the leading leg, her centre of gravity shifting as she started a controlled fall. Using fluids in her middle-ear to gauge pitch, roll and attitude, she recovered her balance and repeated the process again. It took no special skill to achieve this, it required no significant thought, it was an automatic action. She just walked. From a nondescript bed-sit in a nondescript house she walked. Along streets with row upon row of houses, each much the same as the other, she walked. She walked until she was stood by a boating lake in one of the City parks, the boats and pedaloes long since gone as economics and safety rendered them unusable and electronic pastimes deemed them unfashionable. Nature claimed the man-made lake as its own, slowly filling the waters and water margins with wild-life and flora as the years passed. Wind-borne vegetation encroached on the severity of municipal landscaping, fusing it back to the earth, into a semblance of romantic reality missed by its original gardeners as they tried to impose their notions of the countryside on to a city centre. Ashiya stood watching the ducks as they cavorted in their mating rituals. A dowdy-brown female pursued by several gaudy, emerald-headed drakes, sudden frantic darting and insistent quacks as a dominant male came to the fore and the weaker males swam off. Then, a flurry of feathers and splashes water as the female treaded water as the male treaded her back. More like fighting than copulation, it was over in seconds. She shrugged and turned from the lake to look around at the people who were either visiting the park, or just passing through. On a dark-green bench near the waters edge, a young couple, oblivious to their surroundings, were lost in each other. They showed more restrained courting rituals than the ducks, but rituals just the same. 'If they were alone they'd be fucking like rabbits' She thought to herself, with a modicum of envy as the boy nestled his face in the girls neck and his hand strayed speculatively along her thigh.

The sound of juvenile laughter distracted her attention towards the path. Small children followed in the tow of a strutting mother pushing a baby-buggy before her, with her chest held high like a proud pea-hen, she displayed her brood and her fertility for all to see. Subconsciously, Ashiya's hand rested on her stomach, to imagine the feeling of a life growing in her womb, but all she felt was a hollow emptiness. Further back along the path, an elderly couple lent on walking-sticks and each other as they crept along, their progress so slow it was hard to tell if they were moving at all. A young girl swerved around them as she jogged passed. Ashiya watched her pass, mesmerised by her breasts fighting for release with each juddering foot-fall from a sports-bra partially concealed beneath a skimp top. She also watched as the old man become equally hypnotised by her rear as she jogged away. Ashiya smiled a smile of recognition. The old woman scowled in response, feebly lifting her cane to chastise her partner, then smiling too, kissed him on the cheek. The old couple laughed and hugged each others' arms tighter. The sight brought a lump to her throat. She wanted to break down and cry, but her self-restraint held it back, held it all in. For all her independence and love of solitude she had never felt so alone. The succubus that stole into her life, to give her the gift of love without love, had taken something in return. All the pleasures she once took as her own were gone.

Superficial couplings and quick release drugs were no longer enough. Her spectral lover had stolen her life.

…a jumble of thoughts and memories, disjointed and incoherent, racing to the surface to release a cacophonous bubble bursting in an effervescent rush of colour and radiance…

To Rochelle, the World was flat. Not flat in a physical sense, she did not need to go into space to believe that the Earth was a globe, spinning in a vacuum. No, she was perfectly happy to accept that as received wisdom, she was of no mind to argue with four hundred years of science. Rochelle's Flat World existed in a metaphysical sense. The past and present where the only two dimensions of her World. She could measure them. By simply living, she could travel through the present and by remembering she could journey through the past. The future, however, was the third dimension she could only imagine, and then only with inefficient accuracy. Logic told her it existed, but she had no means to measure it without convolving it back in time to the present, where it would quickly slip into the past. And once that had happened she had no way of proving that it ever existed as the future. The more she learnt of the Craft, the more she realised that she had little chance of truly influencing future events, but was more likely to be influenced by them. It was a logical conclusion, in what Rochelle jokingly termed Kismet-hardy, that whatever is happening now has already been pre-determined in the future. For that, the future made her uneasy and she preferred not to even think about it unless she absolutely had to. She looked at her face in the bathroom mirror and felt old. She tried to remember herself younger as she smoothed moisturising cream into the faint tracks that the past was leaving around her eyes, blending her once youthful appearance into the present in an attempt to keep the future at bay. She loathed the thought of growing old and silently cursed both the Craft and the ever secular Science for failing her, in spite their potions and active liposomes. The Blood of Virgins - in this city!? She wished she could have frozen her appearance ten years earlier, when she had frozen her life, discarding the Then and living for the Now. But her Now was rushing headlong into the When, and she was gripped with foreboding. Her limited perception of the future had suddenly become blacker, coloured by a darkness that was more sinister than the unknown. She knew she was being driven by an unnatural desire to find a girl. A girl whose face was quickly consumed by a swirling black cloud whenever she tried to picture it in her mind. Each time this happened, Rochelle would snap back to reality with a jolt that felt like a cold-creep starting at her hair-line, running over her scalp to the nape of her neck and then on down her back. She shivered even at the thought of it.

Rochelle reached for her toothbrush to clean her teeth for the third time since getting out of the bath, then changed her mind and picked up the bar of soap. She looked at the bite she had absent-mindedly taken out of Maud's Fruit Scented soap and gave a short laugh, then dropped it into the waste bin, vowing to buy unscented soap from now on.

…then a fight with a oppressive consciousness, disorientation and turmoil, an overpowering feeling of suppression and domination, confusion and chaos retreat back to safety, a regression into the womb…

Page Thirty: Another Significant Moment

'Saffron' stood at a tee-junction, a minor residential road flowing as a tributary off the main drag that connected one city borough with its neighbour. Behind her was the street that lead back to Philip's simple Georgian house and its complicated owner/occupier, to the left was a small parade of shops, her excuse for leaving the house, and to the right, her true reason, an Underground Station. *Another Significant Moment*, she thought, a moment that affects every other moment from now on. A moment that she will reflect on for the rest of her life: *What would have happened if I had stayed? What if Angels do exist? What would happen if I let Philip get close? What would happen if I weren't such a coward?* 'Saffron' looked up to the heavens for answers and received nothing in reply *Shit! Why is life so fucking difficult?* She wanted to hit out at something in her frustration and anger, remonstrate to an inanimate object for her own failings and short-comings. *I'm not running away, I just don't belong here! This is someone else's life and someone else's problem!* She told herself, trying to appease her conscience. To further enhance her claim, she turned left and walked away from the station, towards the shops - to demonstrate that she was in control of the situation, she was not running away - she was walking.

…the Shadow dispatched tendrils of thoughts, scalding fingers to probe the tender mind writhing deep in the Heart of Darqlands. To further twist the knife another degree, another degree of pain that wracked the soul, piling torment onto torment, adding torture onto torture…

The Sphinx continued to talk after they left the Café, trying to engage the cat in conversation, but the cat had gone very quiet, walking in her shadow, several cat-paces behind.

'You have become very quiet. You are not sulking are you?'. She glanced back at the cat, who walked with his head down, not daring to look at her.

'No, my Queen.' the cat reverently replied.

'Then, have we stopped being friends?' The cat shook its head, but continued to stare at the ground. 'There is no need for airs and graces between us.' She shrugged and then sighed. 'I never had much use for titles anyway. Call me Diana.'

'If you so command. My Qu-Diana.' Diana stopped and knelt down in front of the cat, gently pinching the clumps of fur on its cheeks.

'Oh how I love you, my Lard-arse.' She lent forward and kissed him on the nose. L'Darce sneezed in return and tried to avert his eyes. She sat cross-legged on the warm pavement, and looked down on the cat sat in front of her. 'Am I the same as I was before you knew who I was?'

'Well, I suppose...'

'So let us carry on as before. You be your normal, cantankerous self and I shall be my normal, sarcastic self.'

'It's not that easy. You are Bast and can never be 'normal', especially as you glow in the dark, and I am just a lowly cat.'

'No cat is just a lowly cat,' she scolded, a little more authoritatively than she intended, 'we all are Regal and are not all female cats called Queens?' The cat nodded. 'Have you not been told? 'A Cat can look at a King'.' Diana lifted the cat's chin with her finger so that he was looking directly at her. 'Or a Queen.' She pulled back her finger from his chin, and the cat's head dropped. She carried on looking at the space where his face had been, but her focus was now on her finger. Her gaze traced a line from her finger, along her hand and over the slender bend of her wrist. With her lips pursed, almost pouting, she looked at the bare flesh of her fore-arm, watching it twist as she flexed her hand. 'Am I still glowing?' The cat did not answer. She brought up her other arm to rest along side the first to compare them. 'There must be a lot of loose energy around this city of yours.' She dropped her arms, placing her palms flat against the smoothed paving slabs. 'Nevermind, I only glow for those who can see, so most mortals do not see the aura. In fact most humans do not really see me at all until after I've gone.' Diana thought for a while, in guarded thoughts the cat could not hear. 'I regard you as a friend and in that you are my equal. Assuming you think of me as your friend that is.'

'I said...' The cat started, then changed its line of thought. 'Of course I would be honoured to consider you a friend, but can't we just pretend to be equal?'

'If it makes you more comfortable, then yes. But let us have new names, special friendship names. So we will not be encumbered by a past that my name invokes. What name have you always wanted?'

'Nimrod.'

'Ha. No, not that, too many memories. How about Kipper?'

'That's a dog's name!' The cat indignantly replied. 'Kip sounds better.'

'Okay, Kip, now choose a name for me.' The cat thought for a moment, a collection of images and words that did not constitute conversation, so Diana blocked them out, not wishing to listen to his thought processes. Finally, the cat looked up.

'What was that amazing drink you had last night?'

'Do you mean the electric-blue one?' Kip nodded. 'I believe they called it a Blue Moon.'

'Blue.' The cat's eyes gleamed. 'Can I call you Blue?' She wanted to smile at the cat's renewed enthusiasm and at her little victory, but suppressed it, preferring to remain serious.

'Blue? Okay. Blue and Kip. An unlikely duo.' Blue stroked Kip's head and stood up. 'Like something out of an adventure story.'

'Kip and Blue - it's got a better ring to it.' Kip smiled and Blue grinned back, beaming at him and gestured or him to lead the way. Together they set of down the street. 'That drink.' He thought to her as they walked. 'What's it like?'

'You would not like it.'

'Why, what does it taste of?'

'Bitter Orange Marmalade.'

'Yak.'

'Yak Marmalade, it could catch on.' She joked. They walked some more. The conversation full and animated, but constantly flicking between idle and banal.

…it could sense the soul's uneasy resting, nervously waiting for the next torment, it cold feel the soul reaching out for solace in all directions, the futility of the action adding to its misery. A sudden, unannounced jab of ice-cold needles into its kidneys and the soul will contort in sheer pain. But that is not they way of the Shadow. A quick mental projection of the act and its searing pain into the soul, then stretch that moment so it lasts for ever and the torture begins…

An alien array of eyes peered down while an equally alien brain processed the multiple image into a multiscopic map of light and dark giving massed tactical information. Each distance, velocity and acceleration of the entrapped prey was gathered as it fought against its silken bindings, the tenacious threads pulled tighter, wrapping themselves around its limbs, strapping it firmly into the web. The spider pounced, sinking poison-tipped fangs through the hard carapace into the soft flesh beneath.

…The soul writhed and screamed. And it was learning to hate. Execrating every vile and abdominal affliction it could muster towards its tormentor…

The shop was a small over-filled convenience store that once was called a corner-shop and had subsequently evolved and transmuted over the years until its final decline, bled dry by out-of-town superstores, malls and 24-hour shopping. Now re-invented to inject cohesion into the community, this was a subminiture theme-park to shopping, smart corporate franchising dressed in pseudo-unique originality and factory produced quaintness belying a security system rivalling a major bank as protection from 24-hour mugging and wanton thuggey. An array of mass-modern technology to control and govern the olde-worlde charm of mechanical tills with epos brains and scales with silicon hearts, batteries of atomisers to spray the aroma of crusty baked bread, wax-paper wrapped cheese, wheat-germ and fresh ground coffee at customers as they walked past rows of plastic-cocooned produce. An aged, silver-haired, man in a crisp white apron was stocking shelves towards the rear of the shop, whistling a tuneless and unplaceable refrain, while a young girl, who convention decreed was either his daughter, niece or teenage bride, manned the till and monitored the bank of surveillance cameras. 'Saffron' stood in front of a display of sweets and candy, row upon row of chocolate and sugar-derived confection in garish wrappers with onomatopoetic names, like Spangles, Crunchie and Curly-Wurly. All of a sudden she was nine-years old again, clutching her father's hand, trying to select a 'special treat' from the wonders on show, for being 'Daddy's special little girl'. Ever present was the dilemma of what to buy, one expensive and dreamy designer bar that would taste exquisite but be gone in minutes, or lots of the smaller, cheaper, candy that would last much longer. The choice was overwhelming, it was so difficult to decide: chocolate or gum, mint or fruit-flavour, sherbet or toffee. The longer she took, the less tolerant her father became and the more nervous and indecisive she would become. His grip on her hand growing ever more impatient, his insistent nails digging painfully into her tender skin, until finally he would drag her, crying and empty handed, from the shop. 'Saffron' looked up and saw the young shop assistant stare at her, as if admonishing her for some social indiscretion, before she quickly turned away and busied herself re-stocking shelves behind the counter. 'Saffron' touched her hand to her cheek and realised she had been crying, so she quickly wiped away the telltale tears with her cuff and sniffing back any that were missed. Attracting the assistant's attention with a faint and almost embarrassed cough, she requested a pack of cigarettes and some matches and handed over a couple of crumpled notes in payment. As the girl passed her the change, her fingers lingered, flesh on flesh, for a fraction of a moment and 'Saffron' looked up at the girl's face. The girl looked back with large almond-shaped eyes that reminded her of an adolescent manga characters whose only power was to transmit the world's sadness through her eyes. The faint hint of a purple bruise showed through on the olive-brown skin of her cheek and 'Saffron' raised her eye-brows to question the girl, who answered by throwing a fleeting look towards the old man at the back of the shop and then smiled a reserved smile at her. 'Saffron' smiled back and squeezed the girls hand before releasing it. She then turned to leave the shop, but stopped herself and grabbed two thin bars of flaked chocolate wrapped in bright yellow cellophane. She paid for them from the change she still held in her hand, slipping one of the bars into the breast pocket of the girl's overall before she left the shop and headed back down the road in the direction of the Underground Station.

...The soul learnt to hate with a passion. If the Shadow was ever aware of pleasure, then this would be it...

At one point the cat stopped to scratch an itch. The itch grew more insistent and it attacked the irritant with its teeth, gnawing at it until it ceased. When it had finished, it looked up.

'Blue?'

'Kip!'

'Can you make me human.'

'Why do you want to be an ape? I thought you despised them?'

'It would be nice to be able to talk for a change, rather than have you in my head, reading my thoughts. And I'd like to have opposable thumbs. You know, so I could make things, open my own tins of food and stuff. I'd be much more useful to you if I were bigger, and had hands.'

'Well, I could. But I cannot turn back time. If I made you human, your cat-years would translate into human-years. You would be about ninety-six.' She looked down at him and smiled, 'and plagued with arthritis.'

'So my hands would be pretty much useless.'

'Well, you could just about wipe your nose on the back of them and that is about all.'

'Oh.' Kip thought to himself for a while, so Blue politely blocked it out, taking the opportunity to survey their where-abouts. Occasionally sniffing the air, or cocking her ear to the wind, as if she were searching for something. After a while, she realised that Kip was trying to reach her, so she released the block and raised an eye-brow to him. 'Okay. I'm fed up with pounding the city streets, where are we going?' Blue turned her head, and announced as much to the passing traffic than to Kip.

'Kip, we are going to save the world, just like an adventure story: Kip and Blue save the World.'

Page Thirty One: He ain't Heavy

…the Shadow slipped into the Waking Lands as silently as it could. For the second cycle in succession it had the need to leave the Darqlands when the Waking Lands were not bathed in the concealing blanket of the night. The soul trapped in the Heart of the Darqlands was progressing, but not fast enough. It needed more Despair, it needed something powerful the fuel the hate. Then the Shadow could make its grand entrance, attract as much attention as it liked, but for now stealth was its most useful ally. Stealing along the back streets it picked up minor souls, destitutes and derelicts, too far gone to be a choice source of Despair, but a source nevertheless. Then into the Underground, the oppressive subterranean haven for Despair carved by the sweat and labour mankind. Miles of dank tunnels burrowed beneath the city connecting small caverns of harsh light crammed with people, desperate to be somewhere else. And there, suicide. Sweet suicide, the final solution for the Despairing Soul, the instant release. Not easy pickings, even for the most skilful hunter, to catch the soul before it jumps into oblivion. The Shadow slipped along in the dark gap between glinting silver track and the platform edge, the place where normal travellers never look for fear of being sucked in along with the litter and dust, dead cells shed by the thousands of commuters that stood waiting for a train each day. Jumpers always looked there, longing to be engulfed in the blackness as the unsuspecting train thundered in, and there the Shadow would see them, see the depth of Despair behind their lifeless eyes as the leapt, and there it would wait. In the distance, along the impenetrable black of the tunnel, the distinct rumble of an approaching west-bound train…

…'brother?'…

…the Shadow knew that voice (go away)…

…'old tricks brother?'…

…that voice was dead, long ago (leave me alone)…

…'and in the day-light too?'…

…the Shadow scanned along the line of people poised on the edge of the platform (I'm busy)…

…'the surprise is as much mine as yours I believe, I thought you long dead'…

…there! A tall figure, thin, insectoid frame, wrapped in a long dark coat, only vaguely unfamiliar, but oozing conceit from its predatory face. The same hawk-face, the same hooded eyes, the same smug grin. The clammer of steel wheels on steel tracks was getting louder and the tunnel flashed with electric sparks, illuminating the dark with fleeting flares of lightning…

…'there's no point in hiding down there, come, let us greet like long lost brothers'…

…the Shadow flowed up over the concave lip of platform and slithered between the feet of the waiting passengers like spilt ink filmed in reverse. It slunk into protection of a darkened corner, away from curious eyes and un-poured itself into the semblance of a human form. A violent wind tore along the platform, a vast column of air driven in front of the approaching train. As the beams of the train lights punctured the hole of the tunnel, the Shadow stepped forward, into the light…

…'ho-ho, it's a while since you last did that! I think you need more practice. Nevermind, none of these mortals can see you, those that can, I have convinced otherwise'…

…there was a scream, the Shadow shrunk back in fear of being seen, its near-humanlike eyes darting left and right, scanning the platform. A jumper! Too late! the Shadow lamented the waste. The Angel was smiling…

…'opps! Missed! C'est la guérè, there will be others, I'm sure. Now, well then, its not like you to venture out in the day-light, things must be tough, or are you just getting bolder?'…

…the Shadow shrugged…

…'as talkative as ever I see. I guess I'll be doing the talking for both of us then, just like old times hey? So, what have you been up to? No, I don't suppose you care for small-talk either. Well, I admit I never expected to find you here, I was after different prey. Of a different sort, err, Well, yes. Seen anything of the others?'…

…the Shadow grimaced, as if in great pain, struggling to gain control of its unused voice 'Hecate -' It rasped, a guttural tone that sounded like a slab of pig iron being dragged across the concrete floor of a vast empty warehouse…

…'that old crone! What's the witch up to now? Frightening little children?'…

…'c-atzzz'…

…'ah, that's were she got to, ran off with her familiars to play Queen of the Castle. I thought as much. And what brought her to your attention…

…'killzzz ... Darqnezzz'…

…look, it would be a lot easier of we connected minds…

…FUCKOFFOUTOFMYFUCKINGMINDYOUFUCKINGVAMPYRE!…

…'okay, okay, calm down, I'm out. Whoa, touchy ain't yar! Let me see. The witch is killing your darkness, and I presume you intend to kill her in return. Therefore, I surmise that you are constructing a little nemesis of your very own to defeat her and the hungry little bugger is eating you out of house and home, so you are out now collecting despairing souls to feed it. Am I right, or am I?…

…'yessz'…

…'give me a break! Monosyllabic conversation is bad enough, but one word at a time. I promise not to do anything once I'm in there, just let me in so we can at least have a proper conversation'…

…'no!' the Shadow started to sublimate, the fabrication of form it created simultaneously vanishing in all four dimensions, not shrinking, just going away into the distance without moving. And then it was back in the solitude of the Darqlands, the Angel left standing on the Underground platform, starring at the space the Shadow vacated…

…'well, it's been ... really ... Yar, Gotta go, places to see, people to go. We must do this again sometime, no really. Lunch, let's lunch. Say in another five millennia.' The Angel called out to the departing Shadow, mockingly. He turned round, the Station was in turmoil, huge crowds had gathered around the Jumper, the emergency services fighting their way through, more people cutting across from the east-bound platform to see the morbid side-show. 'Time I was going too.' He thought to himself, calmly walking against the grain, up flights of escalators and into the packed city street. 'Hecate... Attacking the Darqness, taking on my shadowy brother? No, this is not her way.' He walked, as he mused over the possibilities and likelihoods of his siblings and their actions, without realising where he was going. He strolling across a wide busy road as if it were an open field. Taxi's blared their horns, their drivers hailing abuse out of their windows, cyclists swerved to avoid him, raining down more verbal battery. There was a squeal of rubber on Tarmac and a deafening blast of air-horns, he looked up in time to see the horror on the drivers' face as the gleaming gold forty-tonne bus impacted his tall insectoidal body…

Page Thirty Two: Princess Trust

Philip paced the room, hoping that the tempo of his feet against the polished wood floorboards would accelerate the day. He paced over to the window and twitched the curtains; then paced back to the dinning table, to momentarily perch on the edge of a high-backed black-lacquered Mackintosh chair. Nervously, he chewed on the soft flesh of his finger tips and repeatedly glancing up at the clock; before pacing back to the window. He shouldn't have let her go, he knew he shouldn't have, he just knew. She wouldn't be back. She was a runaway, and that's what runaways do, they runaway. He looked at the clock again, over an hour, Philip cursed, she was long gone. He thumped the wall with the heel of his wrist and pushed himself away from the window. So to Plan 'B', he thought, shit! What the hell was Plan 'A'? He found the girl, but she knew nothing, she could not help him find his Angel, so why was he so upset that she had gone? Philip rubbed his hands over his face, trying to wash the weariness away, trying to stimulate the blood-flow that would, hopefully, reach his brain. The coins were the key, if only he knew what they meant. He went over to the book shelves, piles of paper books, data-cubes and ancient CD's littered the shelves in no recognisable order, transcripts of archaic and antediluvian manuscripts mixed with fanciful works of fiction and prized articles of reason. But he knew the answer was not among there, he had already wasted several long nights pouring over them, referencing and cross-referencing, collating eighteenth century romantic poetry with 'lost' pages from the Dead Sea Scrolls to speculative tomes of fiction dressed as scientific fact. He pulled several books from the shelf and dropped them onto his desk. He browsed the pile, mentally categorising them, trying to decide which would be most likely to indicate where to go next. Instead his hand settled on a heavy coffee-table Art book, his fingers traced the edges of the pages, feeling the contrast between those worn smooth and those still sharp and crisp from their original cut, feeling the boundary with his thumb nail he flicked the book open and stared down on the revealed picture. The most perfect drawing he had ever seen, barely a dozen thin lines of hard black pencil on an off-white page, less lines went to make the artists signature, more graphite went into the German words that formed the caption.

…'be not forgetful to entertain strangers for thereby some have entertained Angels unawares - Hebrews 13:2'…

Philip looked up with a jolt. At first unable to determine what he had disturbed him, unable to place the sound he had heard. Knocking. The door! Philip's heart leapt and the rest of his body followed soon after, before he realised what he was doing, he was at the door, his hand on the handle. He took a deep breath to calm himself, '*Probably just the Postman'* he thought, in an attempt to buffer his impending disappointment.

'Miss me?' the girl called 'Saffron' stood on his threshold, looking almost sheepish from behind her scarlet fringe. Philip stood to one side and flicked his fingers absently into the room, indicating she should enter and trying to suppress his surprise and pleasure at seeing her, but over compensating dramatically, appearing beyond cool and nonchalant and heading off into the realms of indifference and impatience. Once inside the house she saw the pile of books on the desk, then turned and looked at him. 'Sorry, I'm disturbing you; didn't you expect to see me again?'

'No, err no that's wrong, I mean Yes, Oh God. Shit.' His resolve broke, he beamed at her like a small boy on his birthday. 'I thought' he could not lie, 'I hoped you would come back.' She stared at her feet for a moment and the held out her clenched fist. She unfurled her fingers to reveal a small rectangle of card with a magnetic stripe on one face, the ticket had been creased in her grip and left white indentations in her palms.

'I got as far as the ticket barrier, but I couldn't go through. I didn't know whether you let me go out on my own because you didn't need me any more, or because you are the most stupid detective in the world, or because you trusted me to come back. Whatever the answer, I couldn't runway again because I think you need me.' She looked into his eyes as she spoke, he could see the truth there, he could feel a tear welling in his left eye, then she cracked a grin to break the moment before it became too sickly. 'So you think they give refunds?' Philip smiled and shook his head, pointing to the 'No Refund' clause on the ticket. She shrugged and stuffed it into the pocket of her coat, which she then took off and threw over the back of a chair. 'Research?' she asked, walking over to the desk and leaning over the open book.

'Err, yes, well ~ no, not really. Most books written about Angels have less than one percent fact and the remainder is pure hyperbole.'

'Hyper-Bollocks...'

'Succinctly.' He replied. 'Well, I intended to look for clues. I'm sure the coins are significant, but as I said, there is no reference to them anywhere. I don't know what to do next, but I keep getting drawn to that picture.' 'Saffron' studied the drawing.

'It's beautiful, so simple, so clever.' She read the words and instantly translated them: "'Paul Klee 1939 - The Forgetful Angel'".

...and one is remembering...

From the boating lake to the flat expanse of grass bordered with perfectly proportioned trees nothing looked natural. Things grew, living things, fuelled by the sun, fed by the soil and nurtured by the rain. Plants that once sprouted from germinating seeds, may be. But now propagate by the skilful hands of gardeners and scientists, cloned in vats for disease-free purity, artificially resistant not for their survival, but for their prolonged beauty. An abomination of nature to please the eye of man. The cultivated hybrids themselves were mocking mankind's' achievements, reduced to a crude caricature of flowers, they resisted the landscape in their bloated distortion, their original genus long suppressed. Ashiya closed her eyes and the park dissolved, its image replaced by an older garden. Not an idyllic pristine garden of lush grass littered with flowers and fruit laden trees, with a frothing fountain feeding three virgin rivers where man walked in harmony with the beasts. Not the garden immortalised in oils through the ages by countless artists, a romantic paradise of the temptation and fall, but a working garden of crops and produce, tended with love and care to feed and nurture. The garden as home and as provider, the garden that took mankind from the animals and moved them closer to the gods. She knew this place, she had been here before. Then, as now, she had been the first to arrive, but it had not been a garden then, just earth, air and water. Ashiya had brought fire to provide light and heat, the others had provided the spirit to create the garden. Together they had built their homes and worked the fields, fields they called Elysian.

…welcome home sister…

The Magpie had seen the girl leave and had not know whether to follow her, or stay and watch the house. It was hungry, so it knew that instinct could not be trusted. But the rain had stopped and the morning sun was gradually heating up the limestone blocks of the church. For the first time in several days it was starting to feel comfortable, and safe, high above the ground away from the cats. So it had chosen to stay and was relieved when she eventually returned. However, the Magpie's relief was short lived, there was now something disturbing about the girl, instead of slouching, she walked with a spring in her step, she even smiled, but more unsettling, was the faint yellow aura that surrounded her. Instinct finally decided what to do: tell someone and tell them now.

Page Thirty Three: Just an Inkling for the Making

…'ohfuckthathurts…

For an instant, Rochelle felt the urge to search for the girl wane. Like a double-take, she momentarily remembered something else, something she should have been doing instead. Then in a blink that was gone and her fingers returned to shuffling through the untidy stack of cards that should have been neatly indexed and filed away, but had never found the time to organise themselves without Rochelle's help. Her mother's axiom had been 'Dreamers don't get things done', but Rochelle always found dreaming far more enjoyable than doing, so the index-cards remained unsorted, scattered across the desk and shuffled into numerous drawers. The card was not there, or at least she could not find it there. She sat back in the chair and stared at the pile of cards, before scooping them into a small pile and sweeping them into the top drawer of the desk. *'No, silly woman'*, she thought, chastising her forgetfulness, *'the girl was new, her card wouldn't be here'*. She got up and went to the kitchen, purposely avoiding direct eye-contact with the mountain of dirty dishes that peered over the edge of the sink. The mornings after her 'little get-togethers' always resulted in a list of household duties to attend to that she would rather not do, a roster of cleaning and tidying that generally got pushed further and further back in the day until guilt forced her to do them. The dishes could wait, they were not going anywhere. Rochelle found the card propped up against the teapot where she had put it after Maud had used it for a coaster. The light brown ring from her mug of apple tea had cause some of the ink to run, but the words were still visible, still readable. The words on the card were faded, looking more like they were written a hundred years ago and not just last night. Rochelle studied at the girl's handwriting, fluid and graceful, almost antique in its style, almost copperplate, as if each word had been meticulously drawn instead of written. The beginning of each pen-stroke was marked by a dark spot of ink where the pen nib paused, with each letter flowing from it like a small stream that gradually grew paler and ended in a faint flourishing curlicue. The colour of the ink reminded her of the black ink the Nuns rationed out at school, ink that had been watered-down so much it was a depressing thin blue-black that quickly soaked into the cheap paper, leaving spreading rings of colour like the chromatography experiments they had done in chemistry lessons.

…slowly shattered shards of bone moved and knitted together, pulling on damaged tendons and ripping jagged pieces of bone from raw muscle. As torn flesh healed over open wounds, skin stretched and triggered the renewed nerve endings to send shockwaves of torture to an overloaded brain that could never lapse into unconsciousness. While displaced and split organs repaired and repositioned themselves every cubic millimetre of his body was aflame. Each single movement within his body infinitely more painful than the act that smashed it in the first place…

'Saffron' stood by the window, her arms folded tightly around her body, hugging herself as if she were cold. The row of houses opposite: a crisp block of pale Georgian terraces, broken only by the gap left for a long disused church and its paltry, overgrown graveyard. The church was the saddest building she had ever seen, the weight of centuries bore down heavily on its slabs of limestone, the once sharp masonry dulled and subdued by the years, its gothic façade carved by the wind and rain into a forlorn expression of tired stonework, it gave the impression of a tragic, tear streaked, clown. As she watched, a back and white shape rose from the base of the steeple and flew off over the city.

'One for sorrow.' She sighed, her mood matching the building. Philip looked up from the large book he was reading.

'Huh? Who is?'

'A Magpie. Like the rhyme, 'One for Sorrow, two for joy..." 'Saffron' walked away from the window, her arms still folded and sat opposite Philip at the table. He looked at her, waiting for her to speak, then returned to his reading, flicking backwards and forwards through the book, scanning the index and glossary, scribbling notes onto the touch sensitive surface of an old and tatty scratchPad. She sat and watched him for a while, then spoke. 'There is a Chinese story about two lovers.' Philip stopped reading and listened. 'A Cowherd and a Weaver. They were stars in heaven, kept apart by the Milky Way and could only meet on the seventh day of the seventh month over the Magpie Bridge. But their love was so strong and eternal that they only needed to be together once a year.' She paused. 'Do you think that could be true?'

'It's probably the other way around - their love is eternal because they only see each other once a year.'

'Cynic. Have you no romance?' 'Saffron' pouted. 'Wouldn't it be neat if today was the seventh of July, then we could look out tonight and watch them meeting, see their loving embrace.'

'I don't know, it seems a bit voyeuristic to me, I think moments like that should be left private. Anyway, since this is August, we would have to wait another eleven months.' Philip saw the doleful look on her face as he said the words, then remembered something. 'Just a minute, it's a Chinese story. That means it's not the seventh day of the seventh month on the Gregorian Solar calendar, but the seventh day of the seventh month on the Chinese Lunar calendar.' Philip reached for the scratchPad and tapped and scribbled, accessing programs buried deep within it's net, finally he looked up, grinning widely. 'It's tomorrow,' he tapped the surface with the pen, and the machine meeped back at him. 'The seventh day of the seventh Lunar month is tomorrow, August nineteenth.'

…the process of immortality was not without its drawbacks and with each excruciating stab of agony, he vowed never to die a violent death again…

Page Thirty Four: Remake: Remodel: Remember

Kip was dozing. The effort of staying awake grew too much. Blue could infused him with another jolt of her energy, but she now felt it safe to let him sleep and recuperate for a while. She was sat on a cold metal bench in a shopping mall, Kip asleep on her lap, the morning shoppers ignoring them as they hurried passed. Blue idly stroked the sleeping cat as she connected with the network of souls, keeping careful watch over the dreaming cat as it cavorted in her Realm. Something had happened, apart from the normal background noise of cats, the Anima Mundi and 'blessed' humans she could no longer feel any other higher spiritual presence in the city, still, she was certain it would be a temporary respite. The 'blessed' did, however, intrigue her. The 'blessed' human presence in the Ether were of three forms. The most common were 'the Enlightened', those who entered the net by their own volition, either seeking enlightenment or by innate ability. From them came 'the Chosen', throughout the ages there had always been a few, picked from the ranks of mortals and elevated to higher levels, as prophets or visionaries, in turn revered by humans as seers, saints or wizards. But their numbers were small and their appearances infrequent. They were never a threat, just an indicator, to show that the Host were still meddling, interfering and watching. Then there were the Nephilim, the scattered offspring of divine/mortal couplings that had survived the pogroms of the 144,000 Powers, the Sixth Choir of Angels. The Angels of Destruction, Punishment, Vengeance and Death led by Camael. His attempt to sweep the 'abominations' from the face of Earth had driven them to hide in the souls of men. The Nephilim had created the perfect camouflage, so completely assimilated into humanity that the Host could no longer detect them. Occasionally, a spirit would be come self-aware, flare for a moment, burning in the firmament like beacon for all to see. An individual Nephilim was of no concern, however should they arise en-masse, then the Host would most certainly intervene and war would be inevitable. She was always vigilant and quick to act: to protect the children of her fallen brothers and sisters (and her own), to invoke their race-memories and send them scurrying back into the shadows. She probed deeper into the spiritual noise, she could sense iridescent sparkles that were not normally there, too faint to determine who or what they were, their residual auras were familiar, but unplaceable, their chaotic shimmerings were uncontrolled and unpredictable. They were not entirely of human origin, nor were they behaving like the Host or the Fallen. A puzzle. Unless… Blue concentrated on the shifting patterns in the firmament. Yes! She could now discern that there were three newly awaken spirits, fledglings testing their new found wings. But who are they? She could not tell, but she must reach them, help them, guide them onto the correct path.

…in the Darqlands existence was less complicated, less confused. The only visitors were the souls lured here to feed the Darqness. The only sound was the dying reverberation of Despair. The weight of recent cycles bore heavily. The concept of sleep unknown, but the Shadow tried to rest, to conserve and rejuvenate. But could not. Meeting its brother lifted scales from its eyes, uncovered memories…

Ashiya was startled and a little disappointed to find herself still in the park, standing erect and motionless like a leather clad statue in the centre of this poor excuse for a garden. Looking around, everything seemed more vivid, more alive, more vibrant. In a single sweep, she could absorb every subtle detail without effort. It was as if she could sense the air crackling with energy emanating from the plants, the trees and the people strolling. She felt she could take a deep breath and inhale the essence of life, infuse her spirit with this power. With this she felt hunger, a manic hunger that would drain all the life she could reach and still be unsated. Like a predatory vampyre charged with blood-lust, she searched for a suitable meal. A crocodile of school children in deep purple uniforms filed passed, each of them gawping with open mouths and craning necks, while the teachers at the head and tail of the procession took no notice of her at all. She flared her eyes at the children, who quickly averted their's in return and moved by with increased urgency. This brought a smile to her face and diverted her attention from the desire to feed. She had wondered if her new awareness had come with any powers, but somehow doubted that the ability to out-stare eight-year olds was much of a gauge. She felt different, she wondered if she now looked different. She looked down to her hands, her pale flesh seemed to be gloved by a dim red glow that sparkled and scintillated. It was as if the air near her flesh had become charged and its molecules, atoms, atomic and subatomic particles reflecting light like microscopic dust motes caught in a sun ray. Maybe only children can see this, perhaps this is why they stared. Ashiya shrugged and, thrusting her hands deep into jacket pockets, turned and left the park.

… First its sister Hecate trying to destroy the Darqlands. Now its brother Meririm, the Prince of Power of the Air, walks the Waking Lands, searching for something, or someone. Not Hecate, no, that surprise was genuine - Meririm never expected Hecate, nor the Shadow come to that, someone else, but who?…

The Magpie had set off in search of the Raven with a clear and single purpose. But now, as the morning passed and with no sign of the Raven, it was beginning to become agitated. It knew something important, but now did not know who to tell. The Magpie was an intermediary, an agent, forever the willing lieutenant, it lacked the capability of creative thought to be a leader. The Magpie flew high, to the tallest building to perch on the highest satellite dish. It knows it should be here, waiting for a call.

Page Thirty Five: Sorrow

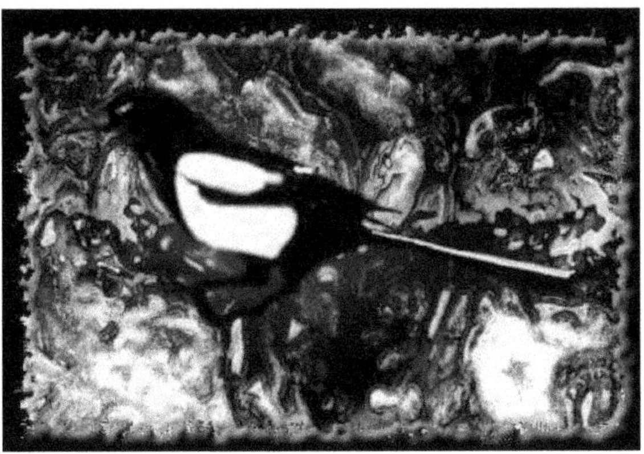

One for sorrow, Two for joy;

Three for a girl and Four for a boy.

Five for silver, Six for gold,

And Seven for a secret that's never to be told.

Chapter Six: Dreamer

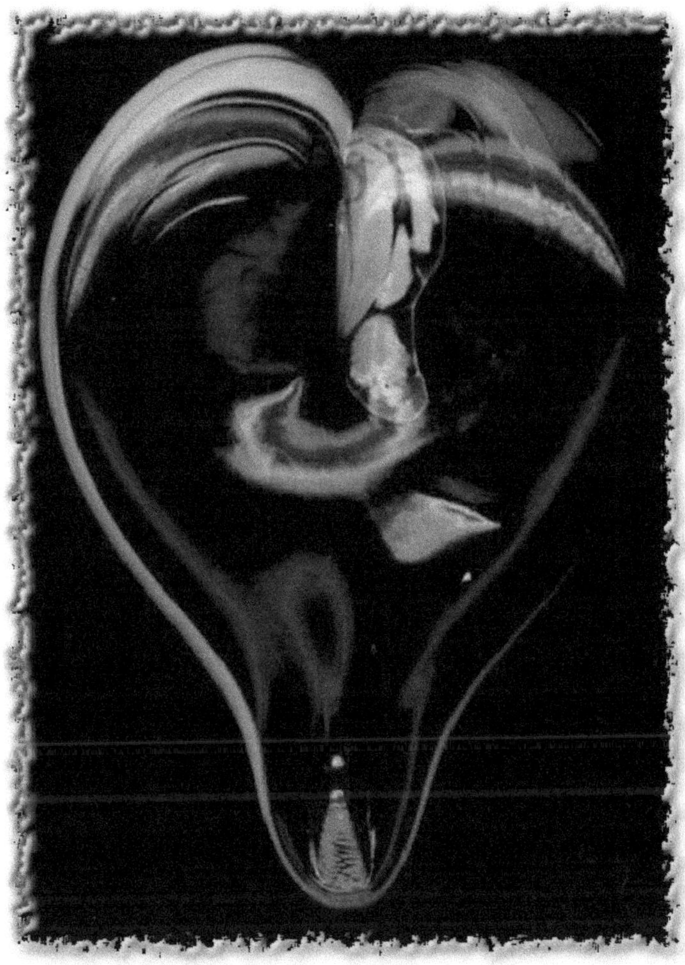

Page Thirty Six: Jeux sans Frontière

The dream-state was more than just sleep with pictures and a disjointed story. It was another existence on another world. Freed from the constraints of the physical and the corporeal, the essence that separates the animate from the inanimate soars through the Ether. The fractional part of the spirit called Imagination has found its element and can create and sculpt landscapes to amaze and terrify. As a singularity, this becomes genius, an isolated thought that can compose an illusion. But combined with other liberated spirits the gift is unsurpassed and the imagined becomes a reality. Here, the spirits of a million cats can form Creation, begetting a Genesis and giving birth to Realm without boundaries. A land in perfect balance where the synergy of infinite thoughts and dreams hold a reality beyond reality, a meta-reality of solidified energy. Running free in the Realm, Blue revelled in his new status, for even in the equality of Bast's Realm there are exceptions: those in Bast's favour are afforded extra respect and reverence.

…there were reasons. Reasons to forget and reasons to remember. The Shadow wandered through the Darqlands, ignoring the mists of Despair that flowed through the Darqness as fragments of memory surfaced and were pushed away…

The address on the index-card was an unimpressive slab of grey concrete layered with a thin coating of glass. Much has already been said about these architects doodles made truth and little of it complimentary. Yet they still stand, defiantly towering against the weight of public opinion. Rochelle had parked her small car in a safer looking neighbourhood a couple of streets away and walked to the building. That way she hoped to return to it and find that she still possessed a radio and a full set of tires. With similar good sense, she avoided the lifts and took the stairs, but even then the smell in the stair-well was of stale urine and festering garbage, not strong enough to make her gag, but unpleasant never the less. All of the flats on the seventh landing had heavy wire mesh stapled to their doors, originally intended as a security afterthought to protect the frosted glass that once filled the frames. Frames now occupied by unpainted sheets of ply-wood hastily fitted after heavily booted feet had discovered that, through repeated kicking, the mesh would bend and the glass would break. As Rochelle walked down the corridor, the light grew dimmer and the dank smell grew stronger. Flat seventy-seven was the last, almost bathed in darkness, she felt an oppressive rush of despair as she approached the door. Hesitantly she pressed her finger against the bell-push to be met with total silence. She pressed harder and the door moved slightly. Through the crack in the door she called out to the occupant and received no reply. She pushed the door open a little more and was knocked back by the stench of decay that greeted her. She put her hand over her mouth and nose and stepped over the threshold into the flat.

… images of Apollyon opening the Abyss…

Even holding her breath, the putrefying stink almost made her want to retch. She had never smelt anything this bad in her life. Forgotten leftovers entombed in Tupperware at the back of her 'fridge would smell better than this. It was so rancid that it stung her eyes and permeated through her closed mouth so that she could taste it. Rochelle felt drawn down the hallway towards what, from the glimpse of terracotta-tile patterned vinyl flooring, she guessed was the kitchen. Warily she moved down the hall, carefully stepping over brightly coloured toys that littered the floor. Her heart leapt when she saw the toys, realising that small children lived in this cess-pit of a home. Rochelle reached for the kitchen door and gingerly pushed it open. Cautiously, she peered around the door. The room was empty. The refrigerator door was open and the light was out, but she could see a trail of dark green-brown slime that had run from a plate of uncovered, rotting raw meat. Running over the off-white plastic, it mixed with the decaying remains of vegetables from the salad tray and then dripped into a large festering puddle on the floor. Rochelle quickly crossed the room and forced open a resistant window. The window opened a few degrees then jammed against the safety screws so it could open no further, however the blast of warm fresh air washed over her face and she took a large draw on the purifying air. She then turned and looked around. It was clear that no one had lived here for some time, and the departing resident had made no effort to tidy up before leaving, the girl had obviously given a false address. But why this one?

…images of the Angel of the Abyss darkening the Sun…

Rochelle started to leave the flat, satisfied that it was empty without the need to check every room, when she was met at the door by two police officers. Later she would reflect on the following hours as if they had been copied from a second rate spook-fi novel, some pulp-fiction story of the paranormal written without care for accuracy or attention to detail. Travelling in the police car with the officers in stone silence, her hands clasped tightly on her lap as if bound by invisible handcuffs, she felt like a criminal. They travelled to the police station where she was finger printed by her own consent. Then she was sat for hours in a small interview room, alone with nothing but a small table and three hard plastic chairs for company. Those, and a solitary vending machine cup of unexplained something - she did not even attempt to taste it, the nondescript colour was more than enough to put her off, whether it was tea or coffee did not interest her enough to find out.

When finally a detective and a WPC arrived, they sat in silence with arms folded as she stared in horror at the three photographs they had pushed across the table towards her. The harsh light from the photographer's flash had done nothing to weaken the impact of the decaying body slumped in the bath, a body crusted in the dried blood that had poured from open veins. The images all to clearly showed how the rotting flesh had started to fall from the bones and where maggots had begun their work. As Rochelle pushed the photographs away in disgust, the detective lent forward and rested his elbows on the table, he spoke in low, deliberate tones. He asked her why she was in the flat, and she told him. He asked who Lilly was, and she said she did not know. He asked to see Lilly's index-card, and she pulled the creased card from her pocket and passed it to him. He looked at it near disinterest, turning it over in his hands before he passed it back. He asked her if Lilly could be the woman in the photographs, and she shook her head, explaining that she met Lilly for the first time the previous evening where she was very much alive. He asked if she knew the dead woman, and she said she did not. He told her that 'forensics' had said the woman had probably been dead for several months, yet the Social Services had visited her in the flat two days ago, where she too, had been very much alive, and she listened without comment. He asked her about witchcraft, devil worship, blood sacrifices and black magic, and she had entered into a long diatribe on how devil-worship was an invention of the Christian Church and nothing to do with Wicca until his eyes started to glaze over and he finally managed to change the subject. (At that point Rochelle glanced to the WPC to catch her suppressing a grin). The interview continued for another hour, meandering into apparent trivia, with earlier questions re-asked and met with the same responses, until there was a knock at the door. A young uniformed officer entered and passed a scrap of paper to the WPC, who read it and passed it to the detective. Her finger prints did not match any found in the flat. They routinely thanked her for her co-operation and she was free to go. As she went to leave, she remembered the toys in the hallway. The WPC then told her that the woman was a registered addict and that Social Services visit had been to take her child into Care. Rochelle's only though was dragged deep from her lapsed Catholic upbringing: an image of the Angel of Death passing over Egypt.

...shattered shards of memory suppressed and forgotten...

'Saffron' looked up from the ancient leather bound encyclopaedia she was browsing and quickly turned her head to see if anyone was behind her, watching. An involuntary cold shudder had caused the muscles in her back to tense and she felt a warm breeze caressing the fine hairs in the nape of her neck, almost kissing her. She cast her eyes around the room to confirm that she was alone amongst the clutter that filled Philip's life. She smiled to her self as she thought that if anyone wanted to ransack his house they would have to tidy-up first. The piles of magazines, books, vids. and data-cubes cascaded from overfull book-shelves onto the floor like a urban version of an Andrew Goldsworthy installation. Every flat surface was covered with something: vases; figurines; an antique transistor-radio in cream leatherette, (that could only tune to wavelengths that once filled the airways with crackling fading music and talk, that were now transmitting nothing but encoded data to non-critical vending machines and automated ticket-mats), lay partially buried under a growing mountain of letters and assorted junk; an industrial strength electric drill lay alongside a heap of brittle china plates and crystal glass. Every inch of available wall space was filled with pictures, obscuring the ancient rust coloured flock wallpaper: fine art hung amid an array of reproductions; post-cards; pages torn from glossy magazines; full-colour print-outs from the net and a young child's heavily daubed painting (she assumed a family scene, a park with flattened swings and slides and three people, large heads with seriously happy grins and small bodies, all holding hands), the thick paint had begrudgingly run and dripped in lava-like flows before coalescing and drying. In one corner of the room, the wall was filled with used ticket stubs from concerts, gigs, plays and art-house cinema shows stretching back in time over forty years, possibly even fifty. They were tacked to the wall in a mosaic of tattered colour that had subconsciously come to resemble a woman's face. Another corner contained several enlarged versions of disc inlays, some were almost double actual size, (roughly 120mil square she thought), a few, preserved in heavy gilt frames behind glass were huge, (easily over 300mil). Some she recognised, most she did not. She wondered if that was what she too had become, just something Philip had collected on the way, to eventually lay forgotten in a heap stuff that he could not bring himself to throw away, or to be preserved forever, thumb-tacked to the wall like a collectors' butterfly. She casually rubbed the back of her neck and shrugged, returning to her reading. Scanning the pages of German, painfully printed in antique gothic script, for keywords and phrases, before translating potentially useful paragraphs on the scratchPad for Philip to read later. But he was right. The factual information was scant, and buried amongst pages of myth and folklore. So far she had come across no mention of the coins and somehow doubted she would.

Page Thirty Seven: Straggler in a Strangeland

…emergence. Back into the Waking Lands. Disoriented. This was not right. Confused. This was not within normal boundaries. Lost…

Across the city, in another large room, a modern Spartan space saying as much, if not more, of the personality that lived, breathed and occupied it as did Mallow's disorganised chaos of him, Ashiya also sensed she was being watched. Not like before. Not her secret lover, gazing at her across a crowded restaurant, or from the apartment opposite. But another. Not baleful, (she felt no menace in the presence), just a benign warmth watching over her. A Guardian, (there was no doubt), she recognised as much and she knew why, (but no more than that), but no who or where. She had no directional ability, (or at least, not one she could remembered how to control), she could not home-in on the feeling, isolate it from the melee of emotions that assaulted her awoken perceptions. The feeling was just one of many jumbled in the furore of noise, but one directed specifically at her, like a magick bullet encoded with her soul-print. She tried to concentrate, focusing her mind on the single emotion, blotting and filtering all others until there was only one. But it was as if the feeling did not want to be found, for as she got close, almost achieving lock, it would phase and shift and disappear back into the background to reappear on a different vector or a different frequency. But still targeted at her. It just wanted her to be aware that it was there. Watching, listening, waiting.

…all around was concrete, the arrogant, ugly stone of mankind that they used to despoil the Waking Lands. With it they desecrated vast open spaces, denuding them of shade, of solace. Creating isolated islands of desolation bisected by bloated ribbons of Tarmac stretching in all directions. On wide arcs of strip-black carved indiscriminately through the landscape journeyed the Pilgrims, the believers, travelling these monstrous aisles of madness, sacrificing the environment on their alter stones of the highway to their demigods of the automobile…

Philip found 'Saffron' asleep at the table, her head resting on arms crossed over the pages of a large book. He stood for a moment transfixed by her slumbering form. Detached from the discomfort of the morning's embarrassment, he admitted to himself that he found this gangly string-bean attractive, even though the obvious age difference between them restrained him taking the thought any further, he had to concede she was a woman, not a child. He carefully and noiselessly pulled out a chair and sat down opposite her. Trying not to breath for fear of waking her, he reached over to pick up the scratchPad, accidentally brushing the touch-sensitive screen as he did. It meeped into life and 'Saffron' instantly awoke as if she was patched into its boot sequence. She abruptly sat up and stared at him through sleep crusted eyes, blinking rapidly to scan in the scene in front of her.

He smiled meekly. 'Sorry'

'Have I been asleep long?' she enquired. He shrugged. She stretched and licked her lips, wiping away the small trickle of spit that had leaked from the corner of her mouth. 'Coffee' she stated, almost as a command. 'I need coffee'. He started to rise, but she waved him down. 'No, I'll make it. I think I can remember how.' She grinned as she left the table and padded into the kitchen.

To the sound of cupboards banging and water running, Philip paged through the data she had translated. As he suspected, there was nothing in the ancient books that had not already been translated, pillaged and plagiarised by later authors and still no references to the coins. The last page was blank. He placed the 'Pad flat onto the table and dabbed his finger onto the [close] icon, but clumsily missed and hit [undelete] instead. The page filled with a list, questions, all of them about him. He knew he should not read them, they were personal, like reading someone's journal, but curiosity got the better of him. He looked up. She was still in the kitchen, the gurgle of the filter-machine was in its dying throws. He quickly deleted the [undelete]d text and the page was once again blank. He now felt embarrassment again, she had feelings for him, she wondered how old he was, she wondered how old his child was, (his eyes rested on his daughter's painting on the wall opposite), she wanted to know what happens next. He was staring into space when she placed the mug of coffee in front of him, his mind wandering over an unknown landscape, through missed time lines and alternate histories.

'A penny for them.'

'Sorry?' He emerged from his day-dream.

'A penny for your thoughts. You were miles away.' She sat back in the chair opposite, cupping her mug in both hands, blowing the curling trail of steam from the dark liquid so the deep aroma wafted over him. 'What were you thinking about?'

'Oh, nothing.' He lied, cradling his own mug in his hands, mirroring her.

She frowned at him. 'I doubt that even a Zen Buddhist can think about nothing.'

'Nothing in particular then, just things.' He said, gingerly taking a sip of the scalding coffee. They sat in silence, contemplating the coffee and the nature of nothing.

'Philip?'

'Mmm.' He answered, concentrating on the eddying bubbles on the surface of the coffee, attempting to will them to rotate in the opposite direction.

'Can I ask you a personal question?' He internally winced and looked up from his drink.

'I change my socks and shorts every day. And I leave the toilet seat up because I can.' He stated. She laughed.

'No, not that. Something else.'

He shrugged, attempting nonchalance, but fearing the worse. 'Okay, fire away.'

'How old are you?'

'As old as my gums and a little older than my teeth.'

'That's what my Grandmother used to say.'

'Mine too.' He returned to the coffee bubbles.

'Come on, seriously. How old?'

'How old do you think?' He asked, deliberately answering the question with another question. She thought for a moment, studying his face.

'I don't know, maybe thirty-five, forty - if you look after your self.' She turned her head and looked around the room. 'Which I doubt, judging by this place.'

'Thirty-five it is then.'

'I'm not that stupid.' Inexplicably, she was getting angry with him. 'I know you are much older than that!'

'How do you mean?'

'The ticket stubs!' She said triumphantly.

'Sorry?'

She stabbed her finger to the mosaic on the wall. 'No one collects other peoples used ticket stubs. They're yours!' She was shaking. She stood up, pushing the chair noisily back and paced backwards and forwards in front of him, arms crossed. 'You went to those shows yourself and kept the stubs as mementoes. You saw The Stones in 1966 for fuck's sake!' She glared at him. 'That would make you at least sixty years old! Probably more.' Tears were running down her cheeks. He put the mug down and lent back in the chair, closing his eyes, raking his fingers through his hair.

He released a long sigh. 'I don't know how old I am. I stopped counting.' She was nervously shifting her weight from one leg to the other, as if she was close to wetting herself. 'Please, sit down. I'll try and explain.' She cautiously perched on the edge of the chair, still distanced from the table, her hands resting on opposite shoulders, hugging herself. 'A long time ago I just forgot to die. I didn't cheat death. I just forgot. Like you forget a friends birthday, or to take a library book back. I was so busy living, I forgot to die. I grew old, bent and grey but did not die. For the next hundred years I hated every second of my life. I was old, weak and feeble. They say life is wasted on the young and it is true, no one wants to be eighty forever, it's like living in purgatory. I couldn't stay in one place, so I became a wanderer, moving from town to town, village to village, living the miserable existence of a hermit. I eventually found the courage to kill myself and I finally died, age one hundred and eighty.'

He paused to take a drink of coffee, giving her time to take in what he had said. She started to say something, but he raised his hand to stop her. 'In my next life I remembered. I remembered being old for a long time. I remembered the misery and the loneliness. So I decided to end that life when I reached thirty, it seemed like the right number, before the body starts to fall to pieces. Unfortunately when I was eighteen I was sent to war and died from a Frenchman's bullet. In the next life I reached thirty-four and took a heavy dose of poison, but sadly not a fatal one. On recovery I was sent to an asylum to save me from myself, which was just another form of hell. Knowing I would stay there for eternity, I forgot to count the years and I forgot to grow old. With time, they forgot about me too and one day I just walked out. I have been thirty-four ever since.

'I have lived a dozen pseudo-lives, never settling, never getting close to anyone, just moving on before people notice that I never grow any older.'

She shot a glance at the child's painting and then turned back to him. 'Ah. Once I met someone and fell in love. Sandra.' He paused, his face taking on a shadow of sad reflection so deep, some melancholic it brought a lump to 'Saffron's throat, after a while he continued, though skipping ahead past undoubtably happier memories, 'Eventually she realised that I wasn't growing older so I had to explain everything. Because of our love, she accepted it. Together we learnt to use theatrical make-up and dye my hair to give the impression that I was ageing so we could live the semblance of a normal life. We had a daughter, Emily. I watched her grow into a woman, leave and have a family of her own. I knew that one day they both would die and I would go on living, forever, and Sandra knew that too. So we lived for the moment and it was wonderful, happy, joyous and fulfilling. Sadly, for all of our plans, she died of TB when she was fifty-two and still young at heart.

'I was devastated. Broken. I moved on and became thirty-four again. This time never getting involved with anyone past casual affairs and one night stands. But now, in these insular times, I do not need to move. I first lived in this house with Sandra and Emily, we bought it just after it was built. Later, when everyone around here who knew us had either died or move away, I moved back in. No one bothers me, neighbours come and go. No one lives in one place long enough in this city for them to realise.'

'What about your daughter, Emily?' 'Saffron' whispered, almost croaking with pent-up tears.

'She passed away in an old peoples home. I used to visit her every week claiming to be her son, though she insisted on telling everyone I was her father, of course the staff humoured her and dismissed it as senility. One day when I visited they told me my 'mother' had died I lost it, screaming at them that she was my daughter. But they just looked at me with that condescending, pitying look they reserve for the newly bereaved.' There were now tears running down his face and he sobbed heavily with eyes closed, blanking out everything around him. He felt her arm resting across his shoulders, her fingers gripping his forearm, pulling him to her. Her other hand stroked the side of his face and gently tilted his head onto her chest. She tenderly kissed him on the top of his head as she hugged and rocked him.

…something had diverted it, dragged it from the Darqlands and left it in an alien part of the City with no defence or place to hide. It struggled and fought, trying to return to the Darqness, but failed. The Shadow now felt Despair…

Page Thirty Eight: The Beast of Butterfly Wings

'Kip!

'wake-up!'

'Shit'n'derision!'

'Have you got a problem?'

'I was about to get fucking laid!'

'Nevermind that, we have got work to do.'

'Blue, have you any idea how rarely I get laid in the Realm?'

'I am sorry, I did not think. Do not fret, I will make it up to you sometime.'

'!'

…marooned in the wasteland. The Shadow shimmered and wavered in the heat-haze rising from the black Tarmac as its energy boiled and vaporised into the atmosphere. Slowly it was being defeated, without a fight. With each moment under the relentless Sun, the solar radiation weakened and sapped its strength. It looked up to the Sun, its long begotten son, and called upon the very essence of Despair, the raw elemental Despair from which all human despair is forged, the Despair that created the Shadow. 'This is not how it ends!' It screamed. 'Destiny will have to re-write her history!' The Despair flew into the air, dragging the dust from the crumbling concrete with it, tearing into the molecules, ripping out base elements, splitting and renting large atoms into lighter elements in controlled fission, absorbing the released energy to further feed the reaction until the Shadow holds a sphere of pure hydrogen in a field of Despair. Then it reverses. As the father once taught the Sun to fuse hydrogen into helium, it now shows more of its power as oxygen pulled from the atmosphere is combined with the hydrogen. A small ball of steam is instantly created that rapidly condenses into a miniature cloud hovering a few meters above the ground. The seed is sown, now chaos is in control, the cloud billows and swirls, and the mist descends, spreading over the landscape. The reaction is self perpetuating, the mist becomes a fog and grows ever thicker. Soon the earth bathed in shadow, blacking out the Sun. If the Shadow had a face, it would smile…

…"And the fifth angel sounded, and I saw a star fall from heaven unto the earth: and to him was given the key of the bottomless pit. And he opened the bottomless pit; and there arose a smoke out of the pit, as the smoke of a great furnace; and the sun and the air were darkened by reason of the smoke of the pit - Revelation 9:1"…

'Hurry, or we will be late.'

'Late for what?'

'Not for anything, just late.'

'Oh great, now it's riddles.'

'Riddles?'

'My first is in "pissed" and also in "off"'

'Kip!'

'What?'

…

Ouch!'

…chaos begets chaos. It is the way of things. The fog engulfs the highway, and the traffic panics. Startled automobiles grind synthetic fibre against steel to the shredding squeal of rubber against Tarmac and the sickening crump of metal against metal. Amid the wreckage and concertinaed carnage, there is life and death, in between them, there is despair and the Shadow responds with veracity…

Gripping the cat tightly, hugging him to her chest, Blue vaporises. Solid matter becomes plasma. The weak bonds between realities are pulled apart like zip-lock and they slip through to instantly emerge into a dense cloud of fog and burning rubber. The air is thick with the cries of the dying, the tears of the dead and the howls of the undead whose souls had been ripped from them. Late. They are too late, the damage that has been done cannot be undone. They drift from wreck to wreck, tending and consoling the injured souls trapped in broken bodies. The cat's spirit guides the uninjured to care for the physical needs of the casualties. In the following days, the newspapers will be full of stories of unbelievable heroism and courage as the survivors are rescued from their crashed cars by other motorists who, blinded by the acrid smoke, tore at the solid metal with nothing but their bare hands. Blue treats the soul-less undead swiftly and painlessly, where she sends them they can never rest, but they will be safe and will have no need to walk the earth. For the dead, all she and Kip can hope for is that their souls found release and are now in whatever heaven they believed in. Blue stops what she is doing and looks to the east. From there, a wind arrives, the cat cannot tell if this is natural or at her command, but slowly the air begins to clear and the full extent of the devastation can be seen. The people stop and stare, some drop to their knees and weep. For miles in both directions the carriageways are blocked with the tangled wreckage of hundreds of vehicles.

'Who did this?'

'Apollyon.'

'Who?'

'My brother.'

'But why?'

'I do not know.'

Page Thirty Nine: A Balance of Questions

…the Shadow vibrated with energy. Despair sparked and radiated in all directions, feeding the Darqness and feeding the Nemesis. The Shadow gloated. It had sensed the crone Hecate's arrival and had silently slipped back into the Darqlands using the same rift she had created for its escape. She had come to gloat over his demise and now it was his turn. Her plan had failed and he was more the stronger because for it. It was simple arithmetic…

It was more than the used ticket stubs. It was the Gift. With everyone she met, she could see into their souls, measure their lives and she knew when they would die. Everyone that is, except Philip. When they first met on the park-bench, all she could see was a line that looped and twisted, stretching to infinity and arriving back at the beginning like an endless mobius strip. At first this had just been a curiosity, he was a soul she could not read, or maybe one that did not wish to be read. Being near him was different, it was somehow thrilling to be with someone and not know when they would die. The gift had distressed her when her mother was alive, knowing every day took her closer to death. Conversely, she had drawn strength knowing that her father was closer to his. She casually stroked Philip's face as he lay sleeping, his head resting on her lap. The mystery was gone. Now she knew when he would die. Never. It was a concept that 'Saffron' easily accepted, even though she struggled to get her head around some of the inevitable consequences. Sure there were downsides and knowing that you would outlive your loved ones must be the most difficult. It must take a strong mind to live with that and not be driven insane. Knowing that you would outlive everything around you, this sofa, this room, this house and even the city they were a part of. To watch them crumble to dust and become buried for thousands of years, waiting for future archaeologists to discover. Still, the thought of immortality was appealing. To be there when they excavate these ruins and listen to them speculate on the civilisation that lived here. To see them recreate their impression of life in the early twenty first century based on the scant remains they dig up. Then to watch that civilisation crumble and die for another future to unearth. She wondered how often this cycle would repeat until no trace could be found of this city apart from myth and legend. Philip moved. She looked down on his sleeping face. There was eye movement behind his closed lids, he was dreaming. A mind that had seen so many things still found the need to create images in his sleep. Was he dreaming of her? Or of someone else, from another life? She smiled at the arrogance of the thought. Philip's head must be full of so many memories, so many wonders, why should she figure amongst them. Hundreds of years of wisdom. Every book he had read. Every skill he had learnt. Did he remember every woman he had fucked? What happens when your brain is full and you cannot remember another thing? Was memory infinite or did the old memories fade with time to make room for new ones? Was memory dynamic, forever changing, forever copying itself, like a remembered word. No matter how many times you use that word, it never runs out, there is always a copy, waiting to be used the next time you need it. Even if you forget that word, one day an unrelated event, a sound or a smell, will trigger it and it will be refreshed, remembered, along with its meaning and a myriad of other facts about that word. You may recall the last time you used it, or the first time you heard it. The word was never forgotten, just the path to finding it was misplaced. No, it did not make sense that all it took to become immortal was to simply forget to die. How do you forget something on purpose? The answer is logical: you cannot. You can remember on purpose, but forgetting is not something you can do deliberately. Perhaps that is the answer. We all were immortal once and maybe we just forgot to live. Philip did not forget, he remembered.

...the elegance of mathematics, the beauty of numbers. The purity of a brush stroke. The same line that can sketch an image can script a poem or construct a formula. All three are powerful and all three can model the Universe, but only mathematics can predict the outcome. A simple formula, the model of light and dark. If both sides are equal, the equation must balance. The left minus the right equals zero. One cannot exist without the other, they cancel each other. Re-arrange the formula. The left divided by the right equals one. If one tries to dominate the other the result will be unity - a stalemate, a stand off...

Rochelle climbed out onto her garden. A retreat from the stone and concrete of the city, a tiny patch of the countryside planted in pots and urns on the flat roof of the kitchen extension that a previous owner had added to the Victorian house. The centre piece of this garden was a shallow box of zinc lined wood that she had filled with soil, like an adult version of a child's sandpit, but planted with grasses instead. Tending this small patch of dirt was a pain, but worth it. With the earnings from her first successful book, she had bought a wooded copse from a farmer only too willing to exchange money for the worthless piece of land. This was where she normally enacted special rituals and celebrated the eight festivals. But the hour and a half drive to get there was too long for her immediate needs. Everything that was happening invoked a feeling of urgency, she had to do this now.

She was within her ritual space, slowly cleansing herself of the filth, purifying mind, body and spirit. She knelt naked, save for an elaborately knotted cord tied around her waist, before the altar. Far below her the noise of traffic rose up so she slowly chanted a mantra to block out its sound, until she was spiritually transported out of the city. Using her *athame*, an ancient bronze knife, she had cast a circle around the area that she had consecrated with the four elemental forces of Air, Fire, Water and Earth. Censers of smouldering incense filled the space with rich smells of spice and resin represented the air. Fire was in the form of a small fire burning at the centre of the circle in a heavy iron hearth, next to it sat a copper bowl filled with spring water she had purified with rock salt. Earlier she had used the *athame* to carve a wand from holly and had fixed a charged ruby crystal into one end. She would need a special wand to fight the forces that assailed her, and holly was a winter tree of deep green leaves and blood-red berries associated with wisdom, hope and Fire. And that Fire energy also brought the energy of Mars, the warrior god. Now the ancient knife lay between two candles on the altar before her, with a chalice of wine and a plate of moon-shaped biscuits. Gripping the wand, she offering it to the gods for their blessing as she channelled her spirit along the fibres of the wood and into the crystal, passing it through the four elements before her as she did. Finally to complete the consecration, she invoked the pentagram of Fire, drawing its shape in the air with the wand, closing her eyes she visualised the ruby crystal, incandescent with energy, moving from Spirit to Fire; Fire to Air; Air to Water; Water to Earth; Earth to Spirit and finally back to Fire to seal it.

The sound of flapping wings disturbed the ritual. She opened her eyes. The pentagram now hovered before her, still glowing red as it had in her minds eye. Unfazed by this phenomena, she calmly banished it by retracing the path with the wand. The energy of the pentagram flowed into the crystal and it began to glow brighter with each stroke. She flung her head back and screamed as she felt the energy being drawn along her arm and into her body. A warmth ran across her shoulder and into her spine where it divided and coursed into the etheric spirit centres of her head and lower back. She felt elation and light headed, as if she were drunk, yet it was more a feeling of power that had recharged her failing spirit. Then it was over. The noise from the city bled back into her world and she heard a metallic tapping noise. Looking down, she saw a magpie perched on her altar, pecking at the biscuits on the bronze plate.

…but. Add an external operator. Nemesis. One side becomes greater, the equation does not balance and the deadlock is broken…

Page Forty: Bittersweet Sympathy

The Magpie sensed a feeling of belonging with this human. From its look-out on the highest satellite dish on the tallest building it has seen the naked woman invoke the powers of nature and was immediately drawn to her. In former times the Magpie had been closely associated with her kind and that link, all be it faint, was still present. The Raven would not have felt that, it was only attracted to darker powers, but the Magpie, like its plumage, was equally attuned with the light and the dark. To the outside world this made the Magpie appear self-centred, however the only true emotion it was capable of was ambivalence. It knew that there were no clear boundaries between Light and Dark, (or good and evil if you will), but a vast fuzzy grey-area, each side had become tainted by the other. Both had become tinged with a malevolent morality that they used to justify their deeds and actions. Even for the forces of Light, there was no action too unspeakable as long as it was directed in the right direction, for the holy cause. It also knew that, like itself, this woman was being used, forces beyond her understanding were directing and controlling her. Distorting and manipulating her beliefs for their own ends. Expendable pawns in a game that contained no rules or codex. And without rules, who was to say that the Magpie could not join this woman and free themselves from this slavery. So, it swooped down to her roof top and waited for the Earth to deliver its gift to her.

Cocoon
The Spider spun and spun.
Thin sticky strands of silk.
Like glass, like steel, like nylon.
Winding and binding.

Binding and winding.
Nylon like, steel like, glass like.
Silk of strands sticky thin.
Spun and spun the spider.
Cocoon

'Ohmygoddesswhothefuckisthat!' Kip screamed at the apparition as it appeared before him. Blue looked up from the soul-less victim she was caring for and saw the Angel, sat cross-legged on the cab of an overturned lorry, watching them.

He spoke first: 'Hello sister, I thought I'd find you here.'

'I might have guessed this was your handiwork.' Blue stood up and faced him, defiant, with ephemeral hands on ephemeral hips.

'Me? This was Apollyon's doing, as well you know. It was you who trapped him here to die.'

'What! Who is this fucker then?' Spat the cat, thinking it was Apollyon who appeared before them. The Angel raised an eyebrow at the cat.

'Can't you keep your little gutter-tongued pet quiet?'

'He is not my pet, or anyone else's.' (Kip winced as an image of the Antique Shop owner opening a tin of cat-food flashed in his mind. The Angel smiled and winked at the cat). 'Kip, this is my brother Meririm. Meririm, this is my friend Kip.' Kip slowly moved back, constantly eyeing the Angel. With the introductions over, Blue continued. 'Now, I assure you that I have no reason to want to trap Apollyon anywhere, least of all here. This Destruction has all your hallmarks. So what is this really about Meririm?' Blue waved an upturned hand towards the lanes of wrecked automobiles. The Angel nodded and sat and thought for a while, then it shrugged.

'Search me. I felt the shock-wave through the Ether and came to investigate. Earlier I met Polly and he told me that you were trying to kill him. So I expected to find one of you here, if not both, preferably with your hands around each others throats.'

'Nice family you've got there Blue, any more like them at home?'.

'Ssh! Grown-ups talking!' The Angel chided. The cat hissed.

'Apollyon spoke to you! Oh come on, he has not spoken since the fall and you would be the last person he would talk to.' The Sphinx stepped closer to the truck. 'I can see the newly healed scars on your body Meririm, you did not talk, you fought and lost. Stop playing games and tell the truth for once!' Blue was getting angry. The air crackled with pent up energy waiting for release.

'Okay, okay.' The Angel held up his hands in mock surrender. 'So the conversation didn't actual flow and it was all a bit one-sided, with me doing most of the talking. However, I did slip into his mind for a brief moment and he, at least, believes that you are destroying the Darqlands and trying to defeat him. These scars,' he gestured to his mending flesh, 'came after we parted, I caught a bus. Sadly, I forgot I wasn't ethereal at the time and the impact shattered most of the feeble bones in this pathetic corporeal body.' Blue shook her head, she felt that Meririm was telling the truth for once.

'If it were his Destiny to be killed by me, then he would be dead already.' She stated. 'So, if neither you nor I trapped Apollyon here, then who did?' She felt that Kip was about to speak-out again, so quickly she put a mental gag on him, preventing his thoughts from spilling out.

The Angel shrugged again. 'I think one of the others has woken up, I haven't figured out who. I though it was you, even though you rarely venture outside your little kitty-litter realm. It would seem that our Shadowy brother is still fixated with you and blames you for everything. So who knows? It could be one of the Seven, I haven't found the other four as of yet. Or it could be any one of the Host, or any of Hell's little demons. Let's face it, all of them have a grudge against us, and against Polly in particular.'

'Or it could be human.' She said, remembering the three new spirits in the firmament. The Angel shook his head.

'Nope. Never gonna happen. I've lived amongst them since forever and haven't met one yet who can hack the power without frying their brains.' Meririm smiled a wicked smile. 'And believe me, I've tried. Had some spectacular failures, spiritual super-nova that have lit up the Ether for weeks.' He chuckled to himself for a moment, but stopped when he saw that Blue was not laughing. 'Well Heccy my sister.'

'Do not call me Heccy, Merri my dear.' Blue interrupted.

'Point taken Hecate, or whatever you are called today. Sheesh! you've got more names than the thing with slightly less names than you. You must have a whole page to yourself in the celestial phone book. Hecate, Demeter, Diana, Inanna, Bast, Kali, Isis, Asarte, Raph...'

'Enough!' Metal rattled and shook at the sound of her raised voice. The Angel gripped onto the side of the truck to steady himself. The fall to the ground would not even have scratched him, but his concern for his safety was genuine, he was fully aware of what the Sphinx could do to him with just her voice.

'Opps. Sorry.' Meririm gave a cheesy grin. 'Anyway, my vote goes for it being one of us, after all, who else can jerk Shady around like a puppet?'

'It could even be him.'

Merirm nodded: 'Sure. He used to be smart enough to be able to pull a stunt like this and carry it off. But now. After all those millennia of isolation in his precious Darqlands…' He pursed his lips while he surveyed the devastation around him. 'He ain't too smart is he?'

'Maybe he is.' Blue lent back against the tangled wreckage behind her. 'What if he staged this to lure us here?'

'And then?' Meririm responded, jumping down from the lorry and landing softly on the ground before her. He paced back and forth like a caged panther as he spoke. 'Where is he? If that was his plan, what next. We're here now and,' he gestured his arm in a wide sweeping arc, 'nothing, nada, zip, zilch. The Greatest no-Show on Earth.' Blue had to admit that Meririm was probably correct.

'So, where are the others?' She asked. 'If they have remembered, then they must have felt this event. That's why you and I came after all. All this emotion release in one go. Absinthium for one would not be able to resist so much Death.'

'Ah, sweet Abby, such a professional.' the Angel smiled as he remembered times passed. 'Truely, if she were still around then she would be here. She would not miss this for the world, or any other planet.'

'And neither would the others. There is even enough Delirium loose here that Ishtarah would have been drawn. No, I am afraid it is either you, me or Apollyon.'

'Or it's the Hell's spawn.' Blue shuddered as Meririm said it.

'Or the Host.' Merirm looked up to the heavens, almost cowering.

'Oh shit!'

'Whatever. Either way, we are in trouble.' While Blue spoke, she could see that the Angel was starting to sublimate, diffusing back into the Ether.

'No. Either way, we're fucked.' With that, Meririm vanished. Blue quickly raise her head to see what he had been looking at to cause him to leave so abruptly.

'Oh shit.' And she too was gone, leaving the cat alone and bewildered. Too stunned by the sudden desertions to move, he continued to stare at the space once occupied by Blue and Meririm. Finally he looked up.

'Oh sh...' He managed to utter just before Blue reappeared, snatched him into her arms and carried him off into the Ether.

Page Forty One: Echoes of Tomorrow

…from deep in the Heart of the Darqlands, Nemesis sensed their arrival. They were not wholly unexpected, but they were not welcome either. Still, it knew they were a necessity. Something it had to do before it could move on…

The years had lain heavily on Philip. Each tick of the clock added imperceptible grams to that mass, the gradual accumulation had been barely noticeable. He had become accustom to their burden, so the relief he now felt went beyond euphoria as that weight was now shared. He felt guilty that he had unloaded it on one so young, but then everyone on the planet was younger than him. What 'Saffron' did with the knowledge was for her conscience, he would not influence her decision but would support her, whatever the outcome. For the moment, she was content to soothe his brow as he rested his head on her lap. He could ask her what she was thinking. He knew that was what was expected, yet the question was superfluous and somewhat redundant. He knew what she was thinking and did not want to start up that particular conversation just yet. She needed time to think. Philip began to doze, drifting off into the in-between world that he occasionally fell into when he was not watching were he was going. From there he could see the visible and the Invisibles equally in the same time frame. The Invisible lived in the real world, but were the forgotten, the people that everyone knew existed, but chose not to see, or do anything about. The homeless, the unemployed, the unbalanced and the infirm. The old, the sick and the lost. 'Saffron' was close to the in-between world; he guessed that she must have been there several times during her time on the streets, disappearing from the eyes of the 'normal' people. Eventually she would have become a permanent part of that world along with the thousands of others throughout the country. Now, he hoped, she had a chance. His day-dream was interrupted by a knock at the door. He started to rise, but 'Saffron' rested her hand on his head and said she would see who it was. She stood up quickly and his head bounced against the hard leather of the ottoman as she left the room. He heard the front door open and a brief, muffled conversation. Then the door clicked shut. When she returned, she was not alone.

'Oh my!' Exclaimed the visitor as she saw Philip. He sat up and looked at the woman stood next to 'Saffron'. A tall firmly set woman. Striking was the word that sprang into his mind. She was head and shoulders taller than 'Saffron', head and shoulders that were adorned with long braided and beaded hair that appeared to have grown through a feather and lace skull-cap she wore so that they had become one. She was dressed in layers of lace and silk in rich dark colours that draped over her tall frame like a wedding-dress that had been dipped in coal-dust. As she moved towards him he could see that beneath the layers she was tightly bound in leather and latex, the material gripping the curves of her body. He recognised the look from years ago, but those had been a mere pastiche compared to this woman, she was the real thing. However, for all her stature and poise, the woman was nervous, so in a effort to put her at ease he leapt to his feat and held out his hand.

'Hi, I'm Philip, this is 'Saffron'. Please come in, sit down.'

'Thank you, er, hello, er, no I mean Hi. Um, I'm Rochelle. Rochelle du Pont.' She beamed widely and taking his hand lightly she almost curtseyed. Then, almost reluctantly, she let it go and moved to the ottoman. She seemed to hover, uncertain whether to sit or run. Philip motioned for her to sit down and she perched too daintily for her size on the edge of the seat, her eyes flitting around the room, trying to take in every detail in one go. Philip and 'Saffron' sat down on the armchairs either side of the fireplace and watched her. Then followed a long silence as all three sat waiting for someone to speak first.

'Coffee?' Asked 'Saffron', almost out of desperation.

'Please.' Rochelle nodded, then shook her head. 'Sorry, no. No stimulants.' There was another silent pause. 'Do you have anything herbal?' She whispered, her voice faltering as if she had committed a gross social error. 'Saffron' shrugged and looked at Philip.

'I've china tea and I think there is a lemon in the 'fridge.' The woman smiled and nodded as 'Saffron' got up and disappeared into the kitchen. Rochelle turned to Philip, still smiling.

'She's an angel.' She said, much to Philip's astonishment at this sudden familiarity.

'She is isn't she.' He smiled back and she nodded, still smiling.

'And there are so few of them left.' She added, looking over her shoulder to the kitchen. 'I suppose it must be like Faeries, when no one believes anymore they just fade away.' Philip stiffened and started to say something, but stopped himself, unsure of the meaning in the words she had said. She couldn't be, he thought, he couldn't get caught twice in one lifetime. No, 'Saffron's' surprise at his Angel story was genuine. There was no way that 'Saffron' could be a real Angel. He relaxed and just watched the woman as she continued to look around his living room. Shortly, 'Saffron' returned with a tray bearing three steaming mugs and a small jug of milk that Philip did not recognise, but assumed must have been buried deep within one of his cupboards. She placed the mug containing a tea-bag on a string before Rochelle and the milk next to it. She then passed a mug that unmistakably contained coffee to Philip and sat crosslegged on the floor cradling the third in her hands. Rochelle looked at the milk and pushed it away.

'Sorry. The lemon was busy creating a new species of life and I didn't want to disturb it.' 'Saffron' said as an apology, scowling at Philip for the state of his 'fridge and Philip scowled back.

'It's okay.' Rochelle replied, removing an ornate silver flask from within her layers of lace, which she uncorked and used its contents to top up the mug before re-corking it and slipping it back from whence it came. Philip shot a raised eyebrow at 'Saffron' who was trying to suppress a giggle. 'Ow, sorry.' She exclaimed, retrieving the flask and offering it to Philip and 'Saffron', who both declined.

'So.' Philip began, leaning forward. 'Rochelle. What can we do for you?'

'The Magpie sent me.' She replied.

'The Magpie sent you.' Philip's heart sank as he slumped back.

'Mmm. He was very insistent . He said I was to tell you two things.'

'What two things?'

'Not two things. Things.' She said, pointing alternately at the pair of them. 'To you two.'

'Things like?' Asked 'Saffron'

'Things like: "The Ophanim are coming".'

…they came. Foolishly, unguided, but with a single purpose. At first they came in ones and twos, to be quickly engulfed and devoured by the Nemesis. Like spinning disks of burning coals they cut through the Darqness, carving and slicing as they came. Nothing resisted their path. There was no plan or purpose in the attack, just numbers. In wave after wave they came, attempting to overwhelm Nemesis by shear weight of numbers. With each it swallowed them whole, without effort, without a fight, growing as it did. As their numbers increased it became proportionally stronger to defeat them. After a timeless eternity, they stopped…

Page Forty Two: Seraphim

Angels & Archangels

'I have this theory,' said a grain of sand to those others of its like that were close by, 'You know they tell us that we wuz once a mountain?' Its closest neighbour groaned, the others feigned disinterest, attempting to ignore this trouble making upstart. 'It's all bollocks! Tha's my theory. I mean imagine that eh? A goddamn fucking mountain! As big as you like. Nah, bigger. Huge!' It was just this kind of free thinking that lost them the mountain in the first place. 'And dj'u'no what they say happened?' Some jostled to move away, the last thing they wanted to hear after years of being pounded and washed by the waves and endless baking by the sun, was a geology lesson. 'We got worn t'nothing by the fucking wind. The wind! Can you believe that! The fucking wind.' But such is the movement of sand, it took hours for them to get out of ear-shot, and often when they had managed it, a wave would come and wash them together again. 'Nah, it's bollocks', continued the radical grain, impervious to its neighbours' efforts to get away, 'It's fucking bollocks, tha's what it is. Everything's permanent, nothing changes. The same old same old. Sand we is and sand we always was. We's always been sand and sand is all we's ever will be. Tha's all, nothing but sand. Sand. And tha's my theory, for all it's worth.' Faith can move mountains. But try telling that to the sand.

'That's a stupid story!' Exclaimed the young blade of grass to the oak. 'Sand cannot talk!'

'Maybe, maybe not.' The might oak replied. 'But did I fail to mention that ten Angels were dancing around on the top of that grain of sand?'

'Ten!' The young blade quickly turned and looked at its Guardian Angel, who had taken a short rest from coaxing its charge to grow while the oak related the tale. 'Ten?' The Angel flexed its translucent wings and nodded.

'…so I have been told. I am new here, but I cannot imagine that they would tell me lies…'

'Dancing on a grain of sand. What's all that about?' Asked the grass. The Angel shrugged.

'…search me, must have been their day off…' The grass nodded in the breeze, fully accepting the answer before enquiring.

'And who are "they" then, who wouldn't lie to you?'

'…the Archangels…' Replied the Angel, hoping that would need no further explanation

'Are they the boss Angels then?' Which it evidently did.

'…well, they are my bosses, but they have bosses of their own above them.' The Angel thought for a moment, 'It is like a ladder: Lowest are the Angels, like me; then the Archangels; the Principals; the Powers; the Virtues; the Dominions; the Ophanim; the Cherubim and at the top are the Seraphim. They are the boss-Angels of all Angels…'

'That's one hell of a hierarchy!'

'…i prefer to look on it as a career path…' Smiled the Angel.

Chapter Seven: Lilith

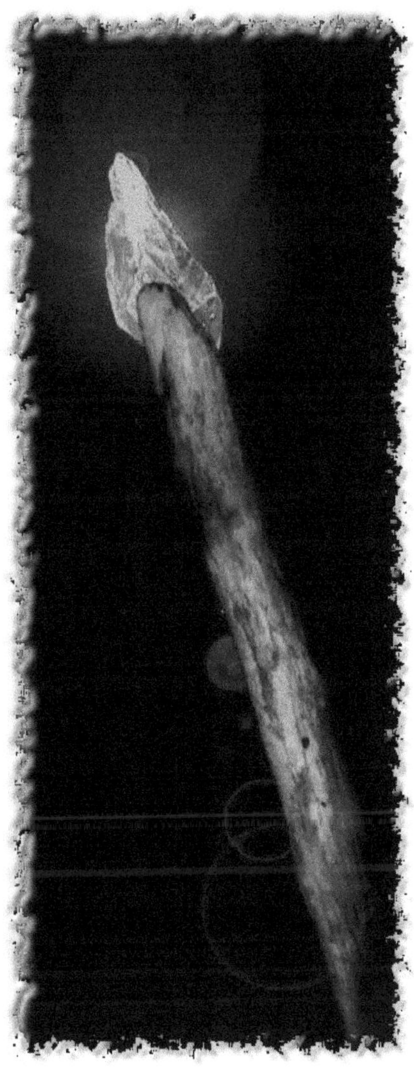

Page Forty Three: The Edge of Tomorrow

The cat crashed into reality. His panicking instinct said *run like fuck!*, but the firm hand grip on the loose skin at the back of his neck said *stay*. And it said it calmly though very, very insistently. The fear subsided, his haunches relaxed, his claws retracted, leaving deep wounds in the ephemeral flesh of the Sphinx's leg, puncturing what passed for skin yet without drawing blood. Kip let out a long sigh of relief and Blue released her grip of his neck and stroked him, as if to smooth out any creases she may have left in his fur.

'You are safe now.' She said quietly.

'I'm safe!' Kip responded indignantly. 'I'm safe! You mean We are safe. You and your scary brother were as frightened as I was, you couldn't get away quick enough. You left me behind, fuck it! Left me with those, with those...'

'Ophanim.'

'...those whirly, burn-y, spin-y things.'

'Ophanim.' She repeated.

'Yes them. What the fuck are they?'

'Ophanim.'

'Yes, so you've said twice already. I'm stupid, not deaf. What the fuck are they?'

'I think that is enough course language for one day; and to be accurate, I said it thrice. The Ophanim are the Ophanim. They are Immaterial.'

'They seemed to matter to you and you brother.'

'No, immaterial, as in incorporeal - without matter.' Blue paused. 'But not without concern.'

'And they are evil motherf-.'

'No, far from it.' Blue cut in before he could finish his profanity. 'They are good. So good in fact, that anyone with even just a speck of bad in their hearts will appear as the foulest demon of Hell beside them.' Kip gulped and looked to the sky, but all he could see was the steel and glass roof of the shopping centre, nevertheless, he cowered.

'And we're safe here.' Kip was far from convinced. 'They won't find us in this shopping mall in the middle of the busiest city in the world?'

'Definitely.'

'Because?'

'They were not looking for us.'

'Then why did we run?'

'When the Ophanim come to earth, you do not get in their way.'

...if pride was an emotion that the Shadow possessed, it would feel it now. Its Nemesis had triumphed and was now even stronger...

Evening had dissolved into night, its charcoal blackness now only a gossamer veil to Ashiya's perceptions as she sat in silence in the darkened room. The light from the windows of the building opposite cast an inverted shadow of her window across the polished wooden floor, illuminating crisp rhomboids of pale beech. The Guardian was here. She could not see him, but she could sense his nearness, feel his concern for his charge. As the night edged towards tomorrow, she was content to sit and wait. Listening to the whine of the clock as its quartz heart counted the seconds that vibrated the solenoid that clicked the ratchet that turned the gears that inched the hands around the dial she could not see but knew was there. At the fulcrum night when today and tomorrow balanced yesterday and today, when the pair of clock hands touched at midnight o'clock, when the distant chimes of long forgotten bells in a long forgotten church marked the beginning of a new day. Ashiya spoke.

'I know you are there.' She said calmly.

Silence.

Ashiya waited.

More silence.

'We are wasting time.' She sighed. A thought came into her head. It was not hers.

...time is not ours to waste...

'And my time is not yours to waste. So, why are you here?'

...I am a Watcher, I am watching...

'Come now, do you take me for some novice, a mere acolyte? I remember more than that. You are a Watchmaker. So, I'll ask one more time. Why are you here?'

…Yesterday. No, I beg your pardon, time marches forward in this sphere, it was the day before yesterday, I was a Watchmaker. I counted time and I measured time. I crafted the instruments that marked the passing of time. Today, however, I am just a Watcher and I am watching you…

'So Mister Watchmaker, do you like what you see?'

…I have pleasure in observing what you have become…

'And what do you like exactly?' She flirted.

…From a little cocette to a little coquette. Quite charming. However, what is more important, do you know what you have become? Do you know who you are?…

'I am.' Ashiya hesitated as she pieced together memories from so far away. 'I am Ishtarah, I am Queen of the Garden. Love of Shem…' Her voice trailed off as she started to speak her lovers' name as if invoking it would condemn them forever. In thought, she drifted back to that time long ago when they were last together, before he was cast out of the Host and she was condemned to walk the Earth for eternity. Memories of that time flooded over her. She felt her skin begin to tingle, a warm creeping sensation that covered her entire body, soaking into the muscle fibres. She was beginning to glow with the same fiery radiance she had seen in the park, only brighter, more pure. The room was becoming bathed in a deep red light that confused her eyes, causing shadows to move and dance. A young boy stepped from those shadows into her smouldering aura. He looked into her eyes and smiled. Then, with a voice that sounded like a thousand choirs singing with the voices of a thousand bells, the boy spoke.

'Not anymore. That was you then, in a different time, in a different world. Punished for your love of an Angel, you have served your penance. I have watched you and I have watched over you. You are now who you have always been. You know who you are…' Ashiya's skin began to split, through the tears shafts of deep red light radiated, piercing through the darkened room, cutting through the walls and into the night sky.

…Uri-el!… She exclaimed as the last shreds of her flesh vaporised, taking with them the boundaries of the material world, into the vanishing-point of perspective. Uri-el now floated free in the Ether, the young Watchmaker-Angel spun and gyrated around her, emanating glee at her release …Where is my Love?… Her thoughts rang out to the music of a million bells. The Watchmaker stopped.

…He waits…

…For me?…

…No. For forgiveness…

Page Forty Four: The Flight of Ashiya

…ashiya. The name was but a memory now, one of many accumulated through countless incarnations and reincarnations. From the first birth into flesh to the last, Uri-el remembered them all. As the angel's soul journeyed down the ages from Ishtarah to Ashiya, all had paid the price for Uri-el's pride. Nefertiti, Helen and Josephine - more memories. Men had fallen under her spell, the 'Great' and the 'Good' had fallen for her charm and their fate had fallen with them. In the Delirium of enchantment, her penance was to cause men to sacrifice all for her love…

The magpie had sent her here. Why the pied bird had singled her out for this purpose was a mystery to her. As a witch, she did not usually work with animals. She did not work with children either, but that is another story. She did not even keep them as pets, animals that is, not children… Well, she did not keep children as pets either, in fact she didn't even keep children as animals or animals as children and absolutely no pets. One thing that amused her was the sign on bottles of bleach that read "Keep out of the reach of small children", she always took this as sound advice and kept well away from children of any size. (Let's just forget about children and just concentrate on animals). There was a cat who visited her on her roof-garden, but it was not hers, it just passed through now and then and would occasionally stop to bask in the warm sunlight. However, the Magpie had chosen her, so here she was. Uninvited and unannounced, invading their privacy because the Magpie had told her to. They were a strange pair, Rochelle concluded as she watched them drink their coffee. Like polar opposite twins, they complimented each other almost too perfectly. Where he was dark, she was light; where he as light, she was dark. There was no single aspect where they matched. The girl was easy to read, her aura shone and scintillated with her every move, the rich yellow making her face glow with the brightness of morning, but she had a serious, dark purpose behind that smile. Yet the man's aura crackled and growled at her in deep hues that transcended the visible spectrum and verged on the ultra-violet. His was an aura that affected people directly, igniting dormant thoughts, creating dreams from nothing. And in that yin-yang relationship there was a bond: as they talked, they would glance at each other and smile; yet they could hardly have sat further apart, like there was a taboo that forbade them from being close. Rochelle noticed that when the girl, 'Saffron', lent forward to speak, the man, Philip, would lean back to listen, maintaining a constant distance between themselves. So, 'Saffron' lent forward.

'Why are the Ophanim coming?' She asked.

'You know of the Ophanim?' Rochelle responded.

'No, I don't know of them personally, but as you can see,' 'Saffron' gestured to the piles of junk littering the room, 'Philip has an extensive library. Most of which is dedicated to Angels, so I know what the Ophanim are.' She thought for a moment, remembering the text she had read that afternoon. 'They are the Third Choir of the First Triad of the Host of Angels. But don't they normally only accompany the Cherubim?'

'No,' Philip interjected, 'not necessarily. They only appear together for the big, dramatic events. The biblical-epic stuff. Often the Ophanim, or Thrones as they are also known, operate on their own. The Ophani-' He stopped as the two women shot him a '*Ssh, Women talking*' look and he slunk further back into his chair. Rochelle made a quiet humph sound and turned to 'Saffron'.

'Why are they here? I don't know the details, but I think the Magpie's former employer has created some kind of 'abomination' and they have been sent to deal with it. It must be small, undramatic one if they are here alone.' She smiled at Philip.

'Let's hope so.' 'Saffron' added, and both Rochelle and Philip quietly nodded. Then followed an uncomfortable and protracted silence as they sat there, sipping beverages, not knowing what to say.

…But only Ashiya found the courage to rebel. Only Ashiya broke the endless cycle of love and betrayal. By denying love and pursuing only hedonism, Ashiya found the key to Uri-el's release…

Philip had finished his coffee but carried on the pretence of drinking, cradling the empty mug in his hands, thankful for the security of having something to occupy himself while they sat there, saying nothing. Their strange visitor, Rochelle, seemed to be studying them, or at least his room, her gaze continually wandered over the stacks of books and collection of bric-a-brac. Until curiosity or impatience got the better of her and she stood up and walked to the wall covered in pictures and other piece of his memorabilia. She stood staring at the mosaic of ticket-stubs, occasionally tilting her head, or leaning forward to inspect a single ticket, or stepping back and squinting. Then unexpectedly she marched across to the door and turned off the main light, leaving the room illuminated by the artificial glow of the fire and a single antique standard lamp. She turned to Philip.

'Sorry,' She pointed to the switch, 'you don't mind do you?' Philip raised his hand in assent and smiled. 'Thank you' she said as she strode back to the mosaic of ticket-stubs. She studied it some more, before turning to Philip again. 'These tickets,' she stated, Philip glanced at 'Saffron', who was staring intently at Rochelle and did not see him, his heart sank. He had not realised they were such a give-away, with regret, he resigned himself to disposing of them soon. 'These tickets,' she repeated, then shook her head. 'No, it doesn't matter.' She turned away from the tickets and move a couple of paces towards Philip before stopping again. 'But they remind me of...' She closed her eyes and pinched the bridge of her nose in an overtly dramatic pose which prompted a small giggle from 'Saffron'. Rochelle opened her eyes, went to the window and lifted the corner of the curtains, letting in a splash of amber street-light to flood the tickets. Her eyes opened wide as the orange glow subdued the colours, leaving a sepia tinted monochrome image on the wall.

'Lilly!' She exclaimed, letting the curtain fall back. Philip's mouth dropped.

'You know Lilly?' He asked, getting up out of the chair and quickly crossing the room. He looked at the arrangement of tickets. They looked like they always had, just a random collection of stubs that he had stuck on the wall, with no thought of design. He squinted at them and still saw nothing. He gave Rochelle a quizzical look and shook his head. She smiled and lifted the curtain again. He looked back at the wall; the sodium glow from the street light had revealed a hidden design in the arrangement of ticket-stubs, light and dark shades showing the outline of a face, a woman's face, that of Lilith.

'Fuck me.' He said very quietly under his breath.

'You're not my type.' Rochelle quipped back. 'And I think there is a queue.' She whispered so that 'Saffron' could not hear. Philip turned to 'Saffron' and pointed at the tickets, who just smiled at him and nodded.

'You knew?' He asked, she continued nodding. 'You never said.'

'I didn't think I had to. I thought you had done it on purpose.' She said, Philip shook his head.

'Do you know where she is?' Philip asked, Rochelle looked down to the floor and sighed.

'Shit. I was going to ask you the same thing.' She said, walking back to the sofa and sat down heavily, almost falling into it. She sat for a moment, dejected, pulling at a piece of black lace from her layered coat. Philip recognised the statement her body-language was making. He knew how she was feeling. He had been there often enough himself. This strong, powerful woman had been reduced to a vulnerable child in seconds. He went over and sat beside her. When she looked at him, her eyes were wet. 'The horrors I've seen because of her.' She sniffed back a tear, wiping her nose on the back of a lace-frilled sleeve. 'I've got to find her. She's screwing my life, fucking with everything I believe in.' 'Saffron' moved from her chair to the sofa, sitting herself down next to Rochelle and taking her hand in hers.

'Why?' She asked.

'I don't know. I just don't know. I met her once, she came to a meeting, then she invaded my meditation and did unspeakable things to me. And she made me eat soap. And then she sent me to a flat, And there was a dead woman, and rotting meat and little children and police. And then the Magpie came and said you would help me.' By now, Rochelle was crying fitfully and 'Saffron' had her arm around her, consoling her.

'That doesn't sound like Lilly.' Philip said, almost to himself. 'Are you sure she is doing this?' She shrugged.

'Who else?' She replied.

'Have you seen a tall man, with a face like a hawk?' He asked. She did not reply, but closed her eyes and lent her head against the sofa back. Suddenly, she quickly sat up.

'The Green Man!' She immediately brightened, as if someone had flicked a switch on her emotions. 'I thought I was dreaming, or delirious, but he was there, in my room, watching me.' Philip was not so elated.

'The Angel -that makes more sense.'

'You think the Angel was using Rochelle to find Lilly?' asked 'Saffron'

'Without doubt. He tried to use me, but must have got frustrated by my lack of progress, so he found someone who had more recent contact with her.'

'Who is this Angel?' Rochelle asked.

'From what I gather, he is sort of the Angelic Secret Police, at least that's how he sees himself.'

'So, who is Lilly, and why is he looking for her then?'

'Lilly is,' Philip paused. 'Another Angel. She calls herself Lilith. I do not know whether she is the Lilith, or just an Angel called Lilith, but if she is the Lilith then,'

'Then she was Adams' wife before Eve and is now the most important and powerful she-devil in Hell. No wonder the Angel's after her.' 'Saffron' interrupted. 'I don't think I want to find either of them.' Rochelle and Philip nodded in agreement. 'So, we do nothing and hope they go away.' she concluded.

'No, they won't go away. He will continue to torment Rochelle until he gets what he wants. And I don't think he is finished with me either. Some how we have to out-smart them both.' 'Saffron' rubbed her eyes and looked at the clock.

'It's three in the morning and I'm tired. I doubt I could out-smart an amoeba at the moment.' She yawned.

'The Magpie said we should talk to the cats.' Rochelle stated as Philip raised an eye-brow.

'First magpies, and now cats. You're not related to Doctor Doolittle are you?'

…now Uri-el was free and she had her coin. The only puzzle now was who gave it to Ashiya and why…

Page Forty Five: Spider, Spider, Burning Bright

The moist morning dew collected on the tacky strands of silk. Vapour condensing into crystal pearls that weighed heavy on the filaments, causing them to drape in slow elegant curves reflected in the flowing lines of Art Nouveau filigree that decorated the roof-top. Seven spider-eyes studied a hundred water droplets trapped in her web. Mesmerising. Enchanting. Seven hundred spider-eyes mirrored back. Hypnotised. Entranced.

...another task my sweet...

There was no honour amongst thieves. This was not a human saying. It came from the Corvidae. Stolen by the Magpie and sold to the humans in exchange for a few sparkling trinkets. Then, there was no honour amongst thieves, so it was only to be expected. The Magpie was never to be trusted. Betrayal was in its blood. Locked in the genetic code that blue-printed that blood. And this was now a blood matter, to catch a thief.

...such a small one as to make no difference, but for the pleasure it would bring me...

The spider moved and seven hundred eyes moved, following her. A stiff breeze rose up from the street, vibrating the web, freeing the larger droplets from their entrapment, sending them crashing to the slate below. The spider watched them fall, dozens of tiny spider-reflections falling to their death. There, a lone fly, a night time straggler caught by the rising sun and caught in the spiders net. A suitable breakfast.

...find her for me, find my tormentor and we shall end this, and end it now...

From the Shadow. From the shadows. It heard the call from the Shadow, and from the shadows it came. Swiftly, Quietly. The hunter and the prey. Quick, Silent. A single darting swoop and the spider was gone. Crushed in large black beak, its bodily fluids flowing down the Ravens throat like sweet nectar.

...for we are ready, my Nemesis and I...

And another black figure, hidden amid the stone gargoyles that stood guard over a disused church, another hunter, watches the hunter devour the hunter that devoured the prey. Smiling, it licks its lips and purrs.

Page Forty Six: Of A Seventh Son

…all twisted and broken: anything remaining of the soul that Nemesis was reaved from bore little resemblance to what it once was, all broken and twisted…

The newly formed triumvirate crossed the city crammed into Rochelle's tiny car. They did consider releasing Philip's car from it's subterranean garage, but Rochelle took one look and refused to get into the 6 meter long limo, (once popular in the first years of the century after the government had taxed 4x4 off-roaders so heavily that they had effectively forced them off the public roads). The journey was thankfully uneventful, apart from the endless complaints from Philip, who had to sit sideways across the rear seat, his head bent down onto his knees so that his shoulders touched the roof.

'Next time we take my car. I don't care how much damn water has to flow over the dam to charge the damned batteries!' Philip protested.

'Look, I said I'll go in the back.' 'Saffron' resolved after listening to his moaning for half an hour.

'No, no, I'm fine, don't worry about me.' He disgruntly replied.

'Okay, have it your way. But stop whining.' She responded.

They travelled the remaining two kilometres in silence, save for the occasional yelp from Philip as Rochelle bounced over the odd speed-hump or two at more than the permitted twenty-five kmph. Once at Rochelle's house, Philip persisted in walking with a pronounced stoop until it was evident he was not going to win any sympathy from either of the two women. Even so, he made a dramatic play of straightening his neck, grimacing as he twisted and contorted it back into its normal position. Rochelle's house was disappointingly normal. Both Philip and 'Saffron' expected to find a witches den of black magic, with crystal balls and jars with labels pronouncing contents such as wing'o'bat, tongue'o'frog and eye'o'newt. They would not have been surprised to find a large bronze cauldron bubbling away in the middle of the living room. But the rooms were tasteful and, well, normal. Rochelle went into the kitchen to brew some tea as they stood looking at the vast ordered array of books that filled a row of pine bookcases along one wall. It was like walking into an occult book store, there were books on every fringe and new-age subject imaginable, together with whole bookcase devoted to Wicca and Pagan religions. On one row, they were surprised to discover that every book was by the same author - Rochelle du Pont. Philip was leafing through a volume on Aura Soma colour-therapy when Rochelle returned with a tray loaded with tea and cakes. He replaced the book on the shelf and they followed her up the stairs into a back bedroom given over to a small but functional office, where they then made their way out of the window onto her roof-garden. Philip was impressed and a little embarrassed, his house boasted a 50 meter run of overgrown wilderness that was easily shamed by this perfect little island of green in the grey city. They sat on the grass, sipping sweet apple tea that Rochelle had laced with a generous dose of brandy, listening to the sound of traffic from the streets below.

'Do you think the cat will come?' 'Saffron' asked Rochelle.

'Oh yes, the Magpie will send him shortly, I'm sure of it.' She replied in a matter-of-fact manner that made it seem like an everyday occurrence.

...all twisted and broken: it's father had six elder brothers, hence grandfather's wealth was thin and watery by the time it reached his blood-line, and hard work and toil brought its slim rewards, so father died all broken and twisted...

'Saffron' liked Rochelle. She sensed a measure of big-sisterly protectiveness about her that appeared as genuine concern and not smotheringly oppressive, so she did not mind and was even a little flattered. Rochelle was severely left of centre, and definitely a borderline flake, restrained by a high degree of intelligence that 'Saffron' found refreshing after the unhinged bag-ladies she had associated with since leaving home. But now she was squatting down on the grass, talking to a cat. Not an impressive witchy cat, all sleek and black with amber eyes that burned like coals. Or a regal Siamese with electric blue eyes and a diamond studded collar. No, she was talking to a stringy, mangy moggy. A feral alley-cat with clumps of missing fur, a half-chewed ear and a badly docked tail. Neither of them spoke as they 'talked', they just stared into each others eyes. After ten or eleven minutes, the cat jumped from the roof garden and was gone.

'What now?' Philip asked. Rochelle seemed not to hear him, but remained crouched down on the grass, with her eyes closed in deep contemplation. From within the layers of her clothing, she withdrew a long gnarled stick with a large red crystal bound into a split cut into one end and held it upright before her. Then she started muttering softly. After a few minutes 'Saffron' detected a repeating refrain and realised she was chanting some kind of mantra. Either by a refraction effect of the moonlight, or neat conjuring trick, ('Saffron' could not tell which), the crystal began to glow and she was as impressed as child at a magic show by the performance. Rochelle touched the crystal to her forehead and the light gradually faded. 'Saffron' was not sure whether this was display was for her's and Philip's benefit, or for her own, but when Rochelle stood up, she strode forward with renewed confidence.

'Now,' she said, 'we go shopping.'

...all twisted and broken: belittled and put down by its own siblings, the smallest, weakest and youngest in a family of seven, wearing hand-me-downs patched and repaired with the shredded remains of other hand-me-downs too worn to wear. The shame and stigma fermenting into a stew of resentment, all broken and twisted...

Kip saw them coming. He knew they were coming, their progress had been tracked and plotted in the Realm and relayed through the network of linked minds in the Ether. He knew when they entered the borough, when they had reached the unlocked entrance to the mall, and when they were about to enter the concourse level that he and Blue were waiting on. They strode towards the bench that he and Blue were sitting on. Blue remained still, sitting bolt-upright, with her eyes closed, legs together and hands resting palms down on her knees; a queen on her throne awaiting the attendance of her loyal subjects. The taller woman bowed, the other two, standing one pace behind her, just stood with heads slightly dipped, uncertain of what to do. The tall woman was about to speak when Blue raised her hand to stop her. She opened her eyes and let out a brief involuntary gasp.

'Do you know me?' She said in an abrupt tone that even took the cat by surprise. The woman started to speak again and Blue silenced her once more. 'You.' She pointed to the man. 'Do you know me?' He shook his head. 'And you?' she asked the young woman, who also shook her head. 'Then all is as it should be. Today, I am called Blue, and this is my friend Kip.' Kip beamed a self satisfied grin at the three strangers. 'So why are you here?' Again the tall woman started to speak.

'I'm Rochelle, this is Philip and 'Saffron'. We need your help.' She waited for a reaction, Blue nodded for her to continue and Rochelle then went on to relate their tale in great detail. The cat found himself oddly relieved to hear that the Magpie had survived, although he was not to convinced that it had changed sides and was not simply baiting another trap.

'Ah, Lilith.' Blue nodded. 'So it is her. I know Meririm is looking for one of us, I assumed it was one of... the others.' Blue stood up and walked up to the human called Philip. She lent forward so that her nose was almost touching his, her eyes burning into his. As she spoke, their lips almost touched. 'The years have been kind to you dreamer, but I would have been kinder.' And she kissed him lightly on the lips. Then she turned to the girl who called herself 'Saffron', and stood before her in the same way: nose to nose, eye to eye, mouth to mouth. 'And you, what do you see?'

Without blinking the girl replied. 'I see a naked woman with a cat in a shopping mall at five in the morning when it should be locked.'

'Look deeper, what do you see Ab-', She hesitated, as if searching for the rest of the name, '-igail?' The girl's eyes widened as she looked into Blue's eyes.

'No.' The girl was shouting, 'I'm not Abigail anymore. I'm not. My father chose that name and I don't use it any more ... I don't want it anymore!' Blue remained unmoved by the outburst.

'What do you see, Saffron?' She asked again.

'Nothing. I, I don't see anything!'

'And that is as it should be.' Blue said as she kissed her and then taking one step backwards, she looked down at her body. 'You see me as naked. Can you not see my sommerfäden?' She said, holding out her whisper thin dress by the hem. Both the girl and the man shook their heads, the girl was blushing. 'Oh well, we had better go shopping for some visible clothing, Kip here will need some new clothes too if we are going to meet Lilith.' All four of them turned and looked at the cat.

…all twisted and broken: the Shadow had chosen well…

Page Forty Seven: Tear Us Apart

What!, Kip exclaimed, And what would I do with clothes?

Wear them of course, Blue replied as she crouched down beside the bench. She lifted his chin with her finger so that his eyes looked into hers. 'I am sorry my friend, but this will probably hurt quite a lot.' She began to purr as she stroked the fur on his back in the wrong direction. The cat felt heat radiating from her hand as it travelled from tail to head. The burning sensation grew stronger until it felt like his back was on fire. Only the soothing sound of her purring prevented him from crying out with the pain, prevented him from running away. He closed his eyes as his bones began to fight against the muscles that held them together. He could feel his skin ripping apart, every inch of his body screamed in agony, sending a continuous flow of stimulation through his nervous system until it overloaded his brain and every thing went numb. The pain subsided. Kip breathed deeply as feelings returned to his body. Slowly he opened his eyes. The world had shrunk. He was still sat on the bench, but his rear-paws now touched the floor. Blue was now as small as he was, they were face to face. She raised her hand and brushed his cheek, he could feel the cool touch of her finger tips. 'Beautiful.' She quietly said as she leaned forward and kissed him full on the lips. He brought his fore-paws up to her face to pull her closer, but reeled back in astonishment as two human hands came into view where his paws should be.

…'what was that!?' She asked, the Watchmaker gyrated and spun around her as the shock-wave hit and then tumbled end over end in its wake, swept along in the turbulence. Uri-el flew after him, riding the wave-crest like a seasoned surfer, her wings flexing and twisting to keep balance, soon she was along side. She reached out and grabbed his shoulder, but inertia won the moment and they both tumbled through the Ether until she managed to counter the spin. 'What was that?' she asked again. 'A star is born.' He replied, adding, 'Nimrod has returned.' 'Is that a good thing or a bad thing?' She further enquired. 'It depends,' he answered without thinking, 'on which side you are on'…

The three stared open mouthed as the Sphinx took the hand of the young man that was a cat just seconds ago and led him to the door of the mall's main department store. Rochelle was the first to snap out of their stupor. 'Come on, quick!' She whispered as she pulled on their sleeves, motioning them to follow the pair into the store.

'I'll wait here.' Philip stated as he went and sat on the bench. 'I hate shopping, especially with a bunch of women.'

'You might cop a glimpse through the changing room curtain.' 'Saffron' joked.

'Seen a few hundred naked butts in one lifetime, you've seen them all. I'll be just fine here.' Waiving them away, he pulled a pack of cigarettes from his pocket.

They had to run to catch up with the others. By the time they reached the door, the Sphinx had already opened it and was holding it for them to enter. Rochelle looked quizzically at the Sphinx.

'Magick.' She announced, Rochelle was hesitant.

'This is stealing.' she said.

'It is not exactly stealing.' Blue replied.

'You know when something is wrong when someone says: "It's not exactly stealing", and then they proceed to explain why using some vague technicality, like how the store owners have been ripping people off for years.' Rochelle stood just outside the shop, with her hands on her hips. 'So, what's the technicality this time?'

'We are not going to steal anything, just move a few items into another time-frame for a while.' Rochelle raised an eyebrow. 'They will still be here in this time-frame. You could say we are just making copies for our personal use.' She beckoned her to enter the shop and Rochelle reluctantly complied.

'It still sounds like thieving to me.' She muttered as she stepped into the store.

The cat was already in the men's department, standing naked in front of a tall mirror, admiring himself. 'No sudden urges to look behind the mirror to find the other you?' Blue asked as she walked up to stand beside him. The cat smiled and she laughed. 'You can vocalise. Try it.' She said.

'Nn-ot ssin-ce I w-wozz a kkit-tenn.' The cat stammered in growling hisses, the tone and loudness of his voice fluctuating wildly as he fought to control his new skill. He turned sideways on to the mirror and studied his profile, running one hand over his flat stomach while the other grabbed a handful of tight buttock. 'Yyou ssaid I wo-ould be o-olldd. Nnine-ty ss-ixs yyou ssaid.'

'I lied.' She shrugged, passing him a pair of leather trousers.

…"And the Angels who did not keep their positions of authority but abandoned their own home - these he has kept in darkness, bound with everlasting chains for judgement on the great Day - Jude 6"…

'Can you spare a cigarette?' Philip looked up in shock to see the Angel stood before him. He had not heard anyone approach and was certain he had all entrances covered.

'Sure.' Philip replied as he composed himself, passing over the packet. The Angel sat on the bench beside him and put a cigarette between his thin lips.

'A little fire?' The Angel said, pointing to the end of the cigarette.

'Huh? oh yeah.' Philip reached into his pocket for his lighter, but the Angel reached over and took Philip's cigarette from his mouth instead. He lit his from it and passed it back. Philip looked at the mangled cigarette between his fingers. 'Funny guy. I bet it was you who pulled the wings off spiders.'

'Every last one.' The Angel smiled. 'Now, what brings you here at this hour of the morning, run out of condoms?' Philip looked towards the store, where Rochelle and three newly attired figures were emerging.

'I came with them.' He said, standing up and facing the Angel.

'Well well, I owe you an apology Mr. Mallow. I think I may have underestimated you.' The Angel stood up and walked towards the approaching group. 'So what have we here Hecate? The lion, the witch and the whore robed?' He said, sounding the "W" in whore to emphasise the pun. Kip hissed, 'Saffron' took half a step back and adopted a fighting pose, but it was Rochelle who acted first and the quickest, catching the Angel by surprise as she lashed out with the wand, slicing the ruby through the flesh of his cheek and connecting with the bone beneath. The cigarette flew from his mouth followed by a spray of blood from the open wound. The Angel spun round, his head tracing the path of blood through the air and fell to the floor in a sprawl, sliding across the polished stone until he came to a rest at Philip's feet. Everyone looked at the glowing wand in Rochelle's hand with quiet admiration as the ruby pulsed and then faded. Rochelle slipped the wand back up her sleeve and walked with the others to the fallen Angel.

'On your feet Meririm.' Blue nudged his ribs with a booted foot. 'Come on. Get up if you want to see Lilith.' She nudged him again and he snarled back at her before slowly rising to his feet. He squared up to them, fists clenched, ready to fight. 'You cannot fight us Meririm. You may have once been able to defeat one, but never three.'

'Three!' Meririm exclaimed. Rochelle nodded as Blue put her arms around Philip and 'Saffron'.

'Yes, three. Now let us go, we do not have much time.'

…'see my precious, my Raven has done well. See, he can sniff out the rot and decay from miles away. He follows the trail of stench through the City to where they gather. They wait for me. A trap? Would that be for me or would it be for them?'…

Saffron watched the Angel relax his stance, flexing his fingers and wiping the blood from his cheek. Blue's firm grip on her shoulders also relaxed, but her arm remained, somewhat affectionately but perhaps protectively, wrapped around her and Philip.

'So, where is Lilith?' The Angel asked.

'I do not know.' Blue replied. 'But if we wait, she will come.'

'How can you be so sure?'

'Because, when we are all here she will have no choice but to come to us. It is destiny.' Saffron saw a wry smile flash across his thin lips. The smile turned into a leer.

'Dear sister, you are forgetting, we are not quorum.'

'I forget nothing, dearest brother.' Blue dropped her arms from Saffron and Philip and stepped back several paces. Everyone turned to face her as she raised her arms into the air and began glowing with an intense orange aura.

Page Forty Eight: Out of the Night

…now!…

The air caught fire in a sharp electric-blue flame that flashed through the shopping mall. Philip went to duck to avoid the flame, but was too slow and was barely in a stoop as the sheet of plasma sliced through his body. Time slowed as fate chose its moment to send him into his dream-state. Stunned, he glanced at Saffron, who was clutching her stomach, her face contorted in a grimace of shock. Somehow, Rochelle had managed to retrieve her wand and was now standing, unharmed, in a sphere of red-mist radiating from the ruby crystal. The Angel and the man who once was a cat were unaffected and just stood, looking at Blue. He slowly turned to see the air beside her twist and distort. A disjointed arm pushed its way through a tear in space, writhing and flaying the air. A warped, deformed arm with a demonic claw of a hand that proceeded to rip into the air, enlarging the tear. Next a leg emerged from the hole and planted its foot onto the polished floor with a wet slap, to be followed by the shoulders and head of a snarling demon. The monster finally pulled the rest of its body into their dimension.

'Nemesis.' The Angel hissed. Philip then heard him mutter under his breath. 'Not now you idiot.'

'Nimrod, it is time.' Blue said as the man who once was a cat stepped forward. 'Your *Shamshir.*' A writhing snake appeared in her hand, which she tossed towards him. As it twisted through the air it became a curved sword that Nimrod deftly caught by the grip. He swung the sword around in his hand, testing its balance before holding it horizontally in front of him. The blade began to rotate along its axis, slowly at first, then speeding up until it went beyond being a blur of glinting metal. He advanced towards the demon, the monster lunged at him with a bolt of electric-blue flame which Nimrod expertly parried with the sword, creating a blinding flash of white heat that ionised the air. Still, Nimrod advanced on the demon. Another bolt was dealt with just as easily, filling the mall with the smell of ozone. A look of panic came over the demon's face as Nimrod sliced through the air with the sword, severing one of its hands. Dismayed, the demon raised the bloodied stump to its face as a shaft of white light burst from the lesion, engulfing its head. The light fragmented into a myriad of spinning discs that sliced through Nemesis's body, dismembering him where his stood. The air became a bloody maelstrom that reminded Philip of the feeding frenzy of Piranha's. Pieces of the demon splattered to the floor in a crimson shower. Then it was over and the Ophanim were gone, leaving nothing of Nemesis behind but a naked Asian youth in a puddle of blood.

Philip phased back into normal time.

He looked down at his stomach. The sheet of plasma had cut through his clothes, the lower half of his overcoat lay on the floor at his feet, together with the tails of his shirt. He nervously pushed his hand under the seared remains of his shirt, expecting to feel the wet stickiness of warm blood and intestines, but was surprised and relieved to find his torso intact and unharmed. He looked at Saffron who, mouth agape and emitting short laughter-like sobs, had made the same discovery.

…no!…

Rochelle felt compelled to help the boy. She rushed over to him, slipping in the greasy crimson slime. He was still alive. He lay in the foetal position, crying, clutching his damaged hand to his chest.

'It's okay, I'm here to help.' She crooned in a soothing voice as she touched his shoulder. The red slime clung to her fingers. 'This isn't blood', she thought to herself. She brought her fingers to her nose and smelt a faint oily, mechanical odour, 'It's some kind of paint.' She helped the boy to his feet and examined his hand. The cut was deep, but had missed all the critical tendons and veins, and judging by the crust of dried blood, it had not been made with Nimrod's ever-turning Shamshir. Removing an outer layer from her coat, she draped it around him and helped him over to the bench, where she sat down beside him and hugged him tightly as he wept.

…the Darqlands were dissolving, the fabric of Despair was melting. The Shadow frantically tried to hold it together, but the Darqness slipped through its grasp like sand and vaporised into a swirling mist. The Heart of the Darqlands was dying and soon there would nothing left to sustain the Shadow…

Nimrod braced himself for another attack as an inky black cloud appeared in the same point in space that Nemesis had used to enter this domain. The cloud swirled and thickened as he raised the *Shamshir* before him, ready to slice into whatever emerged from the cloud. The dense cloud began to spin, creating a miniature whirlwind - a black dust-devil as tall as a human - that sucked up the crimson slime where Nemesis fell, leaving the floor polished and gleaming. Then the cloud vanished and a gold coin fell to the floor in its place. Nimrod walked over and bent to pick it up.

'No, do not touch it!' Blue commanded. 'It is not yours.'

'No, it is mine.' Nimrod spun around to face the owner of the voice and raised the *Shamshir*. 'Put your sword down. You have already defeated me. The Cherubim have ensured I do not have sufficient power to fight again.' A handsome, winged figure stood before him, dressed in flowing robes that radiated a glow of deepest blue. The figure went over and picked up the coin.

'Apollyon?' Nimrod speculated.

'In the flesh. So to speak.' The angel Apollyon smiled and bowed low. He then turned to Blue. 'Rapha-el, Why?' he asked. Nimrod watched Blue bow her head as a pair of golden wings materialised behind her.

…"When they moved I heard the sound of their wings like the sound of many waters, like the voice of the Almighty, a sound of tumult, like the sound of an army. When they stood still they lowered their wings - Ezekiel 1:24"…

She spread her wings, then folded them around herself. She looked up.

'It was not I.' She stepped towards him, but stopped when he raised his hand. 'Micha-el, I loved you, I could never harm you.' He was no longer looking at her, she followed his gaze towards Meririm. 'And do not believe it was him either.' She added.

'Ah, Metatron,' He saw the scars on the Angels body, 'How the mighty have fallen.'

'Will you stop using our Given names Apollyon.' He shot a glance to Saffron and Philip. 'Use our Chosen names.' He whispered. 'Meririm. I am Meririm. And that is Hecate.' He stated indignantly. Apollyon pointed to Philip and raised an eye-brow. 'No, they do not know. And they must not know.'

'Know what?' Philip asked, but Meririm ignored him.

'Don't you see, this is what it is all about.' Meririm held up a gold coin between his index finger and thumb. 'Lilith is after all seven and while they don't know, she can't get us to open them.'

'Know what for fuck sake!' Philip shouted. There was a blinding flash of yellow light.

'I know.' A voice like a million bells came from were Saffron was standing, everyone turned to see her flesh being stripped away by a sliver-yellow light that poured from her body.

'So we see. Welcome back Absinthium. I for one have missed you.' Meririm smiled at the emerging angel.

'Know what?!' Philip screamed as Saffron turned into Absinthium before his eyes.

'Know that these are not coins,' Absinthium said, holding up her coin.

'And now they are all mine.' They all looked up as the disembodied voice reverberated, rattling the shop windows.

'Show yourself Lilith, we have waited long enough.' Hecate shouted to the air. The body of Lilith sublimated from the Ether and strode amongst them, grinning smugly. She walked up to Hecate and stroked her face with long bony fingers tipped with long scarlet nails. Hecate stopped moving.

'You command and I appear sister dear.' Meririm and Apollyon started to move towards her. 'New trick.' She said, snapping her fingers and they both froze in mid-pace. 'Who's next?' She asked, looking directly at Nimrod who was readying his sword. 'Hi, how have you been?' She smiled and blew him a kiss. He too froze. 'How about you, lover-boy?' Philip did not answer, but while she was walking towards him, Rochelle began to remove her wand from her sleeve. 'Let's play - Statues!' Lilith spun to face Rochelle and both she and the Asian youth were also frozen in time. She walked up to Absinthium. 'Nice dress,' She said, walking round her, 'It's so you, so chic, so shear. Do you know I can see right though it.'

'And I can see through you.' Absinthium sneered. 'Cut the charade Lilith. You cannot use the seals, only Gab-' She hesitated.

'Go on, say the name, it won't release him unless he knows who he is. Say the name. It's easy. Gab-ri-el. Gabri-el. Gabri-el.' She looked at Philip, who was looking decidedly puzzled. 'See, nothing. Now say it.'

'No.'

'"Who is worthy to open the book, and to loose the seals thereof?" - I am.'

'What? Is this what this is all about. Religion. You've got religion! You're mad. That was not meant for us. I will not let you do this.' She raised her hand, but was not quick enough. In the blink of an eye, Lilith had stopped her.

'Foolish child. I have been planing this for centuries. You cannot stop me now.'

'No, but I can.' Uri-el materialised from the Ether and snatched Nimrod's sword from his hand. Lilith turned to face her, raising her hand. Uri-el kept coming, unaffected by her powers. 'You made a mistake Lilith.' She plunged the ever-turning sword into Lilith's chest. 'You showed me the way into your heart.'

Page Forty Nine: Seventh Wave

…as a leviathan breathes, swelling the tides,

the Seventh Wave rises in the depths of the oceans.

The kraken that does not wake for it never sleeps,

it just waits…

Darqlands: the Epilogues

Epilogue One - Ashiya and the Watchmaker

...All my Sleeping Dreams are Voices...

...Uri-el stood alone in the shopping mall with the body of Lilith at her feet and the ever-turning serpentine sword in her hand, splattering blood in a wide arc over the polished stone floor as it turned. The other angels, near-angles, humans and meta-humans had one by one left her. Each urged her to come with them, but she declined, preferring to reflect in solitude on the crime she had committed against her last lover. A wall of mist formed in the empty mall, descending like a curtain on a stage at the end of a romantic tragedy. Uri-el watched as an open boat sailed out and glided across the floor to where **she stood. Unseen hands raised Lilith's body** from the ground and floated it into the boat, to be laid on a bed of white blossoms stippled with red splashes her blood. The boat turned and disappeared back into the mist, leaving her alone with her thoughts. But the solitude was short lived. The Watchmaker saw to that.

'Don't feel bad.' He said, walking up behind her. She had not heard his arrival. But his presence at this moment in time did not surprise her. 'She used you.'

'I know that now.' She said softly. 'But I suppose I knew that then. I have used people, humans,' she waved her free arm in the air, 'lovers, for so long that I wanted to be used. I guess I wanted to know what it felt like.' She let the sword clatter to the floor and reverted back to being a snake, before it was sucked back into the Ether, no doubt reclaimed by its Cherubim owner.

'And how did it feel?' He asked. She turned to face him and shrugged. His youthful, angelic face looked back at her with concern. 'So, how do you feel?'

'I don't.' She walked towards him and hugged him tightly. 'That's the problem.' She said into the golden curls of his hair. 'I don't feel anything.' She released the embrace and they both turned to walk out of the Mall, arm in arm.

'Where are we going?'

'Orion.'

Epilogue Two - Kip and Blue Saved the World

...All my Sleeping Dreams are Voices...

…There was nothing left for them to do. They had played their parts. The cat had served his role. After helping Saffron enter the Ether and assisting her in coming to terms with her angelic form, Blue transported herself and Kip back into the Realm. When they arrived Kip stared at her for a while, mouth agape.

You're still human. He thought. She grinned and walked up to him, running her finger-tips over his clothed arm until she reached his hand. She pulled him to her.

And you are still Nimrod. She replied telepathically, since her mouth was busy taking tiny nips of his flesh wherever it was exposed. And I promised to make something up to you. Her hands were releasing the buttons of his shirt and sliding under the fabric, raking her nails across his bare chest. They fell to the ground in an embrace.

…Later. They lay naked on the grass, arms and legs intertwined, her head resting on his shoulder.

Blue? Kip asked, She murmured in response. Why didn't you make me human sooner? She sat up and looked at him, his strong face still bore feline traits that softened the harder edges.

Because I did not want to watch you trying to lick your arse in public. She laughed with the sound of a thousand bells. He grinned back and spoke out loud.

'I must admit, it is tempting.'

Epilogue Three - Saffron

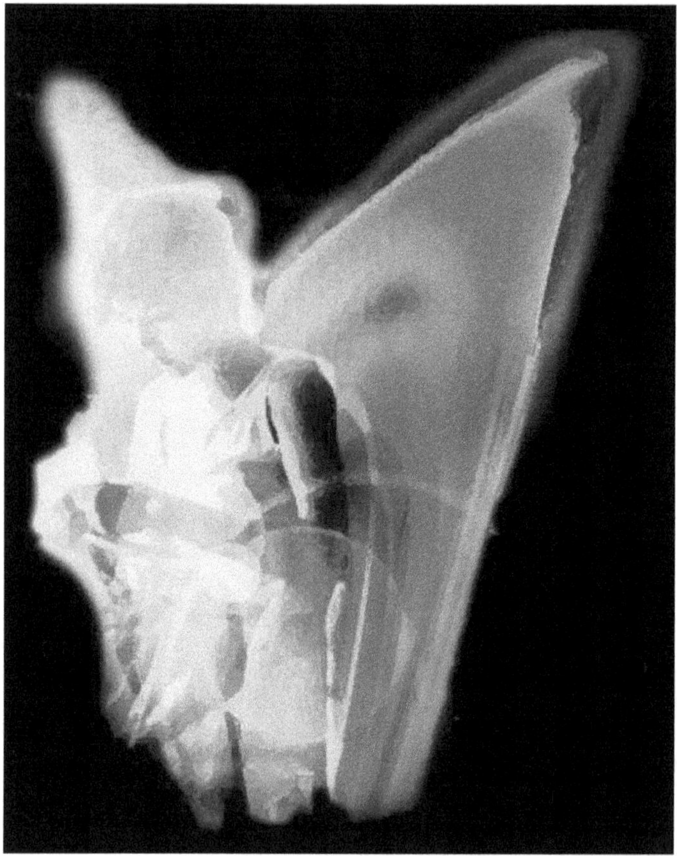

...All my Sleeping Dreams are Voices...

…It did not occur to her until several weeks later that Rochelle du Pont was the Magpie Bridge. She had gone into the kitchen to make coffee when Rochelle first came to his house, but had overheard Rochelle calling her an Angel. Then later, in the Mall, the memories came pouring back and she could no longer contain her true self. The Angel burst from her, compelled by forces she could not control. Confused and bewildered after the confrontation with Lilith, Absinthium was lead into the Ether by Rapha-el (Hecate/Blue) with the Cat (still in human form as Nimrod), where she was allowed to organise and collect her memories under Rapha-el's guidance. Here she learned of her true identity before the fall, that of Sari-el, the Angel of Death, the angel who was responsible for the fate of those angels who transgressed the Law. Unwilling to resume her angelic duties, she soon realised that releasing her angelic form had made her immortal, it meant that she and Philip could be together for eternity, with neither of them having to watch the other grow old. So for now, she chose to keep her human form and return to the Material-plane. To be with Philip true, but also because there was unfinished business here on earth. Ghosts of the past to be laid to rest…

Epilogue Four - Metatron

...All my Sleeping Dreams are Voices...

…oh well, that did not work out as well as anticipated. Metatron mused as he walked along the rain soaked streets of the city. But that's what happens when mortals get involved. The only thing you can rely on them for is to screw things up. An elderly couple walked passed him in the opposite direction, he smirked to himself as their umbrella turned itself inside-out. What's your problem? Aren't your skins water-proof? He crossed the road and headed towards the river embankment with its moorings of house-boats and barges. A floating village that had not moved in centuries. Now, two more of us have woken up. Fledglings! What trouble they will cause? Only time will tell. And heaven knows we have enough of that. At the quay-side, he stopped and rested on a wrought iron bench, watching wavelettes of oily brown river water ripple and slap against the flat hulls of the house-boats. It will soon be night again, then day and then night, the endless cycle continues and we are as trapped as the mortals. A fluttering disturbed the evening air, Metatron grinned as the Magpie settled on the bench beside him. I thought I told you to stay with the witch? The Magpie fixed him with a beady eye. Yes, we are alike, you and I, my pied friend. Neither wholly good or truly evil. But then, we aren't free to choose either. Metatron reached out and pulled a shiny golden coin from under the Magpie's wing. A simple conjuring trick for his own amusement, the Magpie oblivious to the slight of hand. He held the coin at arms length between finger and thumb and squinted with one eye so it eclipsed the setting sun. Curse on Gabri-el for instructing Daniel to make these confounded seals. He scowled as he gripped the seal in his clenched fist. He trusted a mortal to do the job he should have done himself. See, another mortal screws up and we are fucked for eternity, prisoners of a slim disc of metal…

Epilogue Five - Micha-el, the Shadow

...All my Sleeping Dreams are Voices...

…when an Angel walks the city streets wracked with plague and sees the dead and dying lying in their filth while the rich and powerful look on, and the Angel sees them flee to their homes, carrying the spectre of death on their backs and entire towns disappear beneath the soil.

When an Angel walks the battle fields of man, wading through the blood and carnage wrought by sword, bow and axe and gun, bomb and shell, and the Angel walks the trenches, filling its lungs with the stabbing bite of mustard-gas as the youth of nations rot in the mud and mire.

When an Angel walks the death camps with tears in its eyes as the defeated and the despondent file into the gas chambers, and the Angel looks into the eyes of men and sees hatred staring back through the clouded doctrine of propaganda and lies.

When an Angel walks the world and sees poverty, famine and disease as nations starve for another lost harvest, and the Angel sees a neighbour, surrounded by wealth, waste and welfare, look the other way with indifference.

Then an Angel knows Despair…

Epilogue Six - Lilith

...All my Sleeping Dreams are Voices...

…i said it wouldn't be easy. The dark figure of Lilith stood on the bank of the river, trying to skim stones across its mill-pond surface. She bent and picked up a smooth flat pebble slightly smaller than the size of her palm. She weighed it in her hand, feeling its balance and then flipped it into the air, watching it turn end over end before landing back in her palm. Yes. She crouched low and threw the stone at waist-level with all her might. The missile arced several leagues before graceful edging towards the water's surface at the perfect angle. The calculations were correct, the velocity and angles were exact. The stone would skip seven times before crashing into the opposite bank. The River Acheron, however, did not care for mathematics or physics, the stone disappeared beneath its surface without a ripple. Lilith cursed. Countless times over countless millennia she had played this game while waiting for the ferryman to take her home, and each time the River refused to play fair. Still, it passed the time and there was precious little else to do while waiting. She turned the golden seal over in her fingers. I bet this would work; the River would not dare swallow this. But she thought better of it than to risk it on an experiment. I told them it wouldn't be easy. The ferry glided towards her. Still, she smiled; I never imagined it would be this easy…

Epilogue Seven - Philip, Rochelle, Sam and Saffron

...All my Sleeping Dreams are Voices...

Philip helped Rochelle take the boy to hospital. By the time they reached the emergency department, he had slipped in and out of consciousness several times and was muttering incoherently. They had learned his first name and nothing more, so Rochelle booked him in as Sam du Pont and handed over her medical smart-card. They sat in the waiting room, Philip was sipping insipid coffee from a plastic cup while glaring at a No Smoking sign, Rochelle rubbed the sleep from her eyes.

'What now?' Philip muttered, uncertain whether he had directed the question to Rochelle, himself or thin luke-warm liquid in his cup.

'You go home.' She replied. He started to speak, but she continued uninterrupted, 'There's nothing more to be done here. Some overworked nurse will come back in a couple of hours and tell us they will be keeping him in for observation and advise us to go home.' She looked at him. 'I'll be fine.' She patted his arm. 'Look, give me your number and I'll call if anything happens. Now, go home.'

'There's no point.' He said.

'There's every point, now go.' If he had learnt one thing over the past three hundred years, it was never argue when a woman had made up her mind, so he kissed her on the cheek and reluctantly left.

Philip was probably the only person on the planet who could register genuine surprise at finding Saffron sat on his door step. He had always set his sights and aspirations below the disappointment threshold. Of course, he hoped she would be there, he would have been distraught if she hadn't been, however his expectations were low. The gloom of the journey back from the Hospital vanished instantly and was replaced by a grin as wide as Tuesday.

'Hi.' She leapt to her feet and threw her arms around his neck. 'You know don't you?'

He nodded. 'You don't find yourself immortal without wondering how or why. Quite frankly, not having a sudden craving for blood or a fear of day-light doesn't leave too many options.' He reached into his pocket for his key and struggled to open the door while her arms were still wrapped around him. The door swung open and they tumbled onto the black and white tiled floor. With him pinned beneath her, she said.

'I've never fucked an Angel before,' and she kissed him before he had chance to say something really stupid

Addendums: At the End-ums

Why Page: And the Final word is "Why?"

- Why! The Author feels he must justify his action, why? …the Web is a media with a built in lag so attention spans are shorter. No one will read a 'normal' text novel or a 'normal' graphic novel on the Web, it is a promise and a guarantee. They are too long, too slow, too many words, too much input, too much bandwidth. The Darqlands was a Web-novel as an experiment, it was not masterfully interactive or hypertextural. It was just words and images. In the Darqlands, the images are incoherent, as are the paragraphs, sentences and phrases. The grammar was twisted, broken and, in parts, immature ~ this was not an accident. It is the nature of the Internet that permits this, the WWW that promotes this. Only the 'plot' is pure. For there is a story here, amongst the pretentious style-over-substance and distorted grammar, in a plot that threads its way through the text and pictures…

- Why is it so now, long after the web novel had vanished into the ether, consumed by the ephemeral, transient environment of the Internet, that this novel is reborn in the ancient more eternal form of a paperback novel, all be it minus many of the graphic images of the original form and with none of the hyper-active textual links to aid and distract the casual reader? That is the less than subtle irony: that the impermanence of the Web that allowed the novel to be created would be its demise and the more traditional permanence of print and paper would be its legacy.

- Even so, the question - why?… Ah, the immortal question! Once the power of speech has been mastered, one of the first things a small child learns is to ask is "Why?" This is the inquisitive and the mischievous mind working hand in hand on a quest to know more. Every answer is greeted with another "Why?" - A game with a purpose…

- A purpose - why? …this is the search for knowledge of the ever inquiring mind. And children are not unique in this; even animals display this inquisitiveness, the instinctive curiosity. It ensures that the unexpected can be anticipated and dealt with, to flee or fight, to eat or be eaten. It is not a measure of intelligence. It is the desire to know "Why?", a means of survival.

Of man? ~ to eat from the Tree of Knowledge of Good and Evil ~ to see as gods see, forever. To be banished from Eden, forever to know of the darqness.

And what of the others? ~ to eat from the Tree of Life ~ to live as gods live, forever. To be banished from Heaven, forever to live in darqness…

- But why? …seven ethereal immortals sent into the darqness. Displaced and lost through time, they fight to find each other in the darkness of humanity, to survive and to regain what was theirs'…

- Seven? Why? …seven by seven they were, for seven by seven thousand years in legends of time. Seven by seven they were the Lucky Seven, cast in stone as Seven Wonders for the World, writ large in the Heptateuch for the Seven Ages of Man: for his Seven Deadly Sins and for his Seven Sacraments and Seven Chakras in the seven colours of the visible spectrum casting a rainbow bridge over the Milkyway. Created on the Seventh Day in the Seventh Heaven, they were the The Seven Sages, The Seven Endless, The Seven Samurai, The Seven Lucky Gods, The Seven Thunders, The Pleiades and The Septentrions. The Seven Archangels, the Seven Cherubim and the Seven Phoenixes in the Seven Levels of Heaven, the Seven Kings on the Seven Levels of Earth, the Seven Demons in the Seven Levels of Hell. Myths and legends come from somewhere and so they return. Guided by a Seventh son of a Seventh son, from across the Seven Seas by the Seven Hills of Rome to rule the Heptarchy of the Seven Kingdoms. And the Darqlands is as good a place as any other…

- Why? …'Y' is a crooked letter and you can't straighten it…

- Ah, funny. So, why? …Why do you ask?…

The Seven

Ashiya

Ishtarah –Uri-el

Blue

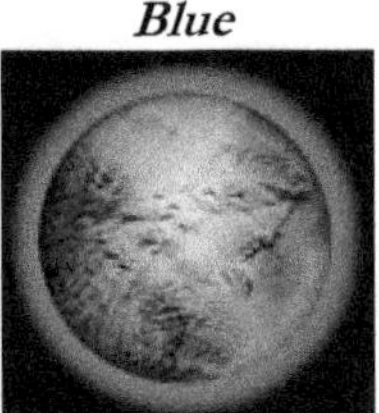

Hecate – Rapha-el

The Watcher

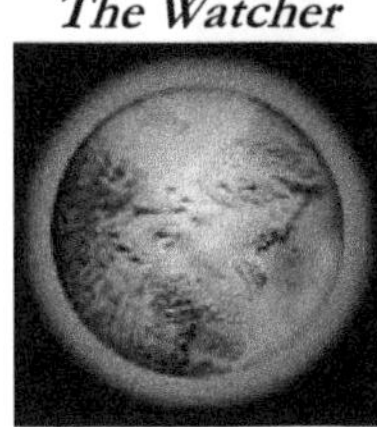

Lilith - Razi-el

Philip

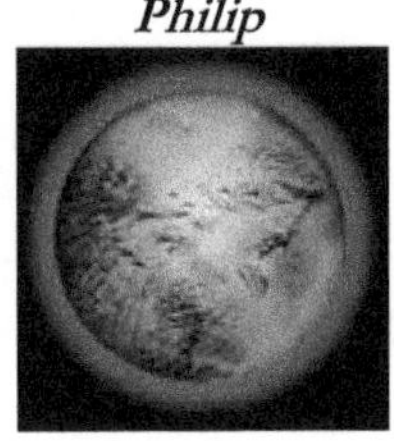

The Dreamer - Gabri-el

The Angel

Meririm - Metatron

Saffron

Absinthium - Sari-el

The Shadow

Apollyon - Micha-el

Ashiya

...Time was and Time will ever be...

Mōnan Dæg's is fair of face: A hedonistic spirit who lives in a constant delirium of pleasure. Through the physical, the material and the chemical Ashiya lives for the instant act of self-gratification. She pursues this with a religious zeal to the extreme so that every waking moment, and most of her sleeping ones, are sensual events. Once governess of the phases of the moon, Ashiya is now governed by them, forever locked in an insatiable madness.

The Sphinx

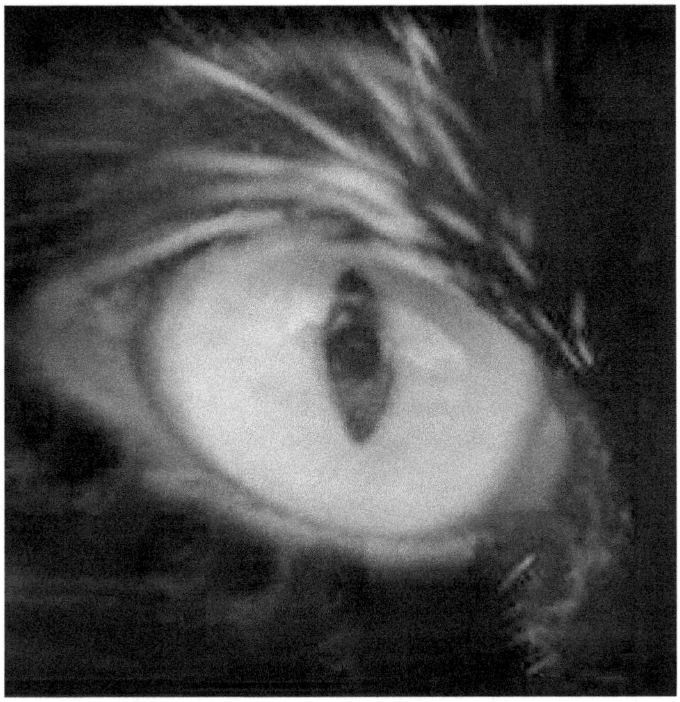

...Time was I was not alone...

Tiwes Dæg's childe is full of grace: A guiding cat-spirit who influences the willing to achieve their destiny. Whose memory is the memory of the future, whose breath changes destiny and whose heartbeat decides fate; Of the Seven, the Sphinx is the only one who lives in the real and the ethereal domains, switching between them with ease, adopting forms in each that best suit its purpose.

'Saffron'

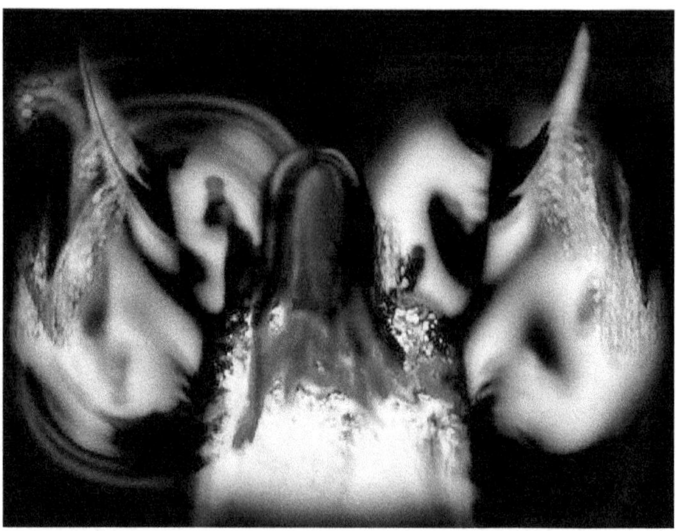

...Time was all there ever was...

Wõdnes Dæg's childe is loving and giving: A lost spirit forever searching, forever to be surrounded by death. The death of family-life, of friendship and of hope. For circumstances unknown, 'Saffron' is a perpetual runaway, running away from her father, her home and herself.

The Angel

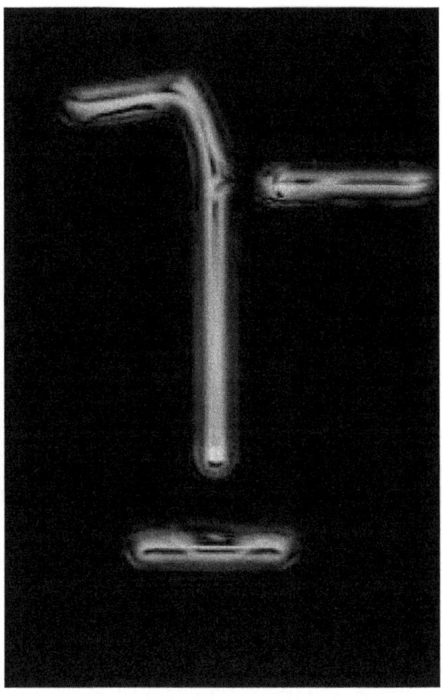

...Time was I walked the skies...

Thunres Dæg's childe works hard for its living: An ethereal spirit of contradictions. Malevolent and benign, bringing forth destruction and rebirth. Of the Seven, the Angel was never lost. Aware of its power and reason to be, ever present and ever vigilant for the misplaced cause and the misguided ideal.

The Shadow

...Time was Shadows cast the Light...

Frige Dæg's childe is full of woe: A dark, primeval and malevolent spirit, Guardian and Hunter for the Darqlands. Creating despair and desolation it stalks the Waking Lands for lost souls to feed the Darqness. The Shadow is the eldest of the Seven, tracing its lineage back to the beginning of time - the Heart of the Darqlands. Some say the Shadow was never cast out of Heaven, some say it was never there, but was created to feed the Darqness. Others say it was the most beautiful of the Seven and the first to Fall, creating the Darqlands out of spite and revenge.

The Watcher

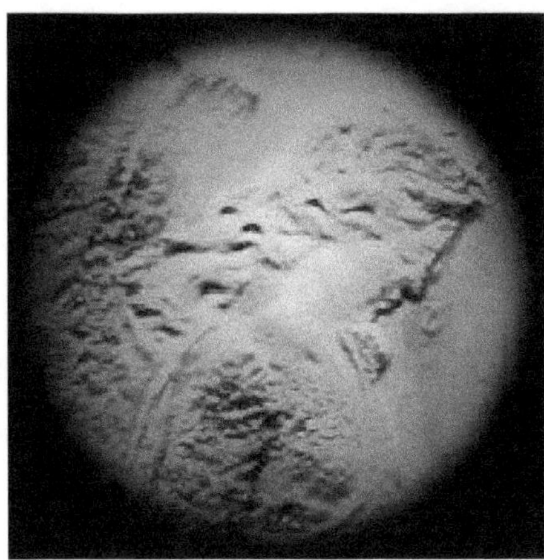

...Time Was I Danced and Sang...

Sæternes Dæg's childe has far to go: A beguiling spirit, enchanting the unsuspecting through desire. The Watcher's quest is to reunite the Seven, awaken the forgotten memories. It tires of drifting the Waking Lands, isolated and alone, it now feeds its own desire ~ to regain the Kingdom and live again as the Guardians of mankind.

Philip Mallow

...Time was and Time will ever be...

The childe that is born on the Sunnan's Dæg: The most lost of the lost. The Dreamer. Unable (or unwilling?) to fulfil his birth-right, he simply lives it. In life Philip Mallow is forever the dreamer. Incapable of achieving his dream, he lives a figment of a life, a pretence of an existence. Forever slipping between reality and imagination, Philip has trouble telling one from the other, for he is unaware that they are the same.

The Somniloquies

Somniloquy One - Ashiya

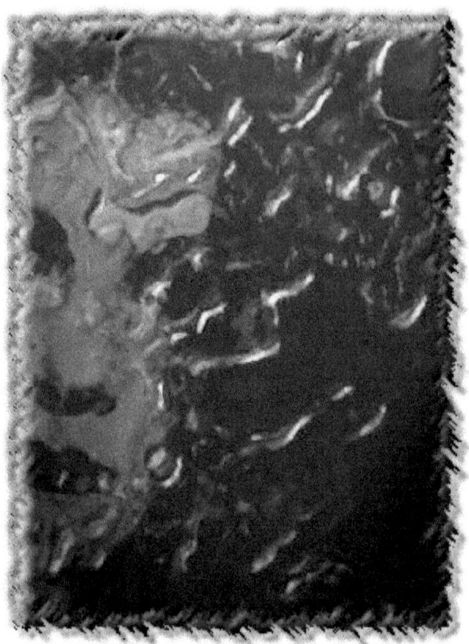

...A Dreamless Sleep...

'Ah! Again. Yes! Yes! Ahhhhhhhhh! No. Yes. Ooooo. Stop. Again. Mmmmm.' [attracted by the æolian calls, the wind breezes in through an open window, raising gossamer thin drapes to billow against the moonlight] 'My love? Is that you? You have come! Where are you? I cannot see you my love, come to me. For I know you are there watching me. Do you see me as I was, young and lithe. Come to me. Kiss me.' [a gentle waft of air caresses her cheek] 'A coy kiss? Is that all I get after all these years? A mere peck on the cheek for some wizen maiden aunt. Do you not love me still? Now I am old and grey and you do not care for me anymore. But once. Once you did, I remember. Gliding over the mountains, hand in hand as one, a pair of lovers of pure orgasmic energy to make the gods quake in their jealousy. Do you remember? Well. Do you?' [the breeze continues to tickle the soft downy hairs on her cheek] 'You do! Liar! It never happened - I made it up. We were never lovers.' [the wind strengthens, insistently pulling at the bedclothes] 'Angels? What? You think me lost in some delirium? No. I do not believe that rubbish. I am not the first, the Heaven nor the Earth. I am not the Light they call Day nor the Darkness they call Night. I shall not send down a hail of fire and blood. That is not reality. I am just an old woman who dreams of being young again.' [the wind ruffles the blankets] 'Or an young woman whose dreams are of an old woman who dreams of being young again? And why would I do that?' [the wind abates] 'Because in dream I remember? I remember nothing! There is nothing to remember! There is no past, there was no future. There will be only now. So come to me my love and we will glide over the mountains.'

Somniloquy Two - The Sphinx

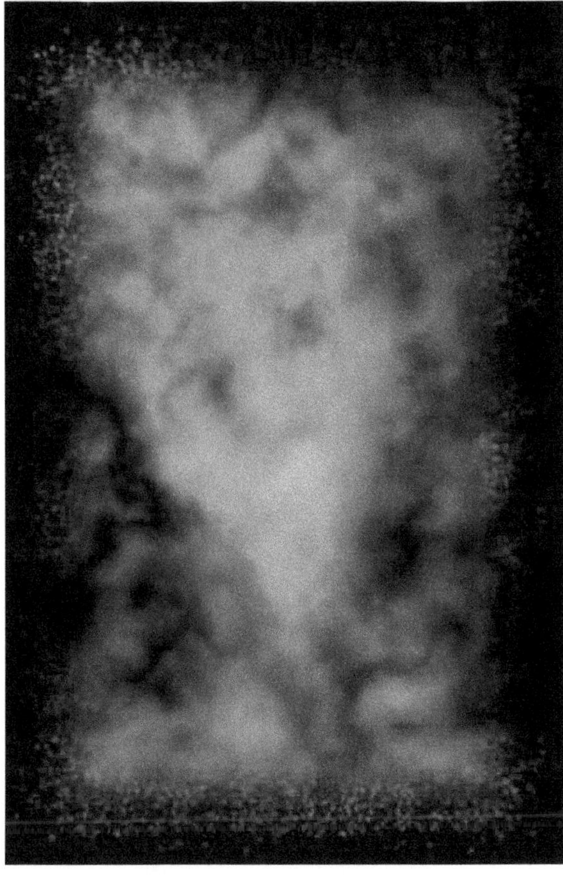

...No chance to dream...

'Look!' [the wind is strangely silent, as if in a sulk] 'Do you see them? See how they squabble and fight. How can they ever get back if they fight so. They should have never left, then they would not have forgotten. I have my realm, I have my power and I have my love. The spirits that follow me are loyal and I love them with all my breath and will protect them with all my strength. This is my destiny.' [the wind attempts to attract attention, stirring the grasses into a gentle undulating sea]. 'Of the others? What of them? What care have I for them? I gave them their destinies and each of them squander it without a care. I care not for them. I am that which divides water from water, but I shall not divide them. I am the mountain that unites fire and blood, but I will not unite them. I will not intervene, I will not help. I only defend what is mine. I only attack that which threatens.' [a small eddy of dust and straw forms, rapidly increasing in speed as it picks up more litter, it swirls and gyrates into a small dust-devil] 'Stop! Who are you to raise your voice to me! Petulant child. Leave. Go, I have much to do. Leave me alone.'

Somniloquy Three - 'Saffron'

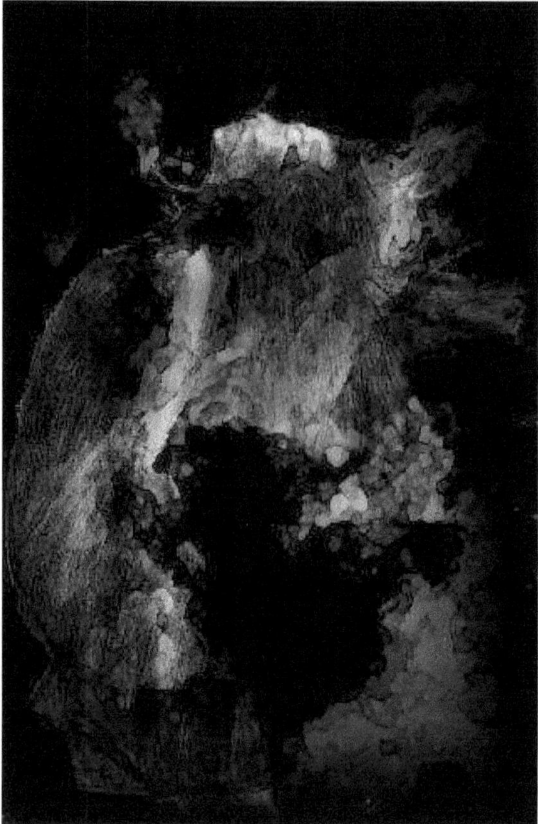

...But lonely voices like the wind...

'Do you hear that? That gentle rushing of waves on the shore. The soft rattle of pebbles in the backwash. Can you hear that? That electric-buzz of static that sounds like the ocean' [the wind rattles dry branches, its discordant chime to be interpreted as words: 'Like when you hold a conch-shell to your ear?'] 'Yes, yes! That sound you hear. That echo of a far away sea.' [the rustle of sun-baked leaves: 'so, what of it?'] 'That is no ocean. That is the sound of your life. The echoes of your thoughts filtering through your unconscious mind. The reverberation of blood coursing through your veins. The rush of time ebbing from your soul.' [the wind blows stronger, picking up more leaves to phrase another question: 'and you know of this?'] 'You mock? Yes I know. I am the third, created as land and sea, the shore to make those sounds. I was created to count the grains of sand that measure your souls journey through the hourglass called life. The third beast with scales in my hand to balance those grains as if they where of corn or barley. I am Wormwood!' [a shallow breeze: 'Absinthium'], 'Now you whisper my name, and I know your life. Water becomes blood, and I know your death. Do you fear me now?' [the wind is still: '…'] 'Silence? Now, now. That is not like you. No smart quip? No witty retort? Come let us embrace. I shall hold you and never let go, for time was all there ever was.'

Somniloquy Four - The Angel

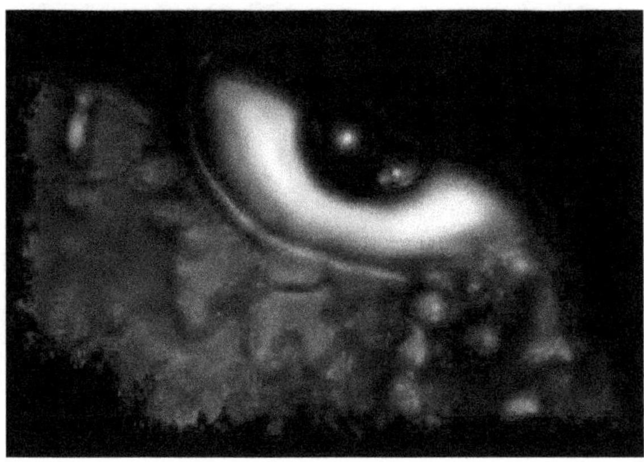

...In my dreaming head...

'…it is written: 'And the fourth angel poured out his vial upon the sun; and power was given unto him to scorch men with fire" [A hollow moan fills the void] 'A lament? Wait, there is more: 'And men were scorched with great heat, and blasphemed the name of God, which hath power over these plagues: and they repented not to give him glory.' So, am I not the fourth? Created on the fourth day, a greater light to rule the day and lesser light to rule the night? And by that, do I not bring forth darkness and destruction and roast the scourge that is mankind? Is that not my vocation?' [the wind modulates the moan, generating tones and sub-tones of discordant harmonies] 'Aye, perhaps you are correct. I do not know anymore. It has been so long. Now, all I do is despise. I despise my siblings for forgetting. I despise myself for not forgetting. And I despise mankind for just being there. Everything is so contemptible. The despiser despises all that is despisable in utter despisal for its despisedness.' [a sharp blast of wind catches the Angel on the cheek] 'Despitefull! Ha! You know nothing of despite! Have you wandered this forsaken land since time began? Have you endured the irresponsibility of mankind as it plunders and defiles?' [another warm blast from the wind strikes the other cheek, less abrupt, but more insistent] 'Of course you have dear friend, I forget, you have always been here, long before even I. Long before the we were cast down and long before the others became absorbed into the fabric of mankind.' [the wind ceases its assault, and drops to a soothing breeze] 'Them? What of them? They sleep. No, that is not true, one of them wakes. Just one of them. I know not which, a sister I am certain, but that is all I am sure of. She walks the Waking Lands searching for the rest, to wake them too. To reunite the family. And then? She will disturb the equilibrium. All that was lost she will take back, all that was built she will destroy. For what? To recover a dream? To relive the past? Pah! It will not happen. Time has made a truth of that. Time erodes more effectively than you my ælean friend. Time creates forgetfulness, in gods and man and angels. She cannot reclaim that which is forgotten. Time was I walked the skies, but now, I crawl the earth…'

Somniloquy Five - The Shadow

...And distant voices like the rain...

'...They say it doesn't dream. Its brother never gave it the blessing. So they say. Then if not dreams, what other name for these memories?' [the wind howls in response and it laughs at that. A loud raucous laugh that rustles leaves and flurries them in minor whirlwinds, conversing with the wind in their common language]. 'But they say it doesn't remember. As old as time, but cannot recall. So they say. But it mastered time, rewinding and replaying. Rewinding to the time before it mastered time, then replaying in spiralling loops and twists. It remembers. Of course it remembers. It remembers. I remember. I remember it all, I can recollect their faces and their names - their secret names. I can recount their tales and deeds, the saga's of ages locked in the vaults of time.' [The thought is picked up like a paper kite, lifted into the air to sail aloft, yet still tethered by a restraining question.] 'No! No stories! Now is not the time for the telling of Stories! Now is the time for creating Stories! A time to write History!' [A violent maelstrom tears at the thought, pulling on the question. Fearfully, the wind drops to a gentle, cowering breeze and the thought settles to the ground to lie amongst the fallen leaves.] 'Please forgive. It forgets itself - I forget myself. You are my guest and I should not shout. There has been too much time, in the past and in the future, when I was alone in the Darqlands with nothing to shout about. So now I shout at the wind, and this is wrong.' [The breeze wafts, soothing and comforting] 'They say I do not regret. For I have the fifth seal, the vial of darkness and that I am the Angel of the bottomless pit whose name is Abaddon, who some call Apollyon. So they say. But am I not the child of the fifth-day? Frige Dæg's childe whose waters brought swimming creatures that hath life, and fowl that may fly above the earth in the open firmament of heaven? I regret many things, but for this I have no remorse. I create, I do not destroy. They cast us out, we did not fall. I became what they wanted me to be, to trap their souls to build the Darqness. I do not remember what I choose to forget, yet in dreams I reminisce and relive all those lost memories.' [Then there is silence and the air becomes still, waiting and listening.] '(One of my sisters is trying to wake me, but I must not, for then I will forget)' [Detecting the change in tone, the breeze picks up and worries the age-old collection of dust, creating undulating patterns of miniature dunes] 'Dreams? Tell you of my dreams? Ha! This is my dream...'

Somniloquy Six - The Watcher

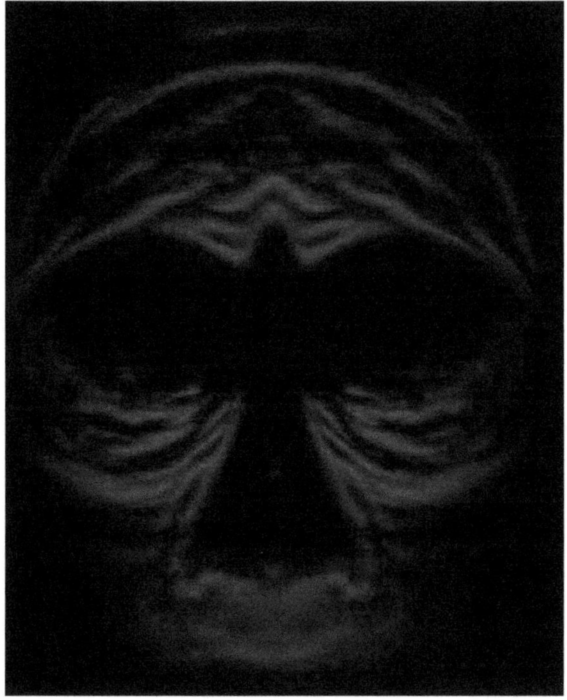

...In my sleepless thoughts...

'Ah, nice of you to come. Come, come, stay a while, it's been so long, please let me introduce myself...'[the wind creates a gentle draft, cooling the air] 'Huh? If you say so, it must be so. Of course, I forget so many things...' [the Messenger cocks an ear to the wind] 'My face? It is the one I choose to wear today.' [listening to the molecules vibrating, one against the other, transmitting a message through the acoustic medium.] 'What? too obvious a derivative, a stereotype! Ha! Oh simple childe, so far to walk yet still not see, but you do see, don't you?' [silence] 'You do understand, do you not?' [more silence] 'You do not.' [then the indignant wind responds with a sudden burst] 'No, no, no, it's just a metaphor, a passing semaphore of - of life and death and afterlife and afterdeath. Nothing more, nothing less.' [the voice to an question is written into the wind, lifting it into the air] 'A common language of imagery? Ah, I See, well, I see we are never too old to learn!

'The story so far... So far ~ so good. A plan, as plans go, a plain and simple plan, but mine own. A plan that goes, well, according to plan as they say. With blood on my hands and hands on my blood.' [the breeze murmurs, muffled and slight, hidden behind the rustle of trees and the whisper of promises] 'Or a taste in my throat? Very good! very well then, 'Blood in my throat, the blood of my Blood'. Yes. My dear brothers and sisters, my sweet siblings: The Lost and The Found, watching and playing, living and not dying. Each playing a game of their own. Of their own design and own invention. None know the rules but I and that is fair - it is just. Is the price to pay - a fair fare for a just justice.' [a momentary gust flurries, picking up partial fragments of forgotten thoughts]. 'Hmm, maybe so, I suppose you're right. But in my own right, so am I. It is my right, my birthright.

'Time was I danced and sang. You cannot comprehend those days. Those joyous days. What fun we had, my brothers, my sisters and I.' [far away, yet so close, the sound of agitated rustling] 'Ha! Yes! Yes! And you too, my Zephyr. They loved us then. Oh yes. They did. Then. And then: Betrayed and banished! Fallen and forgotten! Only wandering and wondering.' [a gentle waft of air disturbs the long forgotten dust]. 'Now? Now they sleep. A long restless slumber of time, a walking sleep through the ages, a … what is that word?' [...] 'Somnambulance! Yes, yes, that's the one. Ah, a such poetic word, the word is a poem in itself - it's own mantra to sleep:

'Som-Nam-Bu-Lance-Som
-Nam-Bu-Lance-Som-Nam
-Bu-Lance-Som-Nam-Bu
-Lance-Som-Nam-Bu-Lance
-Som-Nam-Bu-Lance-Som
-Nam-Bu-Lance-Som-Nam
-Bu
-Lance
~ Ohmmmm...'

'Now they sleep. But not for long, for I have woken them. And when they stir, they will remember. Then what fun we shall have. Is this what you desire? Or what desires you? Hmm? Nothing to say? Cat got your tongue?'

Somniloquy Seven - Philip Mallow

...All my Sleeping Dreams are Voices...

[dream!]

Dream?

[you dream]

I do not.

[everybody dreams,
but not everyone remembers]

No.
I do not dream.

[what are you doing now?]

What do you mean?

[you are talking to the wind,
is this the action of a waking, rational, mind?]

No.
Of course not.
But you are talking to me.
It is you who dream.

[the wind does not dream]

You said it yourself, everyone dreams.
Even the wind sleeps, and once asleep, it dreams.

[my argument exactly!]

But I am not asleep.
I fantasise for the rest of creation.
I imagine conversations and events for every living thing.
I create different worlds and manifest different lives.
But I am not asleep.
So I cannot dream.

[ah, day-dreaming]

Semantics!
Can you see me now?
Are my eyes closed?
Do you see rapid eye movement beneath these eyelids?
Is this r.e.m. sleep?
Am I dreaming now?
So, if not me, then it is you who dreams.

[!]

See, I do not dream.
I am the Seventh.
I am the Voice.
I create the dreams.
I do not live them.

[but, in creating this dream for the wind,
are you not dreaming too]

A dream that reasons?
I must be more skilful than I…

[…dreamt?
see, we both are asleep,
and we both dream]

A compromise?
We both sleep and dream…

The 'Bar Ba Black Sleep' Cocktails Page

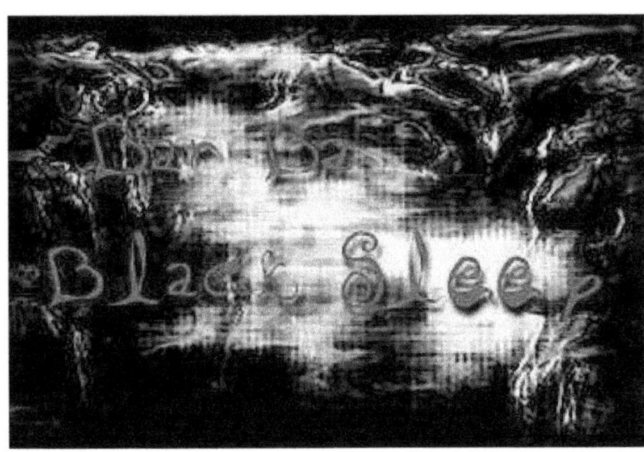

White Lady

Put 2 measures of Gin, 1 of Cointreau, a teaspoon of Lemon Juice and an egg white into a cocktail shaker. Shake well and strain into a cocktail glass. Decorate with a twisted lemon rind and serve.

Red Witch

Basic Snakebite mix (see below), with a shot of Pernod and a dash of Blackcurrent cordial.

Red Kiss

Plonk 3 ice-cubes in a tall timber, add 1 measure of Vermouth, ½ of Gin & ½ of Cherry Brandy and stir. Strain into a chilled cocktail glass with a cherry.

Orange Blossom

Pour Gin, Vermouth & Orange Juice into a shaker and erm, shake. Plonk 3 ice-cubes into a tall glass and pour cocktail over them. Serve with a twist of Orange.

Orange Cloud

Ice, 3 measures of Orange Juice and 1 of Pernod. Stir & serve with a twisted Orange.

Yellow Dwarf

Put 1 egg-yolk, ¼ pint double cream, the contents of 1 passion fruit, a dash of bitter almond essence and a splash of soda into a jug with 4 ice-cubes. Stir, strain, pour down the drain and make a proper drink!

Green Devil

Place the juice of 6 limes, 2 pints of Sparkling Mineral Water and 5 dashes of Angostura bitters into a big jug with a dozen ice-cubes. Stir and pour into 4 tall glasses.

Green-eyed Devil

Add 1 measure of Creme de Menthe to the each glass of the above.

Blue Moon

A few hours before, place glass tumblers in the refrigerator. Half fill each glass tumbler ice. Add 1 measure of Vodka, 1 measure of Tequila, and 1 measure of Blue Curaçao (of course!). The top-up with Lemonade, stir and serve.

Blue Champagne

Swirl 4 dashes of Blue Curaçao into a champagne flute to coat the sides of the glass. Pour in Champagne and drink it.

Purple Nasty

A Red Witch (see above) with an extra shot of Vodka.

Black Russian

Crack 5 ice-cubes and place the debris into a glass tumbler, Add 2 measures of Vodka and 1 of Kahlúa (or Tia Maria) and stir. Top up with coke (optional).

Black Velvet

This is really just a posh Snake Bite, ½ Guinness and ½ Champagne. Cider can be used instead of Champagne - but why bother?

Snakebite

A mix of ½ lager (premium beer) and ½ cider (brewed apple juice). Use the strongest beer and cider available and it becomes an Anaconda (now that's gotta hurt!).

Zombie

(No logical reason for including this, there are no Zombies in the Darqlands - that I know of anyway...) Place a tall glass into the freezer until it is frosted, but remove it before it becomes stuck to your hand when you pick it up! Put 3 ice-cubes in a cocktail shaker with 1 measure Dark Rum, 1 of White Rum, ½ of Apricot Brandy, 2 of Pineapple Juice, 1 tablespoon of Lime Juice and 2 teaspoons of sugar. Shake like St Vitus. Pour into the frosty glass (including the ice). Add sprig of mint, a wedge of fresh pineapple and a cherry. Sprinkle more sugar over the top.

The Angelic Host

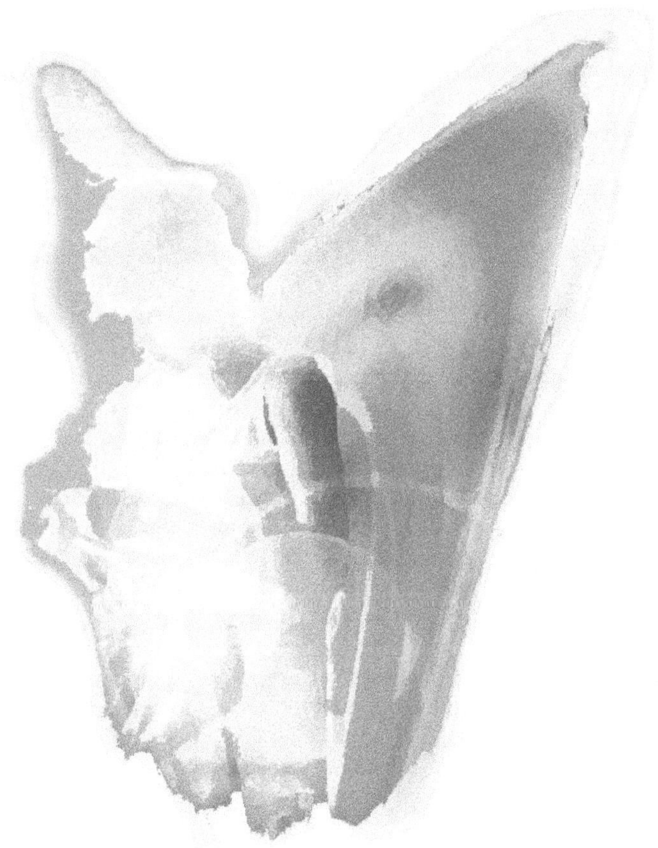

The Host - The Angels

...All my Sleeping Dreams are Voices...

The Angels form the Ninth Choir and are the ones who have most contact with mankind, since they are the Messengers (Angelos is the Greek form of a Persian word, Angaros, meaning courier). Angels are described as being very tall (by human standards) and fair, some have wings, but most it seems do not. From the ranks of the Angels come the ministering angels, who teach and guide. Notable amongst these are the Guardians, who are assigned to watch over each living thing. According to tradition, each blade of grass has an Angel to watch over it. Their close proximity to mankind has been their downfall, since they are the Choir who have been most perverted and corrupted by the sins of man. For example, the Watchers, (also known as the Grigory and the bene ba Elohim) were sent to earth to help create the Garden of Eden, but became captivated by the Daughters of Cain and took them as their wives, (Gen 6:2 'That the Sons of God saw the daughters of men that they were fair; and they took them wives of all which they chose.'), which in the eyes of God was a bad thing in itself. But they also took it upon themselves to teach mankind the arts of civilisation, which was seen as a very bad thing indeed. For their crimes, they were cast down and their offspring, the Nephilim, were destroyed.

The Host - The Archangels

...All my Sleeping Dreams are Voices...

Archangels are an oddity amongst the Angelic Host. As a group they are placed in the Eighth Choir, since they have a human-like form when in contact with mankind. However, as individuals they appear as Seraphim and are the Princes of the Heavens, with each level of Heaven having an Archangel assigned to it. Tradition and scripture has it that there are seven Archangels, but since no two tracts agree on who is a part of that seven, then it is fair to assume that their numbers are either greater, or the make-up of the Eighth Choir is dynamic and ever changing.

The Host - The Principals

...All my Sleeping Dreams are Voices...

The Principals are the Seventh Choir. Being a part of the first level of Heaven, they are the first to be depicted in humanlike form. They are the Princes in charge of the Guardian Angels of great cities and nations. Like the Archangels and Angels in the choirs below them, the Principals are prone to corruption by their proximity to human and many of the Princes of Heaven became Demon Princes of Hell.

The Host - The Powers

...All my Sleeping Dreams are Voices...

The Sixth Choir are called the Powers that protect the higher levels of Heaven from Demonic infiltration and to that end are the Angels who are in charge of our souls - the traditional battle-ground of good and evil. Lead by the Archangel Cama-el, it is the Powers that do battle with the Demon Princes and it may have been Cama-el and his forces that scourged the earth of the Grigory/Human offspring, the Nephilim. However, the largest single defection from good to evil comes from this order of Angels as they are the more likely to come into contact with pure evil and many of their number now rule as Dukes in Hell.

The Host - The Virtues

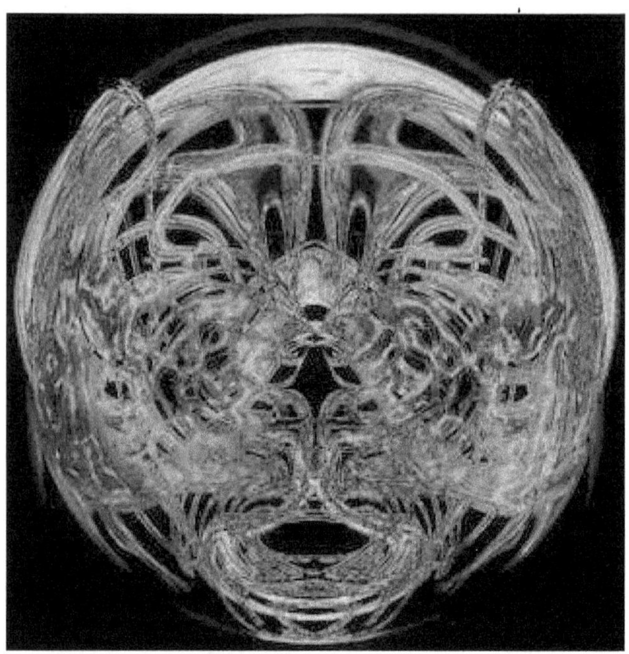

...All my Sleeping Dreams are Voices...

The Fifth Choir, sometimes know as the Malakim, are the Shining Ones who bestow Blessings and Miracles from on high. The Virtues have had many ruling Princes over the ages, including Micha-el, Gabri-el and even Satan-el himself. It would appear that being Prince of the Virtues is a high heavenly honour.

The Host - The Dominions

...All my Sleeping Dreams are Voices...

Little is known of the Fourth Choir, the Dominions, since their sole duty is to regulate the duties of other Angels, they do not come into contact with humankind.

The Host - The Ophanim

...All my Sleeping Dreams are Voices...

The Ophanim form the Third Choir. Often known as the Thrones and occasionally as the Galgallin, the Ophanim are described in biblical texts as being wheels of burning coals, of such height that they cause fearfulness, with a myriad of eyes on their rims. Attempts have been made to transcribe these descriptions into modern references, leading to them being interpreted as U.F.O's in some quarters (Chariots of the Gods). However, since the Ophanim are the first order to exist beyond the material world, occupying the higher levels of Heaven, I favour the idea that this is simply their appearance when they enter our dimension.

The Host - The Cherubim

...All my Sleeping Dreams are Voices...

The traditional view of the Second Choir is a long way removed from the romantic depiction of a Cherub as being a chubby child-like figure with harp and wings, an image lifted from the greek Cupid. The Cherubim are beings of pure light that manifest as creatures with four wings and four faces wielding an ever-turning sword in the material world, however, in earlier scriptures, they were more beast-like resembling sphinxes. The Cherubim are described as Gods charioteers as they often go into battle accompanied by the Ophanim, which are wheel-like in our domain.

The Host - The Seraphim

...All my Sleeping Dreams are Voices...

The First Choir of Angels are the Seraphim. These are the Angels closest to God and from their number come all the Archangel Princes. The Seraphim are beings of pure light and thought, described as fiery flying serpents (dragons?), although when visible to humankind, they have six wings and four heads.

The plug page: 'spunos'

spunos is an album of poorly composed music inspired by 'DARQLANDS' and recorded under the name of The Cacophony Of Light. Like this novel, it is constructed and contrived around the number seven, with seven tracks all of seven minutes in duration, named for no fathomable reason after geological minerals.

character	star sign	rainbow/aura	fallen-angel	arch-angel	mineral / CD track name
ashiya	cancer	red	ishtarah	uriel	galena
the sphinx	capricorn	orange	asarte/hecate	raphael	corundum
'saffron'	aquarius	yellow	absinthium	sariel	gypsum
the angel	sagittarius	green	meririm	metatron	nepheline
the shadow	scorpio	blue	apolyon	michael	trona
the watcher	taurus	indigo	lilith	raziel	obsidian
philip mallow	aries	violet	dreamer	gabriel	feldspar

'...in heaven an Angel is nobody in particular...'

~ George Bernard Shaw

Ultimate Page: Another Afterthought

The Seven Inch Nails

'Millions of spiritual creatures walk the earth
Unseen, both when we wake and when we sleep'

~John Milton, *Paradise Lost*

...the DARQLANDS extended as far as the eye could not see...

...from the depths of a soul to the limits of a mind...

...with the shudder of a broken main-spring this story ended...

...with sporadic irraticism as the muse and inspiration dictated the words and images into the ether...

...there is no more...

... there never was...

ISBN 978-1-4467-8925-4
90000
9 781446 789254

www.ingramcontent.com/pod-product-compliance
Ingram Content Group UK Ltd.
Pitfield, Milton Keynes, MK11 3LW, UK
UKHW012215240726
13966UKWH00003B/767

9 781446 789254